She was bent over a treatment table,
obviously deep in concentration. The curls, light brown and shot with golden highlights, as always, seemed to have a life of their own. He couldn't see her soft lips, but he knew they'd be slightly parted, her teeth unconsciously grazing her tongue. He inhaled her unique scent, a mixture of peaches and vanilla and summer flowers.

He wanted to come up behind her, to press his lips against her soft neck, to rub his raging erection against her round bottom.

Hallie.

He didn't realize he'd spoken her name out loud until she turned. "Baz. What're you doing here?"

The husky words triggered another surge of lust. He fisted his hands to keep from touching her. "I wanted to talk to you." His voice was husky, too.

She turned back to the table. "Not a good time. I'm working."

He moved closer and peered at the creature under her gloved hands. "That's a bat."

"He broke a bone in his wing. I've splinted and taped it."

"You're treating a rodent?"

"The family lives in my attic. He must have flown into something in the dark."

"Bats are supposed to be able to see at night."

"Maybe he didn't read the fine print in his contract."

He smiled. He'd forgotten her delicious humor.

He placed his hands on either side of her rib cage.

"Don't," she said, as if she meant it.

Baz stilled. She was still mad.

About A Baby

by

Ann Yost

The Outlaws of Eden, Maine

About A Baby

Cover Art by *RJ Morris*

The Wild Rose Press, Inc.
PO Box 708
Adams Basin, NY 14410-0708
Visit us at www.thewildrosepress.com

Publishing History
First Champagne Rose Edition, 2010
Second Champagne Rose Edition, 2016
Print ISBN 978-1-5092-1328-3
Digital ISBN 978-1-5092-1329-0

The Outlaws of Eden, Maine
Published in the United States of America

Dedication

To my own babies,
Adam, Ben, and Emily,
who grew up perfectly in spite of me.

Chapter One

Basil Outlaw stopped at Eden's only traffic light and watched last minute shoppers hurry along the sidewalks of Main Street, heads bent against the falling snow. Shop fronts were outlined in white twinkle lights. Evergreen wreaths with red ribbons, a fund-raiser for the Eden High Band, decorated most front doors.

The Presbyterian and Methodist churches, each constructed with Maine's indigenous pearl-gray fieldstone, still faced one another kitty-corner on Main and Cedar Streets like a couple of teenage boys marking their territory. Callaghan's Market still anchored the small business district.

Nothing much had changed since he left twenty years ago, but he wasn't here to see the little town or even his family. He was here to make restitution to the sunny, glass-is-half-full, golden-eyed woman whose hopes he'd crushed one year ago tonight.

It was Christmas Eve, the perfect time for making things right. Just ask Ebenezer Scrooge.

Of course the old guy had been able to do it with some coins, a goose, and a trio of bad dreams. It would cost Baz a whole lot more to re-capture the trust of Hallie Scott. He felt a familiar emptiness in his chest as his fingers tightened on the steering wheel of the rented Malibu.

He was ready to give her exactly what she wanted:

marriage and a baby. He just hoped he wasn't too late.

****

Tiny ice crystals melted on Dr. Halliday Scott's red wool coat as she dawdled along the path between her snug apartment above the Outlaw Veterinary Clinic and the Outlaw family's massive stone house.

She wanted to savor the magical night.

In just a few minutes, all but one of the Outlaw family members would gather around a festive table to enjoy their traditional Christmas Eve supper of clam chowder. It was only because of Basil Outlaw's absence that Hallie had a place in the Outlaw family circle. The man who had filled her heart and crushed her dreams a year earlier was the means of giving her the best Christmas of her life. Just one of life's little ironies.

She sucked in the winter air and took a moment to compose herself. The disappointment that lived inside her would never completely go away, but she'd learned how to work around that. She was happy in Eden. She caught a snowflake on her tongue and mounted the back porch steps to the brightly lit house.

The door swung open, and a familiar wail nearly eclipsed a frantic masculine voice. "Thank God you're here." Cameron Outlaw grabbed her by the wrist and pulled her into the kitchen. "We have a crisis."

Hallie couldn't help smiling at Baz's brother. Surely, the crisis centered on Cam's small, determined daughter, Daisy. She was right.

Another high-pitched squeal and a miniature battering ram hit her at the same time. Hallie caught the distraught five-year-old up in her arms.

"I'm not gonna be in the pageant!"

"What's the problem, kitten?"

Tears streamed out of baby blue eyes and rolled down chubby pink cheeks.

"They can't make me do it. I'm not gonna be a stupid shepherd."

Hallie looked at Cam who shrugged helplessly.

"She's not supposed to be a shepherd," Hallie reminded him. "I talked with the choir director. It was all arranged."

Cam arched a dark eyebrow. Hallie noticed, not for the first time, how much he resembled his tall, dark-haired, broad-shouldered brother. And how little. Basil's rugged face was an unfocused version of Cam's well-defined features. The elder brother carried more muscle on his large form and his hard, cold, gunmetal gray eyes contrasted with Cam's sparkling blue gaze. Cam's openness, outgoing nature, and commitment to family and community underscored Baz's isolation. The latter truly was an island. It had started with the parents' bitter divorce that split the family all those years ago.

Cam's deep voice jerked her back to the present. "The choir director said she was sorry, but somebody's cousin came in from out of town and Daisy's costume was given to her by mistake."

"Get it back," squawked Daisy from her perch in Hallie's arms. "I practiced being a angel. I want to be a angel!"

"What costume did they have left?" Hallie asked.

"Shepherd," howled Daisy, throwing her head back like a dog baying at the moon. "Dirty, brown shepherd. It's a boy costume."

Hallie swallowed a smile. Even if she could have

retrieved the angel costume, Daisy needed to learn to compromise. Her doting father and extended family indulged her on every point, and the little girl had become a tyrant. But she was an intelligent tyrant.

Hallie tried logic. "Is it a boy job to be an animal doctor?"

"You mean a vet?" Daisy quieted for a moment.

Hallie had caught her attention. "Yes. Can only boys be vets?"

Daisy's eyes widened. "No. You're not a boy."

"That's right. And not all shepherds are boys.

Shepherds take care of animals, just like vets do. In fact," said Hallie, warming to her theme, "I bet you could take Wilbur with you." She glanced at the pot-bellied pig lolling on his Miss Piggy pillow. "He can play a lamb who has come to see Baby Jesus."

"Couldn't I take Wilbur if I was a angel?" Hallie bit back a smile. A person had to be on her toes to outwit Daisy Outlaw. "No. Sheep need a shepherd to take care of them. Angels have a different job."

The little girl appeared to weigh the advantages of taking her beloved pet versus the disappointment of the drab costume. "Okay," she said, at last. Hallie breathed a sigh of relief and let Daisy slide to the ground. The child tugged her hand.

"Come on, Hallie. Let's get Wilbur ready."

"Not so fast, princess," said her father. "Eat some supper first. Then we'll give Wilbur the bad news. I don't know how much he'll like hoofing it to the church in ten-degree weather. Besides, his show will be on soon." Wilbur was devoted to cable cooking shows. His favorites were reruns from The Galloping Gourmet. On the screen, the dish of the night was a bacon and spinach quiche. Bacon. Hallie grinned.

Maybe Wilbur wouldn't mind missing this particular show.

Cam's eyes found Hallie. "Think Wilbur will behave?"

"As well as the golden retriever playing a camel."

Cam hugged her.

"I hope I'm not interrupting." The familiar voice struck Hallie's nerves like a sledgehammer hitting a china teacup. Its deep, rough timbre stripped her of a year's worth of hard-won peace. She blinked back tears as pain, sharp and unexpected, ripped through her.

The snake had invaded paradise.

Despite his promises, Baz had returned to Eden.

Hallie forced herself to remain calm as she turned to look into fog-colored eyes. As always, his gaze acted on her like a match to dry tinder. In the past, he'd kindled desire. Now that longing was diluted by pain and anger. And fear. What the heck was he doing here? Maybe if she closed her eyes he'd disappear. She tried it.

He didn't.

Instead, his hard gaze skewered her like a fish on the end of a spear. She noticed new lines radiating out from his eyes, and her heart twisted.

He looked older, she thought, tired and more remote than ever, though, unfortunately, no less devastating. Had he missed her? She rejected the idea immediately. She'd never forget the pea-green color of his face when she'd proposed. He wasn't here about that.

A good thing, too, because it was too late. Much too late.

Her fingers itched to touch him, though. She wanted to smooth the severe planes and ridges of his dark face. She jammed her hands in the pockets of her forest green corduroy dress and ground her teeth.

Twelve months, thousands of miles, and a new life, and yet nothing had changed.

No, that was wrong. Everything had changed.

Cam stepped between them like a boxing referee. "I didn't get a chance to tell you, Hal. Dad invited Baz for Christmas." He spoke as though a visit from his brother was a routine occurrence instead of what it really was: the return of the Prodigal Son.

The question was, why had he come back?

She'd like to believe it had nothing to do with her, but the prickles on the back of her neck and the hollow in the pit of her stomach said otherwise.

Regardless of his agenda, his presence here would disrupt her calm, pleasant life. It already had.

Her Christmas spirit turned as dry and brittle as a discarded Christmas tree. She flashed on the Charlie Brown tree she'd decorated for him last year.

Afterwards they made love on the thick gray carpet in his condo. And then she'd asked the fatal question.

"Aren't you glad to see me, Halliday?"

The deep voice resonated in her lower body as it was meant to, and she lowered her lashes trying to mask both her involuntary arousal and her sudden, violent anger.

He'd promised to stay away.

Her eyes narrowed on him. It was another Christmas Eve. Was he planning to cut her legs out from under her again? She had to remind herself that, when all was said and done, this was his home, not hers. She'd taken a terrible risk coming to Eden.

If it came to a showdown, his family would pick Baz.

She had no choice but to suck it up.

"Welcome, home," she said, tightly. "Merry Christmas."

His eyes met hers; she read the apology in them.

Okay, so he hadn't shown up just to hurt her. It wouldn't matter in the end. Not if he decided to stick around. Suddenly, she had to know. "How long are you staying?"

Something flickered in the slate-colored eyes. "That depends. I have some unfinished business to attend to. You look thinner. Have you been ill?"

She'd looked just fine a few minutes ago. "No.

But thanks for asking."

She watched a muscle work in his jaw. It should have given her some satisfaction, but it didn't. Hallie didn't like being cruel. Not even when someone deserved it.

The doorbell echoed in the big front hall. A moment later the rest of the family burst into the room amid boisterous laughter. Hallie's stomach tightened.

It was Norman Rockwell time.

****

Ezra Cobbs, with his thick white hair and his kind, crinkly eyes, looked every inch the caring country pastor. If he had a failing it was his sermons. They were relentlessly uninspiring.

Tonight he managed to make even the Christmas Story tedious.

Hallie focused on the candles reflected in the arched windows and the magic of the evening service.

7

Wilbur was drugged on sugar cookies. She heard his faint snore in between Pastor Cobbs's words. The golden retriever, after bestowing a tongue bath on the plastic baby Jesus, had curled up next to the manger.

Hallie gazed out at the pews from her seat in the small choir loft behind the pulpit. Over the past year, she'd come to see the familiar faces with a sense of security. Eden had begun to feel like the home she'd always wanted.

Jolene Thompson, owner of the Pink Poodle Beauty Salon, sat next to Hallie in the choir stall. Jo was one of Hallie's two close friends. She spoke under cover of the rambling sermon. "Why's the Prodigal Hunk here?"

"Beats me," Hallie whispered back.

"He can't stop looking at you."

She knew. His intense stare was having its usual effect on her even in church. She was so short of breath she'd had to mouth the words to "O Come, O Come, Emmanuel."

Her friend frowned. "I'll bet you a blimpy burger he's here to get you back."

Most of the bets in Rockfield County involved mouth-watering blimpy burgers from Little Joe's Café on High Street.

"I wish he'd just crawl back to where he came from."

"He came from here," Jo reminded her.

Hallie made a face.

"It took a year but maybe he finally realized he missed you."

Hallie dismissed that possibility. "He never called or wrote. Why would he just turn up on Christmas Eve?

That doesn't make sense."

Jo shrugged. "Who can understand men?"

"Not me. That's why I work with animals."

Pastor Cobbs nodded at the octogenarian organist who launched into "Angels We Have Heard on High." As usual she chose the key of C. The old lady was a purist and didn't believe in sharps and flats.

Hallie stood with the rest of her friends and neighbors. She tried to lose herself in the music, but the heat of Baz's stare seemed to melt her core. She shot him a glance. He was pretending to sing, too. She'd have laughed if she hadn't felt so nauseous. She wanted to shout at him. Why are you here?

Hallie glanced at Baz's father. Dr. Jesse Outlaw's grin outshone all the candles in the little church. The man was thrilled to have his eldest son home at last. Hallie swallowed around a lump in her throat. She couldn't begrudge her boss his happiness. She reminded herself that Baz's visit wouldn't last more than a few days. Seventy-two hours at the most. Surely she could tough that out.

"He's still looking at you," Jolene whispered, as Pastor Cobbs began his long, long benediction.

"Yeah."

Hallie wished she could ignore her instincts. She just knew Baz's agenda had something to do with her.

"Maybe it's just a family reunion," Jolene whispered. "After all, it's Christmastime."

Hallie smiled at her friend. Jolene was right.

She could be worrying over nothing. The organist's fingers struck a series of white notes and the congregation began to sing. Hallie felt the warmth of Baz's intense focus. Against her will, her eyes found

9

his. When he winked her stomach somersaulted.

Joy to the World.

****

It was after nine when Daisy finally agreed to let Hallie tuck her into the four-poster white bed with the Petunia Pig comforter.

"Remember who's coming tonight," Hallie whispered.

"Uncle Baz?"

Hallie wrinkled her nose then tried to turn the sour expression into a smile. The man-who-never wanted-to-be-a-dad had already made a warm impression on his niece.

"I was talking about Santa. Sweet dreams, Sugar Plum. See you in the morning."

Hallie had already declined an invitation to join the family by the massive stone fireplace in the old-fashioned parlor. She slipped down the back staircase, grabbed her coat, and crossed the snow-covered yard to her apartment. This time she ignored the fluffy flakes. Her mind was intent on two questions: how soon would Basil Outlaw leave Eden and could she hang on until he did?

She reached the renovated carriage house that housed the Outlaw Veterinary Clinic on the first floor and her small apartment above it. As she climbed the outside steps, Hallie thought about how much she loved her cozy home with its low ceilings and dormer windows. She always watched the sunrise, fascinated by the notion that hers were among the first eyes to greet the dawn. It was one advantage of living on the East Coast.

She'd decorated her furnished apartment with

Maine handicrafts, including a blueberry basket, seafarer quilt, a stained glass hanging, and a wooden sculpture. She'd grown attached to the people of Eden and their pets. She even loved the small family of bats that nested in the attic overhead.

Eden had become the home she'd always wanted. The tightness in her chest that she'd felt all evening threatened to choke her. Baz held all the cards. It was his family and his hometown. Thank God he'd never live here. His career as head of the large animal department of veterinary science at Pacific University was prestigious, lucrative, and it gave him a chance to supervise exciting new research. He'd never trade that for a small town veterinary practice. The thought calmed her.

He wouldn't come back here. Not permanently.

That was precisely why he'd gotten her the job with his father. He wanted a five-thousand-mile buffer zone between them. She remembered his words: "It's a rural veterinary practice, perfectly suited to you."

It galled her to take anything from the man, but she had needed a job and fast.

"Your dad might not hire me."

"Shit," he'd replied. "Jesse Outlaw would rob Fort Knox if I asked him to. And anyway, he'd be lucky to get you. There's a bonus. You'll never have to see me again."

Gloom settled on Hallie as she flopped on the worn chintz sofa and stared at the twinkling lights on the Christmas tree she'd had such fun decorating.

Was it possible he just wanted to reconcile with his dad? When they'd been together, she'd been after him to do just that. Had he finally realized Jesse wouldn't live forever?

She was probably making herself crazy about nothing. Hallie sighed, got up, and headed for the postage stamp-sized kitchen. She'd eaten very little of the Christmas Eve feast. She figured she'd grab a glass of eggnog and hit the sheets. Just as she pulled open the refrigerator door, something dropped out of the sky and tangled in her hair.

She shrieked and brushed it away with her fingers.

It was warm. It was breathing.

She gaped at the now-grounded flying missile.

It was a baby bat. And it was hurt.

Chapter Two

Cameron, Baz, and their father gathered in the latter's comfortable, book-lined study. The familiar odor of cherry-scented pipe tobacco triggered a flood of memories for the elder son. It had been a sanctuary for his dad in the old days when Evelyn was on the warpath. It had become a sanctuary for Baz, too. He hadn't thought about it in twenty years.

Not consciously, but now he wondered if his decision to go into veterinary science had been tied up in his memories of this room.

Jesse handed out brandies.

"I'm glad to have you home, son." The older man kept his voice calm and low-key, but his fingers shook. Shame clawed at Baz. He'd resented his dad in proportion to how much he'd missed him, and he'd punished them both by staying away all these years.

He'd have continued to stay away if it hadn't been for Hallie.

Cam was studying him. The brothers corresponded occasionally, mostly because of Cam's efforts. Baz knew the younger man wanted harmony in the family and peace for their father.

"Don't take this the wrong way," Cam said, "but I saw the way Hallie reacted to you tonight. I'd like to know your agenda."

Jealousy exploded inside Baz. Fortunately, he'd

had lots of practice concealing his emotions. "You're her protector?"

"If necessary."

"Cameron," Jesse intervened, "this is Basil's home."

Cam's blue eyes didn't waver. "It's Hallie's home, too. I don't want her upset. She doesn't deserve that."

Baz wondered how much Hallie had told his family about their former relationship. Probably not much. For all her openness, she was private about certain matters. He suspected she'd kept quiet about the painful circumstances of their break up.

"When she got here last year," Cam continued, "she was as fragile as an abused puppy. She's in good shape now, and I'd like to see her stay that way."

Baz's heavy brows met between his eyes. "I'm not here to hurt her."

Cam stared at him. "Why are you here?"

Baz shrugged. It was no secret. "I want her back."

"As your lab assistant?"

Baz met his brother's eyes. "As my lover. As my wife."

Cam's eyebrows rose practically to his hairline, and Jesse choked on his brandy.

"Jesus," Cam muttered. "I guess that's blunt enough."

"We discussed marriage last year," Baz went on. He wasn't sure why he was explaining it. For some reason he wanted both his father and brother to know. "I wasn't ready then. Now I am."

"It took you a year to figure it out?"

More like a couple of weeks. But he'd been unavoidably detained during the last eleven months.

14

He'd been married to someone else.

That story he didn't plan to tell Cam. He didn't plan to tell Hallie, either. At least, not until they were married or she was pregnant. Whichever came first.

Baz just shrugged his big shoulders.

"Your timing sucks. She's just started dating the sheriff."

The pain was swift and it left him reeling. "What sheriff?"

"Jake Langley. Single dad with cute twins. He's had his eye on her for months."

"How interested is she?" The question tumbled out of his mouth.

"You'll have to ask her."

Suddenly he was on his feet. The need to see her, talk to her, touch her, was overwhelming.

"Hang on just a minute, Baz," Jesse said. "I want to tell Cameron the rest of our plans."

Baz waited impatiently, and Cam's eyes narrowed as Jesse spoke. When he'd finished Cam spoke. "I know I can't stop you, but I think it's a mistake. If you force her hand, she'll leave.

Underneath that sweet, Rebecca-of-Sunnybrook-Farm exterior there's a spine of steel."

Baz scowled at him. "I'm not going to force her."

Cam got to his feet. "One more thing. Hallie's been damn good to this family. If you hurt her again, bro, you'll have to answer to me."

Baz had to admire the man's protectiveness, but he didn't have to like it. "If I hurt her again, I'll have to answer to myself."

Minutes later he shrugged into his windbreaker and headed for Hallie's apartment. Christ, it was cold. He'd bet the temperature was in the single digits. It had stopped snowing, but an occasional flake drifted out of the trees. He caught one on his tongue. He realized he hadn't seen snow in years.

Not that he'd missed it. Who, in their right mind, wanted to live in an icebox?

He felt a flare of excitement as he climbed stairs outside the old carriage house. He wanted to bury his hands in the soft brown curls that framed her sweet face. God, he'd missed her scent. He'd missed her golden laugh. He'd missed everything.

His palms felt clammy as he balled his fist to knock on the door. He felt like a teenager. He felt alive. When no one answered, he knocked again. Was she asleep? He peered through the sheer curtain.

The living room was empty, and the door to the bedroom stood ajar. She wasn't there.

Jealousy slammed into him, along with a tearing fear. Was she out with someone else? Was she sharing Christmas Eve with the damn sheriff and his "cute twins?"? He bolted down the steps and checked the small parking lot. The green Jeep she'd driven from L.A. was parked on the blacktop that served as the clinic's parking lot. There was a light on inside the clinic, too.

Baz tried the doorknob and found it unlocked.

He shook his head. Eden was a small town, but there was medication stored in there. A bell jingled overhead. He noticed the small fir tree decorated with dog biscuits in one corner of the waiting room.

The sight of the spindly tree sent an arrow into Baz's heart. It looked just like the one she'd bought last year. He flashed on the way it had felt to be folded into her tight warmth and he hardened, instantly.

Light poured through the open treatment room door. He stopped for a minute to admire her silhouette. She was short with gentle curves. While they'd been apart, he'd forgotten how small she was.

He'd remembered her passion, her gentle teasing, her great big heart. His heart raced at the sight of her slender neck, her high, gently curved breasts, her flat stomach, and her shapely legs.

Baz stepped into the room. He barely noted the gleaming white cabinets, cats-and-dogs wallpaper, and the life-cycle-of-a-heartworm poster. She was bent over a treatment table, obviously deep in concentration. The curls, light brown and shot with golden highlights, as always, seemed to have a life of their own. He couldn't see her soft lips, but he knew they'd be slightly parted, her teeth unconsciously grazing her tongue. He inhaled her unique scent, a mixture of peaches and vanilla and summer flowers.

He wanted to come up behind her, to press his lips against her soft neck, to rub his raging erection against her round bottom.

Hallie.

He didn't realize he'd spoken her name out loud until she turned. "Baz. What're you doing here?"

The husky words triggered another surge of lust. He fisted his hands to keep from touching her. "I wanted to talk to you." His voice was husky, too.

She turned back to the table. "Not a good time. I'm working."

He moved closer and peered at the creature under her gloved hands. "That's a bat."

"He broke a bone in his wing. I've splinted and

taped it."

"You're treating a rodent?"

"The family lives in my attic. He must have flown into something in the dark."

"Bats are supposed to be able to see at night."

"Maybe he didn't read the fine print in his contract."

He smiled. He'd forgotten her delicious humor.

He placed his hands on either side of her rib cage.

"Don't," she said, as if she meant it.

Baz stilled. She was still mad. Well, hell. He guessed she was entitled to a little payback. A lot of payback.

"That creature's loaded with bacteria and germs. And probably rabies."

She twisted to look at him, and he lost himself in her golden eyes. "He was hurt," she said.

Tenderness caught him in the chest, and he could barely breathe. He couldn't believe he'd let her go, that he'd waited a year to reclaim her. He damned himself for hurting her. He'd kill anyone

who hurt her now.

He studied her small straight nose and the long, sandy brown lashes that fringed the hazel eyes flecked with gold. He wanted to kiss each faint freckle on her elfin face.

He slipped his hand under the short fall of her hair and against the soft skin of her neck. She protested, but she couldn't control a shiver.

Relief washed through him. At least that hadn't changed. At least he could still make her want him. It was a start.

"I need to give him a rabies shot."

A rabies shot? Oh. The bat. He frowned. "This isn't a good idea."

"It's a good idea for me. I like saving creatures."

He remembered. She'd saved him last year.

She'd coaxed him out of the straitjacket he'd created for himself. She'd led him toward warmth and light, but she'd done it too fast. He couldn't keep up, and when she needed him, he couldn't step up.

He rolled up his sleeves and pulled on a pair of gloves.

Hallie showed no surprise or objection to his cooperation. They'd worked well together before, both in the lab and in his kitchen.

And under his tree.

Baz held the quivering creature while she gave him the injection. He watched as she spread a clean soft towel inside a wire cage that was clearly meant to accommodate the invalid. He hesitated.

"I want him comfortable while he recuperates," she said, reading his mind.

He scooped up the bat and laid him in the cage while feelings raged inside him. She was a nurturer.

Naturally she wanted a child. He contemplated his raging erection. He'd be more than happy to start working on that project tonight. But it was too soon.

He knew it was too soon. He'd need a cold shower tonight. A long one.

"It's late," he said, as she turned on a small nightlight and closed the door. "Christmas morning comes early."

She said nothing as she flicked off the lights in the waiting room and locked the door.

"'Night, Hallie." He leaned in fast, brushing his

lips across her cheek.

"Baz?"

He held very still. Maybe it wasn't too soon.

"Yeah?"

"Why are you here?"

Fear and confusion laced her voice, and he couldn't help himself. He picked up her hands. "I was wrong last year. I was scared and I blew it. I'm different now. My answer's different now."

"What answer?"

He had to be patient and gentle. She was like the small wounded bat. "When you asked me to marry you, to give you a baby. When I said, no."

"Baz," she started to say. He heard the resistance.

"Let's not talk about it now, Hal. Give it some time."

She shook her head. The curls drifted and swayed in the light from the porch. "Time won't make any difference, Baz. I've changed, too."

"You still respond to me. You still want me."

"I'm not talking about that. I'm talking about your answer. It doesn't matter anymore."

She was trying to tell him something. As always, with relationship stuff, he didn't get it. "Why? Why doesn't it matter, Hallie?"

The golden eyes were unreadable. "The answer may have changed, but the question's changed, too."

She paused. "I want you to have a good holiday with your family. And then I want you to go home."

"I can't do that," he blurted. "Not without you."

She looked defeated.

"It's too late," she said.

He had a feeling she was talking about more than

the hour. "We'll talk tomorrow. You can count on it."

She started up the stairs. "Goodnight, Baz."

He waited for the click that meant she'd locked

her door. He waited until the lights went out in the apartment. Then he stood in the parking lot and gazed up at the darkened windows.

"It's too late."

He fought the familiar cold fist that started to close around his heart. "No," he said, hoarsely.

"Goddammit, no. It's not too late, Hallie Scott. You belong to me, woman. And I'm gonna prove it to you."

****

The testosterone had followed her home, and she couldn't get rid of it. She couldn't stop thinking about the feel of Baz's lean hands on her body, either.

The chemistry between them had survived her best efforts to kill it. Good grief. Hallie collapsed onto her single bed and beat her fist into the pillow. A whole year's worth of effort wiped out in a single evening. He was right, she still wanted him. She was cursed. She'd just have to fight the desire that pulsed through her whenever she saw him. Thank God she no longer loved him.

That would have been much harder to fight.

****

By morning, the snow had stopped falling, but the day qualified as a white Christmas because of the fresh layer of clean snow over the old.

Hallie pulled on a red sweater. The image of Rudolph filled up the mirror. Probably just as well.

The antlers and the big red nose distracted from the bags under her eyes.

She still couldn't believe what Baz had said last night. I'm here to get you back. She ran a brush through her curls and applied some lip-gloss. She'd stopped wearing any other kind of makeup. Her hair was too long, too. She'd always worn it about chin length, but it looked much shorter because of the frolicking curls. Lately she'd been too busy to get it cut, and it now brushed her shoulders. She made a face at herself. She looked like a waterfall. She lifted her chin.

"All you have to do is say no," she muttered. It sounded simple enough. The trouble was the concept didn't take into account the way Baz's presence always scrambled her senses. That was why he'd come back, of course. They'd only been together that one night, but it had been like an explosion in a chemistry lab.

He'd missed the off-the-charts sex.

Or maybe he'd missed his friend. The first five months, three weeks, and six days of their relationship had consisted of her coaxing him to go on hikes, to movies and concerts and volunteer activities like the Orange County Spay and Neuter Day.

What had he been doing for friendship and passion for the past twelve months?

Probably better not to know.

She got to the house in time to watch Daisy and Wilbur open their stockings. Wilbur's gifts included an Emeril DVD and a box of truffles. Daisy's included a small, pink stuffed mother pig with half a dozen tiny piglets attached to her underside with snaps. Hallie had seen the toy in a shop in Bangor, and she couldn't resist.

The Outlaws, probably because there had been no mother at the helm, conducted the gift opening like a free-for-all. Twenty minutes of shrieks, ripping paper, howls of delight and yelled "thanks yous" was followed by ten minutes of scrunching the wrapping paper into missiles and flinging them at each other.

Late in the morning, the adults sat on the floor and helped Daisy set up her new Barbie Dream House, a gift from her prodigal uncle. The generosity of the gift didn't surprise Hallie. Baz may have convinced himself that he didn't need a family, but, underneath, he was a warm and generous man. He seemed pleased with Daisy's pleasure in her gift.

"There may be a slight problem," Cam said, rocking back on his heels. "You've got Space Station Barbie and Mermaid Barbie. Neither of them needs a fully furnished dream house."

"The house isn't for the Barbies," Daisy said, seriously. "It's for Wilbur Junior and his babies." She held up Hallie's gift, a plush pig with piglets attached.

"You're naming the pig, Wilbur?" Hallie was touched.

Baz frowned. "You know it's a mommy pig, right?"

"I know."

"Maybe you'd like to give it a girl name."

Daisy's blonde curls danced as she shook her head.

"Hallie said girls can be shepherds and vets and everything. That means boys can do everything, too. So Wilbur can be a mom."

Hallie nodded, gravely.

"I see your point. Welcome to your new home, Mommy Wilbur."

The family patriarch seemed restless as the day wore on. He kept disappearing into his study then returning and joining one or the other of the groups.

Whenever he was in the parlor, though, he couldn't take his eyes off his eldest son. Hallie recognized the happiness in his gaze, but she saw something underneath it. Concern. Her heart ached for the older man. He was, no doubt, anticipating the moment Baz would leave and wondering whether they'd be apart another twenty years.

Guilt slithered through Hallie.

Jesse's fear was Hallie's dream.

Baz was sitting cross-legged on the floor. He looked up, caught her eye, and grinned. Then he rang the bicycle bell a couple of times. Daisy catapulted across the room and threw her thin arms around his neck. His big hands came around her back to support her. Hallie looked away quickly as longing, pain, anger, and despair tumbled through her. The emotions were like clothes in a dryer set on spin cycle.

The Christmas she'd awaited with anticipation had turned into a mockery of what might have been. She'd worked hard to let the disappointment go, to keep from blaming him. His rejection had been prudent under the circumstances, and her infertility was not his fault. But gazing at Baz with Daisy, she imagined him as a father. The picture looked right, but there was no place in it for Hallie.

If he stuck around Eden long enough, she'd tell him that.

The snapshot looked blurry; Hallie realized she was blinking back tears. Daisy bounded over to give her a hug, too. "Thank you for my presents, Hallie.

Wanna play poker? Uncle Baz gived me a special pack of cards."

Poker and a Barbie Dream House. She had to give him credit. He'd disappointed Hallie but found the right answers for his small niece.

"Absolutely," Hallie said.

Soon nearly everybody had joined in. Hallie tried to enjoy the playful teasing between the siblings. Baz fit in remarkably well considering he'd been out of their lives for so long. She was relieved, though, when Asia stepped into the parlor and asked for some help with the gravy.

"I happen to be a world-class gravy maker," she said, jumping to her feet. "Lead the way."

The big, old-fashioned kitchen smelled like roasting turkey and pumpkin pie.

"The gravy's all done," Asia confessed. "I thought you might like a little break from the family."

Asia was the one person in whom Hallie had confided everything. She hugged the wiry housekeeper.

"I b'lieve I'll go on upstairs and put my feet up for twenty minutes. If you need something to do, you can keep an eye on the bird."

Hallie leaned against one of the high countertops and admired the dark green tile on the floor, the granite countertops, and the freshly painted white cabinets. She'd helped Jesse and Asia make decorating decisions when they decided to renovate in here last summer, and she thought it had come together very well.

She looked longingly out the window at her apartment. She would have gladly skipped the turkey for a little privacy, but there was no way she could do that without creating a stir.

She was stuck in the big, warm house, and she'd be forced to eat the perfectly prepared holiday meal.

She grinned at her own foolishness.
"Poor me."

Chapter Three

"Cam must have bought the biggest tree in Maine."

Hallie felt his presence in the room, and she shivered. That rough, husky voice acted like a four hundred-degree oven on her senses. He made her melt.

It was the voice, combined with the memories.

He'd spoken like that when he'd told her in specific, excruciating detail just exactly how he was going to make her climax.

He'd done it, too.

And then he'd told her just exactly what to do to him.

Another tremor skittered up her spine.

"It's a big difference from last year," he added.

You have no idea how big a difference.

"Absolutely."

He stood in the doorway, one big shoulder resting against the lintel. She could see the memories in his gray eyes. That first kiss by the shabby Charlie Brown tree had been tender and sweet. A friend's kiss.

The second kiss dropped her to her knees.

Him, too.

She'd whispered his name, and he'd tried to warn her.

"It'll change everything."

"I know."

The sexual assault was so complete she never had a

chance to change her mind. Not that she'd wanted to. She remembered the way he probed her mouth, wielding his tongue with the precision of a surgeon. He made her sweat and shiver. He made her moan and writhe.

And that was just the kiss.

Inspired, she slid her hands up under his polo shirt, sifted her fingers through the soft hair on his hard chest, and tweaked the flat male nipples.

Eventually she moved south, down to his flat stomach. His breathing roughened.

"If you move your hand one inch lower, Hallie, there's no going back."

She held his gaze and moved her hand. "I don't want to go back."

Then he was opening his pants, and she was cupping the thick, throbbing male flesh. She remembered kissing him there.

Suddenly the world turned upside down. She was on her back alarmed by the expression on his grim face.

"Are you all right?"

"I can't wait any more," he'd gasped.

It had seemed as though he'd gotten rid of their clothing and sheathed himself in a condom all in one fluid motion. Then he was riding her, moving in her, whispering those shocking things in her ear. Soon her attention was focused solely on the sensations he drew from her with his body and his hands. Her breath grew short, and her insides coiled, tighter and tighter until there was nothing to do but explode, nothing to do but convulse, nothing to do but listen to her name shouted as he buried his face inside her shoulder.

If life was made up of moments, that one had been

perfect. At least until a short while later when it had all gone wrong, when she'd asked the wrong question and he'd handed her a one-way ticket out of his life.

Asia's heavy footsteps sounded on the backstairs. The gray-haired housekeeper, clad in one of her interchangeable cotton housedresses protected with a red-and-green-checked apron, greeted them both with a smile. "Time to eat."

Christmas dinner was a feast of turkey and baked ham, sour-cream scalloped potatoes,cranberry potatoes, cranberry sauce, candied yams, pecan pie, pumpkin pie, and homemade ice cream. Naturally everyone ate too much.

"Asia, you've outdone yourself," Cameron complained. "I can't move."

"That's too bad, son," said Jesse, "because Asia's heading out to her daughter's place. As I see it, you and Lucy and I will be cleaning the kitchen."

Baz's chuckle gave Hallie a start. She realized she'd heard it more in the past twenty-four hours than she had in the months they spent together last year. Something had happened to the taciturn loner she'd known in L.A. In the year they were apart, he turned human.

"If you three can get up enough firepower to clear the table, Hallie and I will clean up the kitchen," he told his family.

Her jaw dropped. No one else seemed to realize how utterly outrageous the suggestion was. No one else seemed to realize that Basil Outlaw employed a cook and a housekeeper in his sophisticated Los Angeles condo. She'd bet everything she owned that he hadn't washed so much as lifted a fork in his adult life.

"I'll help, Uncle Baz," Daisy offered. She jumped up from her seat and grabbed his hand. "I love to wash dishes."

"I'll bet you do, pal," Baz said.

He must have known that the tender note in his voice shook her.

His pointed look sent an unmistakable message. Look how I've changed. I can be a family man.

She wanted to scream. Instead she got up from the table and headed for the kitchen to perform the fastest KP duty on record.

Baz's insides churned. He'd watched expressions play over Hallie's delicate features all day. He felt her resistance. She wanted him to go home. She didn't understand yet that his home was with her.

He needed to talk to her, to explain, but the time never seemed right.

And time was running out.

The last thing he wanted to do was blindside her. This was his opportunity, while they stood, hip to hip with soapsuds up her arms and him wielding a dishtowel. He needed to talk, and all he could seem to do was watch Rudolph's antlers move up and down with every dish she scrubbed. He'd spent the day in a state of semi-arousal as he learned the graphic difference between dreaming about Hallie from five thousand miles away and watching her across the room. He squinted at the antlers and realized they'd started to move faster.

Thank God. She was having as much trouble with the proximity as he.

He slid the dishtowel carefully over the blade of the carving knife. Two questions raced through his mind: how the hell could a man explain himself when he had to watch the thrust underneath those damn antlers? And what were the odds of being interrupted if he pulled her down to the green-tiled floor and buried himself in that warm, buttery, tightness?

His slacks pulled hard over his groin, and he bit back a groan even as he heard voices out in the hallway.

The odds were too damn high.

Anyway, he needed to talk to her.

He dropped the dishtowel, stooped to get it. and took the opportunity to readjust himself in a desperate and useless attempt to find some relief. If he didn't get this settled soon and make his way back into her bed, he'd go mad.

"Baz," Hallie said, without turning around to look at him, "at the risk of repeating myself, I'd really like to know why you're here."

He couldn't stop looking at her soft neck and those shining curls. This was the first time in his life he'd wanted a specific woman. Unable to help himself, he stepped behind her, close enough to brush against her backside.

Hallie jumped and turned around. He heard the harsh crack as the china in her hand met the newly tiled floor. Her eyes had turned into gold half dollars. She was Rudolph caught in the headlights.

She strafed his body with those glowing eyes; her attention was caught and held just below his belly.

He made no effort to conceal his erection. "Not much point trying to hide your effect on me."

He reached for her hand. It was wet and sudsy, but he pressed it against his distended fly, anyway.

He felt her shudder.

"Baz, I…"

"Don't argue." He pulled her into his arms and smoothed one hand down her spine until he was lodged securely between her thighs. He ground himself against her then heard a low rumble and realized it had come from him.

The door to the pantry creaked. In less than two seconds, someone would join them in the room. He let her go.

"If you two are done with KP I'd like to talk with you in the study." Jesse's voice trailed off. Did he feel the unnatural stillness in the room? "Everything all right in here?"

He opened his mouth, unsure whether words would come out. "We're good. We'll be right there."

It wasn't loud enough.

"What's that?"

Hallie bailed him out. "We're almost done, Jesse," she said.

Baz heard the door close on his dad and on his plans. He'd fouled things up now. Instead of using their time alone to put a positive spin on things, he'd jumped her like a wolf at mating time.

Well, hell. It was too late now.

****

Hallie sat on the brown leather sofa in the study next to Cam. She tried to forget the way Baz's body had turned her into warm maple syrup and, instead, to concentrate on figuring out why she was included in what was clearly a family conference.

"Hallie," Jesse said, "I'll get right to the point.

I've booked a cruise. My doc says it's time to slow down and I've chosen to do it in the Caribbean. I'll be gone three months."

Hallie's heart contracted. "Are you ill?"

"Just tired. The thing is you'll need some help while I'm gone."

She didn't like the way this was going. "I can handle it alone."

"Not the large animals. It's too much for any one doc. That's why I hired you." He grinned at her. "And you've been better than I could have imagined.

The good news is, Baz has agreed to take a sabbatical from his job. He'll help you with the clinic while I'm gone."

There was no way she could refuse to work with his son, and he knew it. Jesse Outlaw was nobody's fool.

"I know you're happy to have your son back in Eden." she chose her words carefully, "but I'd like to remind you that Baz is a researcher. He hasn't been as near to a cow as a glass of milk in years."

Two of the men chuckled. The other watched her with stone gray eyes.

"It'll come back to him," Jesse assured her.

"Kind of like riding a bicycle. In any case, you're in charge."

"I'm in charge?"

"You sound surprised."

"Have you ever worked with your son? He's always in charge." Anger surged through her voice but she was helpless to stop it. "He would have told Wellington how to fight the battle of Waterloo."

"You know more about running a general practice clinic than I do, Halliday," Baz said, with what she knew was false modesty. "I'll learn at your knee."

Hallie shook her head. "Why? Why would you want to do this? You've got tenure at the university and you're heading for some real breakthroughs.

Why would you want to interrupt your career?" She knew she sounded hysterical, but it was only because she felt hysterical. She could see her entire life circling the drain.

"The tenure means I don't have to worry about my career. It'll be there when I return. I figured it was about time I did something for my dad. Beyond that, I'd like a chance to get to know my family."

Her eyes narrowed on him. Who could argue with a man getting to know his family?

"Baz is doing this as a favor to me. It's temporary. There's no need for you to feel threatened, Hallie." Jesse smiled at her, but there was a glimmer of anxiety in his gray eyes. "You know you're like my own daughter."

Yeah. She was like a daughter, but she wasn't a daughter. This wasn't the first time in her life she'd been hit with the truth of the adage 'blood is thicker than water.' She'd learned the lesson well. She had two choices here. She could work with Baz, or she could hit the road.

She stared at the man whose eyes had never left her face. "Let me get one thing straight. This is really about helping your father and getting to know your family. It has nothing to do with me."

Baz didn't smile. "It has everything to do with you," he said, quietly, unselfconsciously. "I told you last night. I want to marry you and have a family."

Her jaw snapped shut. She didn't say another word. There was nothing left to say in front of Jesse and Cam.

Later, when they were alone, she'd talk to him. She'd tell him not to waste his time in Eden.

She'd tell him the heartbreaking truth. It was too late.

Much, much too late.

"This is your home, Hallie," Cam said. "If working with Baz will be too hard on you, tell us and we'll make other arrangements."

She tried to smile at her friend. It was a wonderful offer, but she couldn't ask the man to turn on his newly rediscovered brother any more than she could ask Jesse to withdraw his invitation to his long, lost son. She could leave, or she could view this as a combat tour of duty.

"It's only for three months, right?"

The other two nodded. Cam's eyes were grave.

She turned to Baz. "I'll do it as long as our relationship is strictly professional."

He nodded much too quickly. Did he think he could change her mind? Probably. Half of her thought that, too. "I'll do this any way you want," he assured her.

That, of course, was what she was afraid of.

A moment later Hallie excused herself.

"I'll walk you home," Baz offered.

"Hang on, son," Jesse said. "I'd like to have a word with you."

Baz gritted his teeth and watched her leave. She was Hiroshima after the bomb. He needed to start in on damage control.

"A year ago I agreed to hire her no questions asked, and she's fit in just fine. Better than fine.

She's like a daughter to me. She's not happy

you're here, boy. I think it's time you gave me the whole story."

It wouldn't be easy. Baz wasn't used to confiding in anyone, and this business was delicate and complex.

Baz tried to figure out exactly how much to tell. If Jesse and Cam didn't know about her fertility concerns, it wasn't his place to tell them. He spoke slowly. "Last year, out in L.A., we became friends and a bit more."

"I assumed the 'bit more' was what prompted you to get me to offer her a job."

Baz nodded. "We quarreled about something, and it suddenly seemed imperative that we separate."

"Hell, boy. I wasn't born yesterday. Explain the phrase quarreled about something."

He hated to do it. He knew it made Hallie look desperate, and it made him look like a fool.

"She wanted to get married and start a family."

Jesse lifted a craggy eyebrow. He not only had the same gray eyes as his eldest son, their faces were similar, bold and square with blunt-cut features.

"I thought I didn't want that. I turned her down and sent her to you. It took about a month for me to admit my mistake to myself. By then, I'd married someone else."

"The hell you say!"

"She was a cocktail waitress, young and in trouble. Her ex-boyfriend's a mobster named Jimmy Dinari. He wanted the baby, and she needed the protection of marriage."

"Jesus, Basil."

"It was always going to be temporary. The divorce was final two weeks ago. Nicole and the boy are well provided for, and I'm free again."

"Have you told Hallie this?"

He rubbed the back of his neck with the palm of his hand. Jesus, he was tired.

"In a strange sort of way I did it because of her. She was always rescuing wounded creatures."

"A wife's not exactly a bird with a damaged wing, son."

"She was only a wife legally. It was a legal arrangement. Hallie will understand that."

Eventually.

"What is your legal responsibility to the child?"

"He's officially my son. I expect to support his mother and him."

Jesse shook his head. "You didn't think this through, Basil. The boy needs more than a monthly check. He needs a daddy. Didn't you learn anything from the train wreck of our lives?"

Baz blinked at him. His dad was right. He hadn't thought it through. There was a perpetual cloud of guilt hovering over his head. Worse than that, he missed the child. "I'm not his biological father."

"You're a fool if you think that'll make a difference to him," Jesse said, sadly. "Or to you."

Fury flashed through Baz. "I can't take care of the whole damn world, Dad. I tried to help this girl, but you can't expect me to spend my whole life with her or her son. I want Hallie. And, whether she knows it or not, she wants me."

Cam finally broke his silence. "Will she want you when she discovers you're somebody's daddy?"

He glared at his brother. As a sucker punch, it was effective.

"You'd better think about this long and hard,"

Jesse said. "Hallie's a damn fine woman, smart and kind with a heart as big as the summer sky. Sheriff's interested in her, and he's a good man. Way I see it, your business with this other woman isn't done."

"I want Hallie, Dad."

Jesse shook his head. "Sometimes wantin' is not enough. You have to think about what's good for her."

****

The next morning the clinic was closed, but Jesse found Hallie in her office catching up on paperwork.

"I didn't sleep well last night," he confessed. "I want to make my boy happy, but I couldn't live with myself if I thought I'd driven you away."

She looked into the anxious gray eyes. He and Baz shared the same color, but the expressions were so different. She'd never seen Jesse's eyes hard and rejecting. She wondered what on earth had driven his wife to seek a divorce. Whatever it was, it had done a number on their eldest son.

"I'm not leaving," she assured her boss. "I love the practice and the town and your family."

"You're part of the family. You know that, don't you? You've brought us so much more than your fine veterinary skills. It's thanks to you that my son's back home."

The slight tremor in his voice reminded her of how much this meant to the older man. She was happy for him, for Baz, and the rest of the Outlaws.

The family circle was now complete. She'd had a lot of experience standing on the sidelines of a real family, and she knew its value. She'd do what she could to help Jesse repair the relationship with his son.

Anyway, she could do three months handcuffed.

She hoped.

"You have a wonderful trip," she told him. "I'll see you in the spring."

Jesse Outlaw pulled her into his warm embrace.

****

Hallie, with Daisy in tow, opened the door to Little Joe's and quickly spotted Jolene and Sharon in one of the booths. The women had agreed to celebrate Boxing Day with ice cream sundaes and gossip.

Her friends wanted more details about Basil Outlaw, but they couldn't talk about him in front of his niece. They restricted their conversation to the upcoming Ice Carnival and their fledgling crafts cooperative because of the little girl.

The Ice Carnival had been a yearly tradition in Eden until ten years earlier when the Milland Outlet store closed and half the town became unemployed.

Cameron Outlaw had been an investment banker in Boston. When his wife died, he returned to Eden with his daughter and taken over Central-Western Bank. He was dedicated to creating jobs in Eden County. He'd already re-established the Chamber of Commerce and the ice Carnival. He was also developing plans with a Bangor contractor to build a luxury resort on land adjacent to the casino on the Blackbird Reservation, twenty miles outside of town.

Inspired by Cam's work, Hallie and her friends were working on a cooperative called the Maine Attraction where local crafts people could market their products.

"Lavinia Cattridge has made up some sample sweaters," Jo reported. "I've already ordered the red alpine cardigan and the royal blue pullover with sunflowers. Janine," she added, referring to her sister who lived in Blue Hill, "wants that sweater with the little pastel Easter bunnies on it, and Aunt Irma asked for one of Mrs. Cat's rainbow vests. Have you seen the vests, Hallie? They're gorgeous."

Hallie laughed at her friend's enthusiasm.

"Sounds like your family alone will keep Mrs. Cat busy. By the way, Harry Finley's set to go. He's got samples of his white pine furniture."

"That stuff will sell like hotcakes," Sharon predicted. The innkeeper knew the sleek lines handcrafted by the reclusive Harry would make a big hit with customers. "Oh, and speaking of difficult men, I'm having a heckuva time with the ice sculpture contest. I got a good price from this guy who runs an ice fishing camp up on Lake Takona, but he's giving me a hard time about everything from the size of the blocks, to the time of delivery."

Jolene blinked at her. "Has he seen you? I've never known a man yet who didn't fall under your spell."

Sharon was tall and slim with long auburn hair and big brown eyes. She was competent, too. She ran the Garden of Eden with class and efficiency. But the best thing about her was her friendliness and warmth.

"I agree with Jo," Hallie said. "A little face time with you will turn him around."

"Heck," Jolene added, "you could close the deal with the offer of your lemon meringue pie."

"I'm not sure he's interested in pie or women," Sharon said, with a laugh. "The guy's a Sasquatch."

She looked at Hallie. "Are Molly's sachets going to be ready?"

Molly Whitecloud, the Reservation's midwife, had

asked Hallie to consult and they'd become friends. In her spare time, she and her mother fashioned burlap sachets filled with dried wildflowers from her summer garden.

Hallie realized she hadn't talked with her friend in several days. Not since Baz hit town. His presence had driven out all other thoughts and enjoyments.

"I love Molly," chirped Daisy.

Hallie understood why. Molly was gentle and patient and breathtakingly beautiful. There were shadows behind her indigo eyes, and Hallie suspected she, too, had some secrets.

"I know you do, Kitten. Could you go to the counter and get us more napkins?"

The child hopped off her chair and headed for the counter. Hallie watched her fondly. A minute later she used one of the napkins to wipe a speck of marshmallow off the little girl's cheek.

"Hallie?"

The voice was male, rich and husky. Tall, broad-shouldered, fair-haired Jake Langley flashed a friendly smile at all the females, but the glow in his gaze was just for Hallie.

Chapter Four

"Sam and Lillie are suffering from post-Christmas letdown," Jake said, referring to his six-year-old twins. I'm taking them to the pond. Anyone up for ice skating?"

Daisy's face lit up. "Me! I want to go skating, Sheriff Jake!"

Hallie considered the invitation. It seemed like a good way to entertain the little girl. Hallie loved to skate. She also loved to watch couples arm-in-arm, teenage girls flirting with pimply hockey players and children wobbling over the ice for the first time. The section of the Eden River designated the "skating pond" reminded Hallie of a picture out of Hans Brinker and the Silver Skates.

As an added bonus, she'd buy herself more time away from Baz. "Why don't we meet you there in half an hour?"

"It's a plan." He tipped his hat to Jolene and Sharon.

The four females, along with the rest of the women in the restaurant, enjoyed watching the sheriff's loose-limbed, coordinated amble.

Jake looked good coming and going.

"I know we've been over this before," Jolene said, "but what's wrong with Jake?"

He isn't Baz.

"I can't think of a thing," Hallie said.

"He's so into you, Hallie," Sharon added. "He's such a hunk. And he's got those darling children."

Sharon and Jolene knew that her most recent lab report indicated her odds for conception now hovered in the single digits.

"He is perfect," Hallie murmured. But not for me.

Jake's number one priority was to acquire a mother for his twins. She understood since having children had been her priority, too. But, as much as she liked the sheriff, she didn't care for the idea of being married to solve a problem. She hadn't even realized it until Christmas Eve when she felt the flames of raw passion. For the first time she wondered if Baz had felt that way. She refused to think about the disastrous proposal. It had happened more than a year ago and was completely irrelevant now.

****

The ancient leather chair in Jesse's office creaked as Baz leaned back into it. He'd skimmed the clinic's files and thought he had a pretty good handle on the large animal component of the practice. There were several farms in the area. It was obvious Jesse visited them on a routine basis.

He'd do that, too. No problem.

He rubbed the knot that had formed at the top of his spine. He worked hard in L.A., but he never felt this guilt-roiling tension. He told himself it had nothing to do with the baby he'd left in California. It was just that he was impatient to get Hallie back into his arms and into his bed. After all, it had been nearly a year since he'd been with her. Hell, he'd only been with her once.

It had made quite an impression.

He shook his head. Her proposal had shocked the daylights out of him, and he'd come up with the wrong answer. As a result, he'd lost Hallie, spent a year with the wrong woman, and assumed responsibility for a child.

He must be nuts.

Baz stared at the walls of his dad's office. It was filled with photos of peewee soccer teams, certificates of appreciation, and childish drawings of animals. Jesse hadn't been in his eldest son's life, but that wasn't his fault. He'd obviously done a good job with Cameron and Lucy, plus he'd been real benevolent to the folks of Eden.

Baz remembered the loneliness of his teen years. He'd promised himself he'd never put a kid through that. He'd promised himself he'd never try—_and fail—_ to build a family. He'd learned to get along just fine on his own.

He closed his eyes. He'd managed to keep to himself for nearly twenty years. He didn't know the neighbors in his condo; he didn't socialize with the assistants in his lab. It would never have occurred to him to sponsor a kid's sports team or to join the Jaycees.

He felt a curious tug at his heart. Maybe the promise he'd made his mother—_ that he'd never step foot in Eden—_ had sealed him even tighter in the cocoon he'd created for himself. For a long time time, he'd kept his promise. He hadn't returned to Eden, hadn't wanted to, until all of a sudden he did. Because of Hallie.

He'd half expected the Outlaw family to blame him for the estrangement. For years, Jesse had been trying to get him to move back to Maine. Cam sent occasional emails. Instead, they'd accepted him as easily as if he'd been on a two-week vacation instead of AWOL for two decades. He wasn't fooled. He was still an outlier. Sharing a set of genes and a name with people did not make them family. He didn't care. The only family he wanted was Hallie.

A knock at the door jump-started Baz's heart.

But it wasn't his golden-eyed partner who opened the door. It was his brother.

"You busy?"

"I'm finished for today."

Cam flopped into a chair opposite the desk.

"Having second thoughts about spending three months pulling calves and inoculating pigs?"

Cameron wore his expensive wardrobe with a casual elegance. He'd undoubtedly always charmed people with his outgoing personality and his intelligence. His saturnine good looks had, no doubt, attracted women in droves. Baz didn't need to be told his brother had been Eden's golden boy.

It would have been natural to be envious of the sibling who'd been allowed a normal childhood and who seemed so comfortable in his skin, but the only envy Baz felt was for the time Cameron had spent with Hallie. Just how close were those two, anyway?

"Calves and pigs seem pretty normal compared with some of the patients around here," he said. "I found Hallie splinting the wing of a baby bat the other night."

Cam chuckled. "I guess you haven't heard about the squirrel that got clipped by a car, or Jekyll and Hyde, the chipmunks abandoned by their mother."

Baz fought the knee-jerk jealousy. "Let me guess. They're all healthy and happy and running around the woods thanks to Dr. Scott."

"Bingo."

"She's missed her calling. She ought to be out on a wildlife preserve. What does Dad think of all this?"

Baz saw his own surprise reflected in Cam's face. He'd used the word "dad" so naturally. Once again he marveled at the way his resentment had vanished. He knew it was because of Hallie. She'd softened his heart. The protective shell was gone forever.

"Oh, she's got Dad wrapped around her little finger. Like all the rest of us."

The comment presented a new complication.

How entwined was Hallie? How hard would it be to convince her to leave her new home and return to L.A.? It shouldn't have been difficult. Not if she still wanted his baby. Not if she still loved him.

But were those things still true?

"She's been like a mom to Daisy and a sister to Lucy."

"What's she been to you?"

Cam appeared to think about the question. He finally settled on an answer. "A friend." A friend could be a lot. He knew. He'd been a friend to Nicole, but he hadn't loved her. He felt something inside him relax.

"I actually came to offer you the ten-cent tour of town," Cam said.

"All three blocks of it?"

"Don't scoff. You were born here, too."

Baz waited for the old, familiar bitterness to fill his veins, but all he felt was a vague wistfulness.

"Thought you might like to go down to the river,"

Cam said, casually. "Hallie and Daisy are down there with Jake and his kids."

She was down on the river with the sheriff?

Baz's gut contorted and he exploded out of his chair.

"C'mon. I'll drive."

The moment Cam closed the passenger side door to Jesse's battered pickup, Baz gunned the motor. He wheeled out of the clinic's parking lot and was halfway down Walnut before he realized he didn't remember where the river was.

****

Hallie secured the laces on Daisy's double-runner skates. She smiled at the feel of the little girl's mitten-encased hand in hers as the two made their way out of the warming shack down the narrow ribbed vinyl runner that led from the wooden shelter to the ice rink.

The temperature had risen overnight, and the skating was sluggish, but Hallie didn't mind. She loved being a part of the community. She loved everything about the small town, including the fishbowl-like lack of privacy. She even loved the grapevine that was more effective than any wire service.

"Dr. Hallie!" Richie Ward, son of the mayor, clutched the hand of his big sister, Fern, and chugged along the slushy ice.

Hallie waved. She'd met Richie last summer at the Fourth of July picnic on the Town Green when he'd found a bullfrog by the gazebo and she'd convinced him not to take it home. She'd rewarded that sacrifice several days later by giving him a kitten. After checking with his mother, of course.

Richie had proven to be a responsible pet owner.

One of the things she liked best about her job was watching the interactions between humans and pets. Animals definitely brought out the best in people. She heard another cheery shout and looked up to see Jake and his kids skating toward her. Sam and Lillie Langley greeted Daisy with friendly enthusiasm.

"C'mon." Lillie grabbed the younger girl's hand.

"We'll skate you across the pond."

"Can I, Hallie?"

"Not too fast."

"We know." Hallie smiled at the little girl. Jake's six-year-olds were fantastic. He'd done a wonderful job as a single parent.

The rangy sheriff was as handsome as Cameron Outlaw, but instead of dark hair, Jake's was golden and his eyes, between long, curly lashes, were the color of twin emeralds. He wore a brown bomber jacket and a scarf of blue, green, and pink. Hallie remembered the scarf. She'd helped Sam and Lillie pick it out at the The Closet, Eden's only clothing store.

"I see you're wearing the Christmas scarf. You look good in pink."

He let out a mock sigh.

"When you're the father of a small female, you find pink invading every aspect of your life. This is no worse than smelling like strawberries because there was only one shampoo in the bathroom."

She giggled, and, before she'd realized what was happening, he'd scooped up her hand and slipped it through the crook of his arm. He hugged it close to his big body.

"I need you to help me balance," he explained.

Hallie laughed. "You don't have to convince me.

I've seen you skate before." They pushed through the half-melted ice. "It's slow-going today."

"Real slow," Jake agreed. She knew he was referring to the progress of their relationship. Her heart squeezed. She'd have to disappoint him, and he didn't deserve it.

"You're pretty good out here," he said, discreetly changing the subject. "I'm guessing you learned to skate as a child." She nodded. "Tell me something else about your childhood."

She shrugged. It wasn't her favorite topic. "It wasn't too exciting. My father died when I was young. My mother, who was a corporate executive, was transferred a lot. I lived all over the country."

"Were you and your mother close?"

"Probably about as close as any parent with a rebellious teenage daughter." Hallie didn't tell him that Art and Felicia Scott had adopted her or that, after Art's early death, Felicia realized she didn't really want the responsibility of a child after all.

"Mom died while I was in veterinary school in California." It felt odd to call Felicia "mom," but it would raise questions to call her anything else.

Jake digested the information. "The holidays must be rough for you with no family."

"The Outlaws have always made me feel a part of theirs."

Before he could reply, a harsh shout shook the air like a sonic boom. "Halliday!"

Hallie's heart pounded against her ribs.

The speaker looked neither to the left nor the right. Skaters scurried out of his way like dried leaves as he made a beeline across the ice. His eyes resembled the winter sky. They were cold and accusing.

Hallie was aware of Jake's hand on her back and she was grateful for the implied protection but she knew it wouldn't be enough. She spread her feet and braced herself. He stopped only inches from her still form.

"What's this all about?" She forced herself to remain calm, reasonable. "You're not even wearing skates."

His eyes glittered and his jaw worked. Before he could speak, Hallie heard an ominous crack. She swung her head around to see flailing arms and a frantic expression on Richie Ward's pudgy face.

Lilly's screech filled the air.

"Daddy! Daddy! Richie's falling in! He's going to drown!"

As the child slipped through the ice in slow motion, everyone froze. Everyone except Baz. He charged toward the child. Hallie's throat constricted when his weight cracked more of the ice, and both man and child disappeared into the frigid black water.

Hallie heard an anguished cry and realized, with a shock, it had come from her. Baz's head surfaced, dark and sleek as a seal. She started toward him.

"Don't go any closer! You'll break the ice," a voice warned. "Lie down and feed this rope to him."

Good grief. She hadn't been thinking. She flattened herself and scooted to within a few feet of the hole. She forced herself not to think about the freezing water or the precious seconds ticking away.

There was a loop in the rope, and she fed that to Baz.

For the first time, she realized he was holding

Richie and that the terrified child was struggling against his chest.

How long could the man tread water before his legs went numb? How long before the icy current

sucked both of them under the black surface?

"Please," she whimpered as she watched the man try to loop the lasso over the little boy's head.

Richie sobbed and wriggled.

"Richie," Hallie called out. "Just hold still and let Dr. Baz tie the rope. We'll pull you to safety."

"I'm scared, Dr. Hallie. I want my mom."

Just them Fern shrieked from the other side of the rink where she'd been chatting with a hockey player.

"I want to get out," Richie wailed.

"Hold still, baby. Remember the bullfrog?"

Richie stilled. "You mean Otis?"

"Right. Otis." Baz had gotten the loop over the boy's head and was securing it around his chest, under his arms. "You need to get back to your natural habitat, just like Otis."

"I'm cold," Richie howled.

"You'll be fine. Just hold still."

"Pull," Baz shouted.

Hallie heard the ambulance in the distance. She hoped Chester Appleton was driving tonight and not Edna Mae, his wife. Chester was nearing seventy, but he was still reliable and strong for his age.

It would take a lot of muscle to get Baz's big body into the ambulance if, for some reason, he was unconscious. Her heartbeat seemed to stop.

Cam and Jake and Fern's friend pulled the rope carefully and pulled the little boy away from the rupture in the ice. Then Jake snagged the child's jacket and lifted him to safety.

Hallie was aware of all that, but her eyes never shifted from the break in the ice. Baz's face was pale under the wet, dark hair. His lips looked purple. He weighed three times as much as Richie, more since he was soaking wet. Could the men pull him out?

Was there time? His legs were probably numb.

"Hang on," she called to him. The gray eyes fixed on her, but she knew he wasn't registering. All his senses were focused on staying alive.

Cam threw the looped rope back to him. His fingers worked, clumsily. Hallie heard someone praying, pleading with him to hurry, and she realized the words were coming from her. Finally, the loop was around his broad chest.

"Pull," she yelled.

The second rescue wasn't nearly as smooth as the first. The first time Baz's two hundred-pound body came up onto the ice, the darn stuff cracked again. Hallie knew she was sobbing, but she didn't realize she was moving toward Baz until she heard Jake's warning. "Hallie, get back. You're compromising the ice."

Another ominous crack.

Oh God.

"I'm sorry," she whispered. The gray eyes were glazed now. Did that mean he had hypothermia? How long could a man stay alive in those freezing waters? "Please hang on," she muttered.

Two more men joined the tug of war. Someone suggested sitting on the ice to narrow the angle, which would reduce the strain on the rope. Hallie was ready to jump out of her skin. She knew they were trying to ensure a quick, safe recovery, but it was taking so long.

Baz tried to hoist himself up onto the surface of the ice. Hallie heard another horrifying crack. She whimpered.

"Stay still," Jake shouted. "Let us drag you."

Apparently the command in the sheriff's voice reached him. Baz did as he was told. She wished she could enjoy seeing him obey someone else's orders.

She prayed she'd get a chance to see the familiar arrogance. What if he died? This was so much worse than the break up. She couldn't bear to see him leave this world.

Finally, Baz's big body was hauled onto secure ice. He was wearing a shearling jacket, probably not his, and he looked like a big beached sheep. A wet, beautiful, beached sheep. She held back tears as the rescuers tugged him along until he got to the edge of the river where the ice was stronger. Dozens of hands reached down to pull him up onto the snow-covered grass.

"That's Jesse Outlaw's oldest son," someone said. "He moved like Batman to rescue the boy.

Faster than a speeding bullet."

"That's Superman," someone argued. "He was like a Navy Seal."

"A hometown hero," someone else said. "Lucky thing he was in town."

Chester pulled up next to the river. Baz insisted on getting to his feet. Cam put his shoulder under one of Baz's arms while Jake took the other side.

"Let's get you in the ambulance," Cam said.

"Don't need it," Baz growled. It was hard to understand him. His teeth chattered like castanets.

"Your lips are blue," Chester pointed out. "You got hypothermia." He sounded tentative. Hallie didn't think the ambulance driver/paramedic would force the issue, and she couldn't blame him. Even soaking wet and half frozen, Baz was intimidating.

"T-take the b-boy," Baz told Chester. He stuttered like Elmer Fudd. "Hallie can d-drive me home."

"No way," she put in. "Chester's right. You need to go to the hospital."

"Drive me h-home," he repeated. She gazed at him. Be careful what you ask for. She looked to Cam for help, but the other Outlaw son just shrugged. She was on her own. She realized, suddenly, that's where she wanted to be. She wanted to take care of Eden's newest hero. She dug into the pocket of her white parka and found her keys. Chester wrapped Baz in a blanket while she retrieved the Jeep.

"Pretend he's an injured squirrel," Cam muttered to Hallie. "I'll take care of Daisy." She flinched. She'd completely forgotten about the little girl.

"You, okay?"

"I'm fine," she said, but it was a lie. She couldn't feel her face or her legs. Her heart seemed to be in a cage.

She felt someone tugging on her feet, and she looked down. Jake. He was untying her skates.

"Thanks," she murmured.

He pulled them off. "Anytime."

She drove back in her stocking feet.

"Aren't your feet freezing?"

She could barely understand the gruff words.

She didn't answer. She was trying to figure out the fastest way of raising Baz's core temperature.

Hot tea? A bath? Damn. She should have asked Chester.

She pulled onto Walnut Street.

"What's the m-matter?" Baz clacked.

"I'm thinking."

"You're not thinking," he chattered. "You're crying."

She touched her face. He was right.

"I'm okay, Hallie."

He was already minimizing his part in the rescue and her very understandable reaction to it.

"Yeah."

"It's not that big a deal."

She didn't argue with him. She didn't tell him it would have been a very big deal to her if he'd been swept under the ice.

"It's a big deal. You rescued Richie."

"If I hadn't, someone else would have."

"No one else moved fast enough. You're a hero."

"Shit."

She thought she understood. He'd spent so many years as an island it had been a shock to reconnect with family. He wasn't ready for the town to regard him as a hero.

She pulled up into the yard behind the back door. She helped him out of the car and clasped her arm around his waist. He might be weak and frozen, but his body was still hard and flat and so masculine.

As soon as they got into the mudroom, she stopped and pressed herself against the length of him. His arms came around her.

"It's all right, h-honey," he stuttered. "I'm all right. The boy's all right."

She buried his face in the opening of his sodden jacket.

"Hallie? Can you help me get out of these clothes?"

Oh God. She was an idiot. She stepped back and began to peel the heavy material off his shoulders. It took forever to work his sweater up over his head.

They didn't talk. Only the chattering of his teeth filled the silence. Finally, he leaned against the dryer, exhausted, his wide, hair-sprinkled chest clammy and white.

Her gaze dropped to his boots. The laces were frozen.

"What's wrong?"

"I don't know how to untie your boots."

"Get a knife."

She hurried over to Asia's wooden knife block and selected a cleaver that could have brought down an oak.

"Maybe something a little less lethal," Baz said.

Good grief. Where was her head? She found a steak knife. Its sharp blade slid easily through the stiff cords.

Baz got his belt undone and his pants unzipped, but he couldn't manage to peel off the soaked denim.

"Sorry," he said.

"No problem." She couldn't help the rush of heat that hit her as she tugged the water-soaked jeans down his muscular legs. His briefs came with them.

She had to tell herself not to stare. This was an emergency not a sexual romp.

"Let's get you upstairs and into the shower," she said, briskly.

"Take your clothes off."

She halted. "What?"

"You're wet and freezing, Hallie. Strip."

He didn't add that she'd drip water all through the Outlaw home, but it was true. That would be unfair to Jesse and Asia and everyone else. Besides, he was in no condition to take advantage of her nudity.

She opened the door to the kitchen and led him up the back stairs.

"Jacuzzi," he mumbled.

"Good thinking."

The Jacuzzi was in Jesse's bathroom. She knew because of last summer's renovations. She and Cam and Lucy had had to talk the older man into buying the fancy bathtub.

She helped him down the steps then turned on the jets after making sure the temperature setting was lowered to warm. She didn't want to send his system into shock by bombarding his cold body with hot water. She tested the water with her fingers.

"How does that feel?"

He didn't answer, so she looked at him. His face was so pale it was almost green, but the stone-colored eyes glittered as they swept her unclothed body.

"Get in with me."

Chapter Five

She couldn't believe how badly she wanted to join him in the hot tub. "I don't think that's a good idea."

"Get in, Halliday."

It was a mistake. The only excuse for getting into that tub would have been full-blown hypothermia, and she wasn't even close. She was shaking, but it was half residual fear and half excitement. She wanted to be next to him, touching him, surrounding him. She wanted to assure herself that he was alive. She gazed into his pale, rugged face and knew her feelings hadn't changed during the last twelve difficult months. She was still in love with Baz Outlaw.

"Get in, Hallie."

She got in.

A few minutes later, despite the heated water lapping and bubbling around them Baz was still shivering. She held the back of her hand against his cheek. "You're still too cold. I think we should go to the hospital."

"You can warm me up."

She tried. She soaked a washcloth and smoothed it over his face, neck, and chest. He was so muscular, so hard. And still shaking. He grabbed her wrist, and she dropped the washcloth.

"Use your hands."

Hallie's eyes narrowed.

"This better not be some lame attempt to get me into bed."

"It's the most efficient way to warm me up," he said. "We both know you can get me hot faster than anything else."

She considered pointing out that they'd only made love once. They didn't know much at all about their mutual chemistry. Except that it was explosive.

She couldn't argue with that.

He didn't stir as she stroked his chest and rubbed his arms and legs trying to jump start his circulation. He just watched her. After a few minutes, she thought she'd made some progress but not enough.

"Use your mouth," he said. His throat sounded dry.

"My mouth?"

"On my body."

She had to sit on his lap to get close enough. It felt kind of awkward but definitely warm. She leaned in to press her lips against his neck, under his ear.

"Like that."

"This is good?"

"Mmmm."

Mmmm.

It was the sound he'd made repeatedly that night by the light of the Charlie Brown Christmas tree. It was a sound of pure masculine need. She moved her mouth to his.

"Good," he said, finally, breaking the contact.

"Go lower."

She looked down his powerful torso. Where to start? There were so many enticing possibilities.

"Nipples," he directed. He dropped his head back and closed his eyes. She was relieved to see that the shakes were calming down. His skin color was pinking up, too. She climbed onto his lap and used her tongue to flick one of his flat, copper-colored nipples. His chest hair got into her nose and she sneezed.

"Bless you."

She laughed and shifted on his lap.

"Mmmmm." His fingers touched her sides, her back, the bumps on her spine. Strong fingers threaded themselves through her wet curls. He pulled her against him, her cheek flattened on his chest. She tensed as she felt his erection, thick and hard coming alive under her buttocks.

"That's a good sign," she murmured, swallowing hard.

"A very good sign. But not at all unexpected. You'll be able to make me hard when I'm dead, Hallie."

A shudder ran through her body; his eyes held hers. Then he leaned against the tub surround. "I want you, baby," he said.

His blood was no longer cold. It was boiling hot, and it was all in one place. It was like the corpuscles had decided to hold a meeting in his groin.

He fought to control the urge to take the choice away from her, to lower her on top of him, to fill her and pound into her until the veins popped out on his forehead. He had to remind himself this wasn't a one-night stand. He wanted her for keeps. He was playing for deep stakes.

He had to be careful.

But she was warmth, and he'd been cold so long.

He felt as if he'd spent the last twelve months in the icy Eden River.

"Hallie." Her name came out on a groan. She didn't answer him in words. Instead she held his gaze and worked her hand down his body.

She closed her fingers around him and squeezed, gently. He moaned.

"Inside you," he whispered. He should have known she wouldn't deny him.

This wasn't a referendum on their relationship. It was about the rescue, pure and simple. And about her generosity. The sex could backfire, but maybe it could show her that what they had was real, that they could still connect on this level, that they still belonged together.

Her hands were on him now, and he shuddered as she joined their bodies. He looked at her through lidded eyes. "That feels good." His voice was hoarse.

"So damn good."

It was more than good. It was perfect.

His head fell back against the rim of the tub as she began to move on him, slowly, relentlessly working the sensitive tip, then sliding down the pulsing thickness. Jesus.

He cupped her face and pulled it toward him so he could fit his lips on hers. The sensation was so exquisite, the relief so profound. He never wanted this to end, but it would end. Soon. It was time to remind her of last December. He slipped his fingers between their bodies then he gently rubbed the female flesh where it was most sensitive. She let out a satisfying little sound.

"Yeah, baby," he whispered. "That's right. Come for me."

Her small, inner muscles gripped him and milked

him as she moved to create the almost unbearable friction. He was too close. His thumb pressed harder. He felt her body tense, then she shrieked and came apart in his hands.

He got only an instant to enjoy the intense satisfaction. His own climax came at him like a shotgun blast at close range. He groaned heavily and convulsed. He felt her arms around him as he spent himself inside her.

His face was buried in her shoulder. She stroked the muscles of his broad back while he struggled for oxygen. He was definitely warm enough now. His skin burned her fingers.

She couldn't touch him enough. It felt like an addiction. She didn't want to stop touching him. Not ever. She threaded her fingers through his wet hair.

Baz.

He felt so good. He smelled so good, soap, sure and aftershave, but mostly he smelled male.

Hallie hadn't even realized how much she'd missed it. Missed him. She pressed her lips into the folds of his neck.

He'd been a genuine hero today, but he was also a healer and a searcher. He sought new ways to treat animals and to feed them. He ran a research lab at a large university, but he could vaccinate a puppy with gentle care. The man had so much to give. Not her, of course. She knew that. This was a moment out of time. But she felt a rush of gratitude that he'd come east to reconcile with his family. Because that was why he was here. He just didn't know it yet.

"Hallie?"

She'd pulled his head against her breasts. His

breath tickled her bare skin in the most tantalizing way. "Mmmmm?"

"We're together now."

She sighed. "Let's not talk about this now."

"We have to talk about it, sweetheart. You came to me with your eyes open. I want you to know this time you won't be disappointed. I'll never send you away again."

She tried to keep her voice even. "This was a special circumstance, Baz. It was about the moment,about the cold. Let's just enjoy this time together, okay?"

"I can't enjoy it until you admit this is a new beginning."

He wasn't going to give up. Big surprise.

"It wasn't a new beginning. I told you before. I like my new life. I'm not going back to L.A. There's nothing you can say or do, Baz." She kept her voice gentle. "I've made up my mind."

He leaned back and regarded her from underneath his long lashes. "You may not have any choice. In case you didn't notice, we failed to use protection. You might be pregnant as we speak."

She held very still for a long moment. Then she carefully peeled herself away from him. At least she tried to. He was still inside her and, as far as she could tell, he was, once again, growing hard.

"Hallie? Did you hear me?"

"I'm not deaf. I've got to get out of here before Cam and Daisy get home."

"You can't leave."

"You're warmed up now." She grabbed one of Jesse's fluffy yellow towels and wrapped it around herself.

"My core temperature's still low."

She twisted on the hard length of him. "I doubt that."

"I'm not sure I can get out of here by myself."

She thought he probably could, but she wasn't taking any chances. He'd lost a lot of energy this afternoon what with the battering accident and the industrial-strength climax. She reached down to help him out of the Jacuzzi. She tried not to look at all that masculinity. It wasn't easy.

"Here's a towel." She flipped one over to him.

"I'll get you a flannel shirt out of Cam's closet. Your golf shirts aren't going to keep the heat in."

"I know a better way to keep the heat in. We'll go out to your apartment and climb into bed."

"I don't think so." She hurried to find warm clothes for him. She borrowed a sweat suit from Lucy's closet for herself.

"You seem to know your way around here."

He was right. It had felt like her second home until he arrived.

"I've spent some nights here, you know, watching Daisy, hanging out with Lucy, and playing pinochle with your dad."

A shadow crossed his hard features, and her heart twisted. He was thinking about the way she'd enjoyed his family while he'd been alone in California.

"Cam and Daisy will be home any minute," she said, as she hurriedly tidied up the bathroom. "If you need me, for some reason, call my cell."

"I need you now."

She shook her head. "Get some rest."

"Hallie."

"Yes?"

"I know it's too soon for me to regain your trust, honey, but I meant what I said. I'll make it up to you."

"I don't want to talk about this right now."

He continued as if she hadn't spoken. "You won't be able to ignore it if you turn up pregnant."

Pain turned to fury.

"Why are you doing this, Baz? Why show up here out of the blue? Did you think I just waited around for twelve months? I got on with my life.

You're going to have to get on with yours, too."

"I want to get on with it, only I want you with me. Last year you said you loved me, Hallie. You asked me to marry you and give you a baby. I know I'm late, honey, but I'm here now. Let's do it. Let's get married. Let's have a family."

Anger took away her breath. She was amazed she could find the words.

"It's too late."

"How can it be too late? You're single. I'm single.

We're not a hundred and five. We lost a year, but we'll make up for it." He grinned his lopsided grin.

"We'll make up for it starting immediately."

She closed her eyes and called on the last of her reserves. "People are allowed to change their minds.

I've changed mine."

"I know I have to regain your trust, honey. I understand that. But surely you haven't changed your goals. Having a baby was the most important thing in the world to you last year. Are you trying to tell me you don't want to do that anymore?"

She stared at him. "I'm trying not to tell you I can't

do it anymore. But there's no point. The baby ship has sailed, Baz. That's the long and the short of it. It's not on my radar screen anymore."

"Is this about that damn sheriff?" His eyes flashed dangerously, and he waved his arms. The towel slipped on his slim hips. "He's got a couple of kids so you don't want to go through a pregnancy?

''Cause I don't believe it. I won't believe it. You couldn't have changed that much in one year."

She was raw and hurting, and she just couldn't fence with him. She couldn't face three months of repeating this conversation, either. She knew Baz Outlaw. He'd decided he wanted her, and he'd never give up until he fully understood that there wasn't anything to want.

"You asked some questions, and I'm going to give you the answers. Please listen carefully, because I don't want to talk about this again. I don't have a boyfriend. I don't want to marry anyone. I can't marry anyone." She kept her voice even and reasonable. "I'm not pregnant. I will never be pregnant. I can't get pregnant. I told you last year that I had a small window of time when I had a good chance of conceiving. I am now clinically infertile.

The endometriosis sprinted to the finish line. My window is now as closed as this conversation."

She started for the door. She heard a startled hiss.

"You can't know that for sure that you're infertile."

"I've got a lab report that says otherwise."

He cursed, harshly.

The back door opened and closed. Cam's and Daisy's voices wafted up the stairs. It was time to leave.

"This isn't over, Halliday."

She didn't bother to respond. It had been over for some time now.

Hallie's feet were frozen by the time she ran barefoot across the courtyard and climbed the outside steps to her apartment. She remembered she'd left her purse at the house along with her clothes, so she had to fumble for the extra key under the outside mat.

She slipped in the door. The dusk of early evening turned the furniture into lonely, ghostly shapes, but she didn't turn on the lights. She didn't want to encourage visitors tonight. She picked up the Storm-at-Sea quilt, designed and sewn by Jolene's Aunt Rhonda, pulled it around her shoulders, then she curled into a corner of the worn chintz sofa.

Tomorrow she'd rise with the dawn and rejoin the human race. She'd take care of Eden's pets, cultivate her friendships, enjoy the home she'd found in this small town. Tonight, though, she wanted to be alone to mourn again the loss of the child she'd wanted, and the man she'd loved.

I wouldn't be a bit surprised if you were already pregnant.

Her eyes stung and she closed them.

****

Baz stood very still as water dripped down his body and pooled around his feet. There was a hundred-pound bowling ball on his chest, and his brain waves resembled a television screen full of snow.

He felt more helpless than he had in the icy river. What the hell had happened? The answer to that was almost too painful to face.

It was too late.

She'd said so repeatedly since he arrived on

Christmas Eve. He just hadn't realized she meant it literally.

Too late.

For some reason his mind flashed back to their first date some eighteen months ago. Oh, they hadn't called it a date. They were co-workers, and Hallie had made it her mission to coax him out of the lab and into the real world. She'd gotten him to agree to a picnic, and, despite the thunderstorm outside, she'd shown up at his condo with a basket of tuna sandwiches, chips, fresh fruit, and pink lemonade.

He still remembered the pounding thunder and the lightning flashes. He still remembered watching the horizontal rain smack against his tall windows.

She'd insisted he take off his shoes and sit on the quilt she spread over his carpet. As soon as they'd eaten she'd produced a deck of cards.

"Poker?" he'd asked, hopefully.

She'd flashed him that million-mega-watt grin, the one where her hazel-golden eyes shone brightly enough to warm his insides. "Crazy Eights."

He'd scoffed. "That's a kid's game."

Her grin widened. "I know."

He didn't know why he'd agreed to it. He'd have preferred to watch the rain and listen to Bach, just as he'd have preferred wine and paté for lunch but, somehow, he couldn't bear to disappoint her. He watched her deal. What kind of a woman kept a deck of cards in her purse? The question startled him. He never probed into the past.

"Did you play cards as a kid?"

She nodded and spoke without losing count.

"When my dad was alive, we played Poker and Go

Fish, Slap Jack, Canasta, and Seven-Up."

"And after he died?"

She laughed her musical laugh. "I tried to play both hands for a while. Eventually I got a library card."

"No playmates?"

"I had a nanny for a while then a housekeeper until I went to boarding school."

"I went to boarding school, too." He paused. That was another thing he never did. He couldn't remember the last time he'd volunteered information about himself.

"Any sisters and brothers?"

He didn't want to open that can of worms, but he found himself loathe to see disappointment in those friendly hazel eyes. "One of each," he said.

"What kinds of things did you do together?"

He found himself telling her about the forts he and Cam used to make under the sheets hanging in the backyard and the way they'd get cookies and milk from Asia then take it up to the tree house in the backyard where they'd pretend they were stranded on a desert island.

He told her about the big stone house in Eden and his dad's practice in the clinic out back.

"What about your sister?"

"She's younger. She was just a baby when I left."

"When you left?"

He cursed himself. The conversation had become much too personal. "My folks divorced when I was fifteen. My mother and I moved to Colorado. The others stayed in Maine."

"I'm sorry." He heard the sincerity in her tone. It was as if she understood the devastation of a family break up. "Did you visit your dad in the summer?"

Baz thought about his mother. Evelyn Outlaw had been a hard woman who'd discovered infidelity in her marriage and had decided to punish her ex by splintering the family. He realized, for the first time, just how selfish she'd been.

"No. I haven't been back."

"And now?"

The golden gaze was full of empathy.

"I have no plans to go back." Too much time had passed. The Outlaws weren't his family anymore.

"Ah, Baz."

Something gave inside him. Suddenly the Pandora's Box opened, and the bitter memories spilled out. They somersaulted through him, stinging, hurting, wounding. It was like he was stuck in a nightmarish film reel until he felt her warm fingers on his wrist. The memories faded from black and white to gray until they were nearly invisible, until he felt exhausted but relieved. He felt her hand on his arm. He'd forgotten she was there.

"Don't give me any advice," he'd growled.

She'd nodded, solemnly. "Just remember, blood is thicker than water."

She was as good as her word. They never again talked about Maine until that morning he'd sent her into exile there. He wondered now about his motivation. Had he known, on some level, he'd come after Hallie? Had he wanted an excuse to see his father again?

Father. He winced at the word. He didn't know his father, and now he'd never know his son. Thanks to him Hallie wouldn't get to have a child, so he'd never be a father again. Robert was his only chance.

And he'd left Robert.

Baz had gone over and over this. He'd always planned to leave Nicole. It was part of the bargain.

But it was one thing to tell a woman who was barely pregnant that he was leaving. It was something else to walk out on a month-old child.

He'd provided for them, but he knew, better than anyone, that money wasn't enough. A kid needed caring parents. Robert had a teenage mom and no dad, and it was his fault.

What about Hallie? All she'd wanted was a child of her own, one person with whom she could share blood ties. Last year he could have given her that.

Now it was too late.

Hallie would never be a mother to a child of her own. She'd never share blood ties with anyone.

She'd probably never forgive him. He sure as hell wouldn't forgive himself.

The door burst open. Daisy rushed in, followed closely by Lucy and Cam. "You're a hero, Uncle Baz," the child said. She wrapped her arms around his knees.

"Everybody's talking about it," Lucy said. "It's gonna be the lead story in the paper next week. I just know it."

"How's Hallie?" Cam asked. "Did she go back to the apartment to change before supper?"

"She's beat," Baz said. "I think she's gonna eat something over there and go right to bed."

"I wanna see her," Daisy yelped. "I wanna tell her about the coloring book Lillie gave me."

"Tomorrow." Baz picked his niece up in his arms. Even though she weighed next to nothing, he was sort of surprised he'd found the strength. "Let's let Hallie get some rest."

"You sure she's all right?" Lucy asked.

She wasn't all right. She'd never be all right, and it was his fault. The least he could do was give her some privacy.

He forced a smile.

"She's fine. C'mon. Let's go down and find something for supper."

"You know, Baz," said his newly rediscovered sister, "you really are a hero. You risked your life for a perfect stranger."

She had him nailed. He'd risk everything for a stranger. But for the woman he cared about he couldn't do a goddam thing.

It was too late.

Chapter Six

The next morning Hallie pulled on chocolate brown corduroys and a fuschia pullover with an asymmetrical collar. When she'd arrived in Maine last year, she'd needed winter clothing. She'd figured bright colors would cheer her up. As result her closet was a rainbow.

She gazed into the mirror, and, while brushing her rich brown curls, she searched for the upside.

There was always an upside; usually she could find it.

It had been something of a relief to tell him.

Now that there were no more secrets since he understood her position, he'd leave her alone. He'd stay the three months because he was a man of his word. After that he'd return to L.A., and she could return to her life in Eden.

Except it wouldn't be that easy. It was pretty obvious Jesse wanted Baz to stay or, at least, visit on a regular basis. How could she handle that? Could she bear to see him meet someone in Eden, marry and reproduce? Probably not. Could she deal with seeing him and his family a couple of times a year?

She made a face in the mirror. It didn't help that she'd climbed all over him like a cat in heat last night in the Jacuzzi.

"Stupid move, Hal."

She shut her eyes and remembered the feel of his strong fingers on her skin, the sense of controlled power in his big body despite his harrowing adventure and the euphoria as they'd experienced a mutual release. He'd felt it, too. That part of their relationship definitely worked.

They'd do it again. She could tell herself to stay out of hot tubs with him but she knew, in her heart, within three months they'd make love again. A new thought struck her. Maybe he was turned off by the infertility. Man was designed to spread his seed. It was against biology for him to keep returning to barren ground.

Whatever. Her job now was to keep some distance between them. More contact could only result in more heartbreak. She put on her crayon-red parka and plunged out into the weak winter sunshine.

Asia's kitchen was, as always, full of light and the scent of baking bread. Cinnamon rolls and fresh coffee awaited Hallie. She smiled at the housekeeper. She held onto that smile even when she felt Baz's gun-metal gaze upon her. She issued a general greeting that included him along with Cameron, Daisy, and Lucy.

"Want anything from Boston, Hallie?" Lucy asked.

"You're going to Boston?"

"Yep. My roommate, well, my ex-roommate, Miranda, wants me to visit through New Year's."

Lucy Outlaw had graduated from college the previous spring, but she hadn't settled down yet.

She'd taken on a series of part-time jobs while waiting to get an offer from a newspaper or a magazine.

"You'll miss the Grange Hall dance," Cam pointed out. The annual New Year's Eve celebration, Hallie knew, was practically the only Eden tradition that had survived the area's economic downturn.

She watched Lucy's delicate features twist.

"No harm done. I didn't have a date, anyway."

She looked at Hallie. "I guess you'll be going with Jake."

Hallie felt Baz's eyes boring into her. She glanced at Lucy and thought she caught a flash of jealousy on the young woman's pretty face. That was unlikely, though. They were separated by thirteen years and a sort of simmering hostility.

Cameron changed the subject. "How'd you sleep after your ordeal last night, Hal?"

His voice halted the progress of Hallie's coffee cup from the saucer to her lips. Her ordeal? Last night? Had he found out about the lapse in the hot tub?

Baz's deep emotionless voice chimed in. "He means the business at the river," he said, his voice gravelly.

Good grief. She avoided his gaze. Instead, she addressed Cam.

"I slept fine. The adventure belonged to your brother."

"He was the hero, all right," Cam said.

Lucy's eyes twinkled. "We were so proud of you, big brother." She leaned over and hugged him.

His body tensed. It was an odd reaction from a man who'd enjoyed as many women as he. But, he'd had few sisterly hugs. Very few. Lucy was a baby when he'd last seen her.

"Richie almost drownded," Daisy reminded everyone. "But my Uncle Baz saved him."

"I had lots of help, Sunshine." He grinned at her,

and Hallie's heart turned over. She knew he was hurting, filled with guilt over the infertility, but he was able to find a warm smile for his new little niece. In the space of two days, the man who'd been an island had allowed his sprite of a niece into his heart. He was well on his way toward becoming a family man.

All he needed was his own family.

The little girl hopped out of her chair and climbed up on her uncle's lap. "You feel good," she purred, putting her head against his massive chest.

He closed his arms around her, and Hallie looked down into the still-full cup of coffee.

"Ready for your first day as a country doc?" Cam asked his brother.

"He looks ready," Lucy said.

He did. Baz had forsaken his customary hand-tailored suits for low-riding jeans and a brown-and-white flannel shirt. He looked comfortable and right.

She couldn't help hoping he wouldn't like it too much here. Her peace of mind in Eden, Maine, depended on Baz's return to L.A.

"I figure this is the proper attire for roto-routing critters and pulling calves."

Hallie reminded herself she should be grateful to have a large animal expert close at hand. She didn't feel competent to tend the farm animals. That was Jesse's department. And now, Baz's.

"That reminds me." She cleared her throat. "I need to talk to you about a mare out at the Meadows' place on M-15 near the Rez. She's about to foal, and your dad's a little worried about the situation."

Baz nodded. "He mentioned that."

Well, naturally, he had. Jesse was far too

responsible to go on a cruise without making arrangements for his patients.

"I'll drop in on them. Maybe you could come, too, since the farmer knows you."

"Of course." Hallie's spirits lifted, marginally.

They were both professionals. Maybe they could work together, after all. "Would tomorrow work for you? Today is booked solid since we were closed for the holiday."

They walked to the clinic together. Hallie prayed he wouldn't refer to last night or to her baby bombshell. Apparently the prayer worked because they only discussed the weather.

Hallie's attempt to introduce Baz to the elderly receptionist proved unnecessary. She remembered him from his early teen years when he and his mother still lived in Eden.

"Oh my goodness me." She studied him. "I haven't seen you in donkey's years, Basil. You grew into a fine man. My stars, you look just like your father."

Hallie saw his face tighten. He didn't want to think of Jesse as either his father or a role model, but he was gallant to the old lady.

"You, on the other hand, don't look a day older than the last time I saw you."

"Pshaw. You're a smooth one, Basil Outlaw."

"Just call me Baz," he advised with a wink. "It won't scare the clients as much. Basil makes people think of vampires and zombies."

Hallie stared at him. Where was all this charm coming from?

He sat at the desk in the office. She grabbed the smock decorated with colorful paw prints. She didn't put it on though, until she went into one of the two treatment rooms. It seemed so intimate to dress in front of this man. She rolled her eyes. Too bad she hadn't had those feelings last night.

The bell over the door jingled, and she heard Baz introducing himself to the clients. Most people in town knew who he was but not merely because he was Jesse's son. The talk was all about yesterday's rescue of Richie Ward.

Hallie was surprised at how comfortable and easy he sounded. In the L.A. lab he'd been efficient, remote and occasionally, mildly impatient.

The newcomer said something amusing, and Baz's rare laugh reached Hallie's ears. Her chest felt tight. Maybe this was his natural habitat.

In spite of the tension between them, she appreciated his help as the day wore on. He restrained Hap Heller's big rottie, Antoinette, while Hallie clipped the dog's toenails, then he listened to Hap grouse about a proposed second stoplight in town. He helped vaccinate a litter of puppies, and he smiled at ten-year-old Tina Barber as she told him each of their names and personality characteristics.

He helped Hallie calm Laura Wilkins who was hysterical about her balding parakeet, Petey. He even agreed with Hallie's diagnosis: molting.

The first clash of the day occurred just before lunch. Mrs. Ingersoll's Pekingese, Ralston, had developed a shortness of breath. Again. Baz took one look at why the dog's belly brushed the floor, and he delivered a short, harsh lecture to the old lady. Mrs.Ingersoll and Ralston left in a huff.

"You were a little rough on her," Hallie pointed

out. "She pretended to be angry, but I saw her eyes tear up."

"She deserves to cry. She's killing her dog with those table scraps."

The good-natured, laid-back country vet routine was already getting old. Hallie felt a flash of relief.

"Mrs. Ingersoll's children have moved away. She's only got Ralston. She thinks she's making him happy by sharing her meals."

"He's happy all right. He just can't breathe."

"I know. Mavis and I are working on a weekly get together for some of the elderly pet owners."

"Lessons in nutrition?"

"I was thinking more of a support group in the guise of a canasta group or a book club. If they had more friends their own ages, they'd be less focused on their pets."

His gray eyes narrowed in disapproval. "Listen, Halliday. It's our job to take care of the medical problems of animals, not the psychological problems of their owners. We are not a lonely hearts club."

She shook her head. "You've been in a lab too long. You've forgotten that pets and their humans are intertwined. I can protect Ralston's interests best by watching out for Mrs. Ingersoll, too."

"Don't you ever get tired of trying to rescue people?"

She gaped at him. "Look who's talking? As far as Eden is concerned, you're the new Batman. I'm just doing my job. I know you're more accustomed to anonymous white mice than companion animals. Maybe if you named those little suckers you'd get more attached."

His stern mouth twitched, and there was amusement in his eyes. His gaze remained on her though, and she couldn't look away. The bell jingled signaling another client, and Hallie swallowed hard.

"You'll have plenty of years to teach me the finer points of companion animal medicine after we're married," he said, softly, deliberately.

Hallie went perfectly still as he strode past her with his hand outstretched.

"Harold," he said, greeting the village treasurer."Who do we have here?"

"This is Pinkie. She's a teacup poodle."

"So I see. A fine specimen, too."

Hallie swallowed, painfully. He still wanted her?

She hadn't expected that.

That single reference to the future was the only one. She began to think he had backed off and she started to relax.

The following afternoon they drove Jesse's battered pickup out to the Meadows' Farm. The house was in need of paint. Icicles clung to its sagging roof but the barn was spacious, clean, and heated.

Hallie told Baz that Ralph Meadows was attempting to hold onto his family's acreage by selling his tractor and developing a quarter horse breeding program. The pregnant mare, Blue, represented the foundation of that program.

Ralph greeted them and showed them into the barn. Hallie watched as Baz examined the sleek, chestnut-colored animal. His hands were thorough but careful, and Blue tolerated his touch very well.

Hallie didn't blame her. There was something so seductive about the combination of strength and gentleness in his big hands.

Ralph brought her back to the present with a comment. "She doesn't have much pep." His words were tinged with anxiety. "Normally she's chomping at the bit to get out in the fields."

"She's resting up for the big event," Baz explained.

"It's called nesting," Hallie chimed in. "It happens with human mamas, too. Just ask Janie."

She felt Baz's eyes on her, but she refused to look at him. This wasn't about him or her. It was about the mare.

Ralph invited them into the shabby farmhouse.

Hallie wondered whether Baz would be put off by the young couple's obvious poverty, but she got her answer when he graciously accepted an invitation to stay to supper from Ralph's very pregnant wife, Janie.

The stew was plain but hot and filling, and Janie had made fresh biscuits to go with it. It was followed by homemade peach cobbler.

"This is delicious," Hallie said. "Did you can the peaches yourself?"

"Yes. I've got shelves and shelves of them down in the cellar," Janie said. "You should take some along. We couldn't eat them all in five years."

"I've got a better idea. A group of us are opening a crafts cooperative in the spring. The Maine Attraction. We figure it'll get a lot of traffic when summer tourists start heading this way to looking for a place to cool off. How about providing us with peach cobbler? We can buy it from you direct then serve it to our customers. We could pay a couple of hundred dollars a week to start. If we get more traffic, we'll buy more. And if you'd like, we can take orders for you."

"That would be great." Janie flashed a huge smile at her husband.

Hallie noticed a nick between Baz's dark eyebrows. He didn't approve of the plan. She couldn't imagine what kind of objection he'd have.

"The cobbler's certainly tasty," he said, smiling at Janie. "I don't know when I've enjoyed anything this much."

"Janie's a fine cook," Ralph said, with satisfaction. "Just like her mom and sisters."

Baz nodded. "Have you thought about baby names?"

Hallie blinked, more than a little surprised by the question. Despite their earlier talk, it was hard to conceive of Baz and baby names in the same conversation. He really had changed.

"We didn't need to spend much time on that subject," Janie replied. "It's going to be Ralph, Junior."

"Fine choice." Baz's comment earned an appreciative look from the young dad-to-be.

"Of course, it could be a girl," Hallie pointed out.

"Not a chance." Ralph grinned at his wife and laid a protective hand on her mounded stomach. "We specifically ordered a boy."

Hallie felt Baz's eyes on her, and she had to fight down the fury that uncoiled in her stomach. She knew it wasn't possible to avoid all references to babies, but he didn't have to throw her infertility in her face by looking at her like that.

When the meal was finished, Janie struggled to her feet.

"Let me clean up," Hallie started to say but, Baz cut her off. "Why don't you gals relax in the parlor while Ralph and I clean up?"

Once again Hallie gaped. She didn't know which shocked her more, Baz using that lazy country drawl or Baz offering to clean up the dishes. But the biggest surprise was yet to come. Janie propped her feet on an ottoman and told Hallie about her preparations for the baby. Suddenly a pair of male voices reached Hallie's ears.

"What on earth?"

"That's Tennessee Whiskey," Janie explained.

"It's Ralph's favorite. He always sings it when he's doing chores."

"I'm a little, er, surprised that Baz knows the words."

Janie shrugged. "He grew up around here. Even if he's been gone for a good while, Eden County's his home."

The farmer's wife was right. Baz's roots were here in west-central Maine. The signs that he belonged here were everywhere. All she could do was pray he wouldn't see them.

She decided to do a little investigating on the way home. "I didn't know you liked country music," she said, with what she hoped was an appropriately casual tone. "You must have gotten that from your mother. I've never heard Jesse listen to anything but classical."

"My mother loved the symphony. That was the one thing she and my dad had in common."

"Why did they get divorced, anyway?"

It was dark in the cab of the truck. Hallie could only see his rugged profile, but she felt him tighten up. "Infidelity."

Hallie stared at him. "Hers?"

"His."

She shook her head. "That doesn't sound like Jesse."

"It was a fluke. A one-time thing. From what I could gather, she was somebody's visiting sister-in-law.

She saw Jesse and targeted him like a pointer picks out a fox. Eventually she ran him to ground."

"Your poor mother."

He was silent a moment. "In retrospect, I think she was just waiting for an excuse. She hated it here in the sticks. Jesse's lapse gave her the opening she was waiting for."

"I wouldn't call infidelity a lapse."

His head turned swiftly, and his voice was harsh.

"Life's messy, Hallie. It can't always be divided into neat categories. People make mistakes, and they hurt each other."

Jesse Outlaw and his ex-wife had certainly hurt their son. She thought about the boy exiled from one other parent, his siblings, his family home. No wonder the man's heart had been frozen for so long.

She just wished he would keep it from thawing until he got out of Maine.

"I'm sorry."

"It's ancient history. What was all that about the peach cobbler?"

"You mean buying it for the co-op? I think it's a great idea. Who wouldn't want to browse around a shop full of unique gift items and enjoy homemade cobbler at the same time?"

"I thought the co-op was supposed to be nonprofit. Can you afford a couple hundred dollars a week?"

"We'll figure something out."

"You're going to pay Janie out of your own pocket, aren't you? You offered her the job because you know they need money, but you forgot one thing."

She was sick of defending her actions to this man. "What?"

His voice was very quiet. "You forgot you won't be here in the spring. You'll be in L.A. With me."

His words stripped away the thin veil of protection she'd started to build around her heart.

"Look. Let's get something straight here. I told you my story so that you'd let up on this. I do not want to keep having this conversation."

It was as if he hadn't heard her. "About that lab report. I'd like to take a look at it. There might be something the lab technician or the doc missed. If there's a way for you to have a baby, we'll find it."

"You're the most stubborn person I've ever met," she replied.

"I am when I'm sure something's right. This is right. You and me."

She shook her head. "You don't understand. I've lost my chance to have a baby of my own."

"And you blame me?"

"Yeah. Yeah, I do. If you'd given us this chance last year things might be entirely different. Timing is everything, Baz. Your timing's off."

"You can't really blame me. You're a scientist.

You have to know that the endometriosis was growing back then. It's probably been growing for several years. If it's true that you can't get pregnant now, there's every likelihood that you couldn't have gotten pregnant last year, either."

"If it's true?" Her voice scaled two octaves.

"Like I said. I'd like to get a look at that report."

"You know what? It doesn't matter. Nothing you say and nothing you do is going to matter. This isn't about a report, and it isn't about science. It's about you letting me down when I needed you. You think it isn't fair or logical for me to blame you? Tough.

We're talking about my feelings here, not my brain.

In my head I know you're making sense.

In my heart, I blame you and I'll never, ever be able to forgive you."

They drove in silence for the next thirty minutes. Hallie felt nauseous with guilt. She hated hurting people. She hated hurting Baz. But she'd told him the truth. When he'd turned his back on her she'd accepted it. When she'd gotten the news about the infertility, she'd accepted that, too. But he'd come back expecting her to be ready and available and that was no longer the case.

She didn't feel the same way about him. The sooner he understood that, the better.

She finally spoke when they turned off the M-15 and onto Main. "Could you drop me off at the bank?"

"Why?"

"There's a town council meeting tonight. I'm supposed to make a report on preparations for the ice festival."

"I'll come with you."

She thought about sitting through a two-hour meeting with those gray eyes boring into the back of her head. "Not a good idea."

"Why?"

"You'd be bored. Anyway, it's going to be short. I

can get a ride home with someone."

"Like who? The sheriff?"

She shook her head. She doubted Jake was even speaking to her anymore after her crazy behavior at the pond.

"Like your brother."

Chapter Seven

Baz checked his watch and groaned. Five minutes had passed since the last time he looked.

Not even five. More like four and a quarter.

He scowled as he paced the perimeter of the room. The study was too damn small. He wanted to stretch out his stride, to eat up the ground under his feet. He wanted to go for a run on the beach. What he really wanted was to shake Hallie until she changed her mind.

I blame you and I will never, ever forgive you.

Fear trickled down his spine in the form of perspiration. What had he expected? It was his fault she hadn't had her shot a year ago. It was his fault he hadn't come to reclaim her until last week. It was his fault she wouldn't get to be a mother. While he squandered her chances, he'd helped another woman become a mother.

He couldn't wait until she found out about that.

No wonder she wouldn't forgive him. Hell. He'd never forgive himself.

Damn. Damn, damn, damn.

He'd never had any knight-in-shining-armor instincts until he'd met Hallie. If he hadn't known her, he'd never have helped Nicole. If she hadn't known him, she'd have been involved with some other man and probably a mother already, or at least someone who would have had the brains to say yes when she asked.

He thought about Robert and the miracle of his

birth, and he clenched his fists. Hallie would never have that. His jaw tightened. She could blame him from here until doomsday, but it didn't change anything. She belonged to him. He'd never been so sure of anything in his life.

Baz stared out the window into the black night.

It was never this dark in L.A. The city lights kept the sky the color of charcoal. In the daytime, it was mostly a lighter shade of gray. This past year he couldn't remember seeing blue sky. He couldn't remember seeing bright colors. It wasn't L.A. It was Hallie.

God, he'd missed her.

He checked his watch again. She'd said it would be a short meeting, and it had already lasted ninety minutes. Was the sheriff there? Probably. If Baz had been in his shoes, he'd have been at that damn meeting.

He needed to do something. He grabbed a jacket and headed for the street. If nothing else, a run in the sub-freezing night might release some tension.

"We've received official permission from the Bureau of Indian Affairs," Cam Outlaw told the town council. "Weather permitting we can break ground on the resort as soon as we get the go-ahead from the Tribal council."

Everyone knew Cam and his partner, Bangor developer Nate Packer, didn't need permission from either the B.I.A. or the Blackbird Reservation's Tribal Council, but it was important to maintain friendly relations with the tribe, especially since the Blackbird Casino was the lure that would bring tourists to the luxurious Sunrise Resort and Spa scheduled to open in early summer.

All of central-western Maine needed economic development. The resort would create jobs for construction workers and hotel employees. It was a huge asset to the casino enterprise. Tourists would come to gamble, and they'd find luxury. They'd stay for longer periods, and they'd come again. All of that meant more money flowing into Eden County.

The only real objections had come from a small but vocal group of young men from the Rez who claimed Cam and Packer were planning to exploit the Native Americans. They were deaf to the argument that the resort and spa would complement each other, which meant more money for the Rez.

Hallie knew how badly the tribe needed every cent it could get. Her friend, Molly Whitecloud was a certified midwife, the only medical professional at Blackbird. Molly's dream was to build a community clinic for her people.

Cam's report reminded Hallie she had a message for him. She delivered it on the way home.

"I spoke with Molly just before Christmas. With all the uproar of the holiday and everything, I forgot to tell you. She said the council elders will vote at their meeting next week. She expects them to vote unanimously in favor of the project."

Cam's square jaw seemed to tighten as he guided his maroon-colored Mercedes through the dark, quiet streets of Eden. Hallie had seen that reaction before when Molly's name was mentioned.

It was as though Cam stepped back from the conversation. She wondered why. Was there some bad blood between Cam and Molly? They were about the same age. Had they known one another before he went off to college and then Boston?

Hallie wanted to ask but she didn't. Molly Whitecloud was a good friend. If she wanted to confide in Hallie she would. And she certainly wouldn't invade Cam's privacy without asking. Baz's brother had shared his family including his darling daughter with her. She liked and respected him too much to pry.

But she really wanted to know.

"Oh, there's one more thing. Molly said there might be a demonstration at Tribal Council meeting.

You know, those hotheads who don't want the lines between whites and Indians blurred."

"Okay."

"She's afraid there'll be trouble. They plan to have police at the meeting. Jake's jurisdiction doesn't extend to the Rez. She must mean the tribal cops."

Cam glanced at her. "Tribal cop."

"What?"

"There's only one,. Davey Tall Tree. He weighs about three hundred pounds and likes to wear bedroom slippers with his uniform. Oh, and he's a big fan of Wayne's World. Need I say more?"

Hallie grimaced. "Maybe Jake could come as an observer."

"Probably a good idea. He looks real intimidating in that uniform. By the way, what's up between the two of you? I thought there was something developing in that direction."

"We're destined to be friends. For some unknown reason, sometimes things that seem obvious to everyone else just don't work out."

"Baz?"

The man was entirely too perceptive. "He's a

complicating factor but, honestly, I'm not the right woman for Jake. He'd have figured it out sooner or later."

"So what is up between you and my brother?"

She noticed he'd neatly deflected the conversation away from Molly. "He wants to take up where we left off last year. I don't."

"C'mon, Hal. I saw the way you came apart at the ice rink. You still have feelings for the guy."

There was no real reason not to tell Cam about the infertility. He'd be sympathetic and closemouthed.

Maybe it would help him understand what was going on in his family circle. She gave him the thumbnail version.

"Shit."

"Yeah. Well, stuff happens. I'll be fine. Baz will be fine, too. All we have to do is get through the next three months."

"I know from my brief marriage that three months can seem like an eternity."

It was the first time Cam had confided anything about his past. "Do you think you'd have been divorced if she hadn't died?"

He shrugged. "Hard to say. I didn't realize how miserable I was until it was over. Then there was Daisy."

Hallie smiled. She always smiled when she thought of the little tyrant. "You are so lucky."

It was nearly eleven when she finally fell into bed. Sleep, for once, came quickly and blessedly, but when a harsh buzzer awakened her sometime later, she didn't feel refreshed. She opened one eye and peered at the bedside clock. No wonder.

She'd only been asleep nine minutes.

Hallie slammed the pillow over her head, but she could still hear the irritating buzzer. It took a long minute for her to figure out it was coming from the doorbell outside the clinic.

Emergency.

She shot out of bed, pulled on a pair of jeans and a sweatshirt, and pounded down the outside steps.

Her heart contracted at the sight of the small group huddled around the clinic door.

"Hi, gang," she said, her voice soft and sympathetic. She touched Marge Gregory's broad shoulder and smiled, gently, at each of the three children. "It's time?"

She phrased it as a question but it really wasn't.

The Gregory's little white poodle, Snowball, had made it to the impressive age of sixteen. Even though the dog still looked like a puppy, he was the equivalent of one hundred and twelve in human years. He'd had a great life.

It was never easy to lose a loved one. "Come on in," she said, trying to maintain a professional attitude in the face of their obvious sorrow.

This was the part of her job she hated. With the shock of Baz's presence and her fatigue, her coping skills were scraping the ground. She ushered the soon-to-be-bereaved family into the waiting room and winced at the Christmas tree decorated with ribbons and dog biscuits.

"Why don't you all have a seat out here. I'll be back in a minute." Hallie moved to the examining room and flipped on the lights. She'd started to prepare the syringe of pentobarbital sodium when she heard Baz's low voice behind her.

"What's going on?"

A shiver ran down her spine.

"What're you doing here?"

"The buzzer rings in the house, too. I figured I'd find out what's up."

The gray eyes were steady on her face. She knew he could see exactly what she was feeling because he put a steadying hand on her shoulder.

The tears were very near the surface now.

"Euthanasia?"

"I've got it covered. You can go back to bed."

He swore. "You're exhausted, Halliday. Let me do it or tell them to come back in the morning."

His comment didn't indicate heartlessness.

Euthanasia was routine for most vets. But it was never routine for the family.

"I can't do that."

"Why the hell not? You're out on your feet."

She looked into his flashing silver eyes. He was trying to take care of her. Did he think that, since he'd failed to give her a baby he could make it up by helping her with office stuff? "I told Marge I'd do it

when they finally got adjusted to the idea. They got adjusted tonight."

"Your hands are shaking."

She couldn't swallow around the lump in her throat as she went to the waiting room to retrieve Snowball. Each Gregory gave their pet one last kiss.

"Sit down," Baz commanded, as soon as she returned to the treatment room. He held the syringe in his hand. He took care of it with calm efficiency. It was all over quickly and, in spite of herself, Hallie felt grateful.

Baz cleaned up the room then he stood in the doorway and listened to the soft words of comfort Hallie gave the family. She was too damn softhearted for this job. She needed someone to protect her, to soften the risks inherent in the profession. He should have seen it last year but he'd

been too busy protecting himself.

Tonight he'd give his soul to be able to drive away her pain. A night of hot, over-the-top sex might do it, but that wasn't an option. He should've kept his hands off in the Jacuzzi, too. He had to find a way to show her he understood her disappointment. That he shared it.

The bell jingled as the family left. Hallie's slim figure was silhouetted in the arched window. Her disheveled curls gleamed in the low light. She had her arms wrapped around her waist as though she could draw some comfort from her own embrace.

He moved behind her and slid his arms around her, cocooning her with his body. He thought she'd protest, but she didn't. He stood there a long, long time letting his warmth seep into her until her stiff body relaxed against him.

She fit him so perfectly. He lowered his chin to rest it on top of her brown curls, and he stroked his hands up and down her arms. She trembled, and he felt his blood pooling in his groin. He still found it hard to believe she always had this effect on him.

One touch and he was ready to launch. Sometimes all it took was a look.

He felt his brain stand down as desire streaked through his body. Dimly, he heard her voice.

"It was the right time."

"What?" His voice was thick with need, but she didn't seem to notice.

"For Snowball. It was the right time to do it."

Snowball. It took him a minute to figure out she was talking about the late, lamented poodle. "Oh. Yeah. Yeah, it was."

"They loved him so much." Her voice broke, and he felt her sucking in deep breaths, trying not to cry.

He turned her in his arms and pressed her head against his shoulder hoping she would feel his warmth and compassion and not his arousal.

"Life and death, Hallie. That's the cycle. Come on." He drew her over to the sofa and down on his lap.

Hallie didn't protest. Sitting down she fit him perfectly, too. She leaned her head back against his shoulder and let out a little sigh. He tried to ignore his physical response and provide her with the comfort she craved.

When she snuggled closer, though, she rubbed against his fly. His erection flexed against her.

"Baz," she said.

"It's an involuntary response." He knew he sounded like a kid making excuses.

She turned toward him, her face reflecting amusement. "I know what it is." She placed a soft hand on his cheek. "Thanks for helping me, partner."

"You're welcome." He waited to see if she'd say anything else, but she didn't. He needed a neutral topic. Something completely non-sexual. "How's the bat?"

"I put him back in the attic. He might fly a little crooked after this."

Baz smiled. He started to lower his head. He could almost taste the sweetness of her mouth, hear the soft little sound she'd make. He knew she wouldn't protest.

Instead, he gathered himself and brought them both to their feet. "It's late, Hallie. C'mon. I'll walk you home."

She said nothing.

He tensed. Did she think he was making a pass?

"I meant I'll walk you to the stairs."

"Hush. I knew what you meant." She placed her forefinger on her lips and pressed it to his mouth.

He stifled a groan, left her at her door, and limped back across the yard. This couldn't go on much longer. He'd waited way too long for Hallie. A full year. He couldn't rush her though. Time was his friend in all this. Time and luck.

He'd really need the luck.

Hallie was a warm, loving woman. She'd probably forgive him, eventually, for the whole infertility debacle. The business with Nicole, however, would take a helluva lot of explaining especially since he kept having doubts about Robert.

Should he have left the baby with his flighty mother? Would the kid be all right? He missed the boy like the devil. Oddly enough he wanted Hallie to meet him, but that was unlikely to happen. Robert was the living proof of Baz's treachery. Every time she looked at the baby, she'd think about the baby she couldn't have. Anyway, Robert belonged to Nicole.

Baz scrubbed a hand down his face.

What a damn mess.

****

The next few days represented a period of détente. Hallie tried to enjoy the peace, but it wasn't easy to relax. She spent most of the day with Baz, her resistance to him wavering dangerously. Not only was he pleasant and helpful around the practice, he seemed to be a hit in the community.

He'd joined the ice festival committee, too. She didn't know whether it was that community-minded gesture or his hero status, but every client greeted him with real enthusiasm.

He fit into the small town. Not the way she did, because she lived here and worked here. She had joined the community. Baz belonged in a more fundamental way. He'd been born here as had his father before him.

He would always belong to Eden.

She tried not to dwell on that and to focus only on the improved relationship between them. Baz seemed to have gotten the message. She felt equal parts of relief and disappointment about that.

****

The day before New Year's Eve, Baz and Hallie drove out to see Blue. The little mare looked ready to pop. Baz told Ralph to call the minute labor started.

The directive startled Hallie. Was he anticipating trouble?

Janie looked different, too, more uncomfortable.

Her belly seemed lower, which probably meant the baby had dropped. Hallie caught Baz giving her a quick, professional look and realized he'd noticed it, too. A familiar emptiness filled her. She would never be round and ripe with his child. She would never hold his baby in her arms. She forced herself to smile at the young couple.

"I'm hoping Blue's foal and Ralph, Junior will both show up before midnight on New Year's Eve,"

Ralph joked. "I could use the tax deductions."

Hallie heard the nervousness in his voice. The Meadows lived some thirty-five miles from the nearest hospital. They were probably ten miles from a neighbor, and December in Maine could be unpredictable. Hallie couldn't blame Ralph for worrying a little. "Do you two have any family coming for the birth?" she asked. She kept her voice soothing and casual.

"My mom can't come for another week," Janie said. "She's with my sister. Clara had her first on Christmas Day. She named her Noelle."

"What a lovely name," Hallie said.

"Janie's not due till January sixteenth." Ralph's tone implied he expected that date to be solid.

"You know you can call either of us any time," Hallie said. "Both of you."

Baz glanced at her after they'd climbed into the pickup. "'You can call either of us any time at all?'"

"They just look so scared."

Baz's mouth formed a straight line. "They're smart to be scared. They're way out here to hell and gone. If there's a snowstorm and an emergency, they'll be in real trouble."

"Well, let's hope there's neither one. First babies take a long time coming."

"Not always."

She glanced at him. "You have experience with that?"

"I'm a doctor. I've seen a lot of births."

She couldn't argue with that. A large animal doc got in on the action a lot more often than a vet who specialized in companion animals.

Hallie peered anxiously at the lowering skies overhead. The wind had been whipping pretty hard around the barnyard, but as far as she'd been able to find out, there were no storms predicted until after the New Year. The heater inside the cab felt good.

She realized, though, that Baz hadn't moved.

"What's up?"

"There is more than one way to have a family Hallie. There's adoption, for example."

For an instant she froze. The comment had come out of nowhere, and she hadn't been prepared. "No," she snapped at him.

"Why the hell not?"

"I'm not interested in adoption." She remembered, vividly, that day she returned from camp the summer her dad had died. She'd overheard her mother telling her friend Pauline that she planned to put Hallie in boarding school in the fall.

"I've come to the conclusion that I'm not really mother material," her mom had said.

"It's natural you should feel that way, Louise.

It's not as if she were your real child. And it was really Harry who wanted to adopt."

Hallie considered that summer a turning point. She'd been only thirteen, but from then on, she'd seen her mother only on holidays and vacations.

She'd remained dutiful right up until Louise Scott's death, but she'd found comfort in the prospect of one day having a child of her own. In her opinion, adoption didn't work.

"I'd think you of all people would understand that a kid is a kid. After all, you were adopted."

She rounded on him. "I was adopted. You know

what I learned from that experience? Blood is thicker than water."

"That doesn't even make sense."

"It does to me."

He shook his head. "I'm not letting you off the hook with some enigmatic epigram. If you've got a prejudice against adoption, you'd damn well better tell me what it is."

She seemed to be telling all her secrets these days. This one was especially sensitive. Her mother hadn't loved her. It made her sound like a monster.

But it was clear now Baz wouldn't give up easily.

Maybe if he understood just how inflexible she was on this point, he'd leave her alone. She sucked in a breath and gave him the Cliff's Notes version of the overheard conversation.

He stared at her for a long minute. "Well, hell,"

he said. Then he put the truck in gear. He didn't speak for several miles. Finally, he said, "Blood isn't always as strong as you might think. My mother abandoned two of her children, and she used me as a weapon against my dad. Every case is different."

"I'm sorry about your mom, but that isn't the point. Since I was thirteen I've wanted to have a biological tie with someone. A baby." She felt emotion crowding her windpipe. In another minute she wouldn't be able to talk. "Adoption won't work for me, Baz. I don't believe in it, and I don't want it."

The words were harsh, but she couldn't regret saying them. They were true.

Chapter Eight

For the next couple of miles, she thought she'd ended the discussion. Then all at once he spoke.

"You know what your problem is? You don't get the concept of parenthood, Halliday. It isn't about frilly outfits or cute teddy bears or picking baby names.

It's about pain. It's about taking responsibility for another human being and discovering you've made a lifelong commitment to worry and fear and, if you do your job right, to loneliness. You don't get a kid for life. You get to participate in raising him for eighteen or so years, and then you get to watch from the sidelines while he either sinks or swims. Blood has very little to do with that."

She fell back against the seat and gaped at him.

"My God, Baz. No wonder you didn't want to be a parent. What about the hugs and smiles and the way they turn your heart to mush? What about Daisy.

Do you think Cam would send her back if he could?"

Baz said nothing.

"What about your dad? Do you know how often he talks about you? He's so damn happy to see you back home he was willing to give up his practice for three months."

"Speaking of my dad, I heard him tell you several times that you're a member of this family."

"It's a figure of speech. He didn't mean it. Do you think for one minute he would have chosen my comfort over yours? Do you think he'd have canceled his trip because I asked him to?"

"He thinks he owes me."

She shook her head. "It isn't that. He loves you.

Your happiness means more to him than anything else because you're his son."

He didn't try to argue with her. They rode back to Eden in silence, but, unlike the other night, it wasn't hostile. They'd each learned something about the other, and the new knowledge made it even clearer to Hallie that they had no future together.

Finally, he pulled into the Outlaw garage and stopped the truck. She popped open her door, but his hand on her arm detained her.

"Go to the Grange Hall Dance with me tomorrow night."

It was tempting. She'd like nothing more than one last evening of being held in his arms. But it would be foolish and, besides, she had a prior commitment. "I can't. I'm going with Jake."

His hold tightened on her wrist. "Break the date. Tell him you're going with your lover."

"You're not my lover, Baz."

"Are. Were. Will be again."

She stared at him. "Is this the way it's going to be for the next three months?"

He nodded. "This is the way it's gonna be until you come to your senses. I came here to get you Hallie. I'm not giving up."

She let out a half-shriek of frustration and he let go. She shoved open the door.

"Hallie."

She turned around. She squinted her eyes and shook her head. "You just don't get it. I don't want you anymore. Not for keeps. The past is dead, Baz. It has to be. I told you I'll never forgive you."

"You already mentioned that."

****

I'll never forgive you.

For the first time Baz felt a jolt of real panic.

Not that he planned to give up but never was a long time.

He refilled the tumbler of golden whiskey for the third time and stared at the books in his father's study. The house was quiet with the silence that comes only after midnight.

He'd been so sure he could convince her to give him another chance. Last year she said she loved him. Did love die? Had he killed it with his poor timing and ill-conceived gesture toward Nicole? He didn't know. His experience with love was minimal.

All he knew for certain was that he couldn't face a life without Hallie. He slumped in his chair. He hated this feeling of helplessness. She resented him for what he'd cost her, well, dammit, he resented her, too, but he hadn't held it against her. She was the one who coaxed him off his island. She was the one who lured him into the human race. She was the one who penetrated his carefully built fortress and made him long for life. For her.

And she thought this was over?

Not a chance in hell.

She still needed him. She still wanted him. She still loved him.

She just didn't know it.

The room swayed before his eyes. He needed a plan. He'd always been good with plans. He'd come up with something. He felt his eyelashes against his cheeks. He'd come up with a great plan.

But first, he'd get a little rest.

****

The next morning Hallie sat in the Outlaw's empty kitchen and sipped coffee doused liberally with milk. She'd have preferred to have breakfast in her cozy apartment today, but she wasn't letting Baz force her into hibernation. She wasn't letting him push her out of her own life.

The door from the butler's pantry swung open.

Baz and Cameron entered together. Each was devastating in his own right. Together they were enough to hot-wire any woman's hormones.

"Happy New Year," she said, forcing a bright smile.

Cam echoed the greeting. Baz grunted and headed for the coffeepot. He poured himself a cup and stood looking out the kitchen window into the snow-covered courtyard. He drained the cup in one long swallow.

"Good grief," she said. "Why don't you take it in an I.V.? It'd be faster and wouldn't cauterize your entire digestive system."

Cam poured some for himself and took a seat at the table. Baz said nothing. He poured more coffee and made his way to the table, his gait careful, his face tight.

"Brother Baz overindulged last night," Cam explained. "Celebrating the New Year early."

Baz shot him an annoyed look as he lowered

himself into a chair. He did look kind of pale.

Without thinking Hallie reached over to touch his wrist. "Are you all right?"

"I'm dandy," he growled. He didn't pull away, but he didn't look at her either.

"Somebody got up on the wrong side of the bed," Cam teased.

"Somebody got up in the wrong bed," he muttered.

Hallie went very still. Surely he wouldn't refer to their physical relationship right here at the breakfast table in front of God and his brother.

Cam lifted his eyebrows at Hallie, but he didn't speak.

Baz chugged his coffee then he turned to Hallie.

He moved his head as if it were a prize piece of china he was trying not to jostle. "I'll check on the farm stock."

She studied his face. How hung over was he? Would he be all right driving down the twisty country roads in his current condition?

"I'll go with you," she offered.

"No. Thank you." His response left no room to maneuver.

The sheepskin coat he had taken into the river hadn't been cleaned. Baz shouldered into a bright green parka that was at least a size too small. A minute later he was gone. They heard the truck's engine turn over then the sound of Baz backing out of the driveway.

"What do you think the chances are he'll hit the mailbox?" Cam asked.

"Seventy-five percent? He's pretty coordinated. Whose jacket was that?"

"I have no idea. One of Lucy's college boyfriends

probably left it here." Cam seemed to study her face.

"Something new happen between you, two?"

"Not really. Another heated discussion. Your brother doesn't take no for an answer."

"His stubbornness is well documented. Look how long he held out before he came to Maine. Twenty years. For most of that time he was alone, Hallie. I think he'd gotten used to it. When you came along, it must have given him a hard enough jolt to re-wire his circuits. I can understand why he wants you back."

She probably shouldn't have been surprised at Cam's perception. She'd seen the same quality in his father and his brother.

"He'll find someone else." She spoke with a lightness she didn't feel.

"Are you sure that's what you want?"

She nodded. Baz's presence just reminded her of what she'd lost. There was another consideration too; she'd realized last year that he needed a family.

He needed children of his own.

She smiled faintly. "Sometimes I think the hardest person to build a relationship with is an ex.

It's like all the bridges were burned or something.

You've got proof that you don't work as a couple."

A shadow passed over his well-defined features.

"I hear you."

She was more than ready to change the subject.

"Who're you taking to the Grange Hall Dance tonight?"

"Leila Gunderson. She married one of my high school buddies who was killed in Afghanistan."

"Wow. That must have been so hard."

"I'm sure it was. I was down in Boston at the

107

time." He smiled at her. "You're going with Jake?"

"We made the date a couple of weeks ago." She didn't know why she felt it was important to point that out. She'd just told him she wasn't interested in his brother.

"Save me a dance?"

"Absolutely."

Hallie found the clinic's waiting room full. Everybody, it seemed, was intent on getting their problems solved before the office closed for the holiday. She worked her way through the list.

Fred McGee suspected his two German shepherd pups had ringworm (they did.) Gladys Miller was worried about her pedigreed Persian's sudden weight gain (pregnancy). Barney Smith, who probably hadn't visited a dentist himself in five years, brought in his mutt, George, to have the tartar cleaned off his teeth.

Late in the morning Daisy arrived with a leashed Wilbur. The leash was just for show, of course. Wilbur, the laziest of pigs, was most unlikely to make a break for freedom. He was smart, too. He stayed glued to Daisy's side.

The twosome had brought freshly baked pig shaped sugar cookies, and, in between patients Daisy, Hallie, and Mavis conducted a hasty tea party.

Jolene surprised her by calling around lunchtime.

"Aren't you busy?" The Pink Poodle was Eden's only hair salon.

"Frantic. I just wanted to check a couple of things with you. You are wearing the red dress tonight."

It wasn't a question.

"I guess."

"We picked out that dress especially for tonight,"

Jo reminded her.

"I know."

"You need to get down here and let me do your hair."

"My hair's okay. You've got to be swamped."

"Look, girlfriend, you've got two of the hottest guys in town sniffing at your door. The least you can do is look your best."

Hallie didn't tell her friend that both those hot guys would soon be on the market again. "Aren't you busy?"

"Busier than a stud bull in mating season.

Everybody in town's coming in here to get a 'do,' but I've got time for you."

Hallie couldn't refuse. Outside of the Outlaw family, Jo and Sharon were her best friends. She knew they'd been worried about her since she received the diagnosis. Jo probably thought a beautified, sexy Hallie would inspire Baz or Jake to make a proposal that would make it up to her for not being able to have a baby.

"This has nothing to do with the Prodigal Hunk," Jo said. "I just want you to look your best.

After all, New Year's Eve only comes once a year."

"Okay, okay. I'll be over in a bit. Daze and I are just finishing some of Asia's incredible cookies."

"Bring one for me. Oh, by the way, I saw Jake yesterday afternoon."

"Did he come in to get his hair done, too?"

"Very funny. No, he was out on the sidewalk yelling at Lucy Outlaw. Something about illegal parking. You know, it's weird. He's unfailingly polite with everyone else. Anyway, he said to tell you he'd pick you up around six. Apparently he's giving Sharon and her date a ride. We'll meet you at the hall."

Hallie hung up the phone. She'd really looked forward to the Grange Hall Dance. It fit right in with her fantasy of a close-knit small town. She'd bought the racy red dress and shoes to match, and she'd looked forward to spending a romantic evening with Jake. She sighed.

Instead, thanks to Baz, she'd have to let the sheriff know she was no longer interested. Damn.

She realized, too late, that she'd forgotten to ask about Sharon's date. The tall, stunning redhead was determinedly single, and Hallie knew Jo intended to fix her up with somebody.

She shrugged. She'd find out soon enough.

The day continued at a whirlwind pace, and by the time she returned to her apartment to dress, she was exhausted. There was just enough time for a quick, power nap, but, despite the alarm, she overslept.

"Curse the snooze button," she muttered as she bolted into the shower and turned on the spray.

Too late she remembered her newly coiffed hair.

"Nuts!" She slammed off the shower, but the bouffant "do" was gone forever.

Great. Now she'd look like a drowned rat. A cranky drowned rat.

Hallie towel-dried her hair. Immediately, the curls Jolene had worked so hard to subdue reappeared. She rubbed vanilla-scented moisturizer onto her skin and slid into the flapper-style fire engine red dress. It had fit perfectly when Jolene convinced her to buy it last month. Now it was a little loose.

Stress would do that to a person. Her eyes

narrowed. Another sin to lay at Basil Outlaw's door.

She studied the mirror. From the front, the dress looked sleek and sophisticated with its high neckline and spaghetti straps. What made it distinctive was the back. It consisted of a series of narrow crisscrossed straps that ended at the base of her spine.

Hallie hadn't been sure about the frock, but Jolene said it was sexy and provocative while remaining tasteful. She'd liked it and she'd bought it.

Now she wondered whether she should wear it at all. Would Jake get the wrong idea or worse, think she was a tease? Maybe she should just put on the black sheath she'd worn to every formal occasion since college. But then she couldn't wear the adorable strappy red shoes.

Hallie heaved a sigh of exasperation. Wardrobe was so much more complicated when there were men involved. She applied a little blush, some mascara and lip-gloss, and glared at her reflection in the mirror. Her hair looked like seaweed. She'd just plugged in the hairdryer when she heard Jake at the door.

Well, dang. He was early. At least the seaweed hair would offset any inappropriate message sent by the red dress.

She swung the door wide, an apology on her lips, but the man standing tall, dark and impatient on her doorstep wasn't the sheriff. She gasped at the sight of the perfectly cut black tuxedo that hugged the masculine lines of his body. His gray eyes blazed and the lines around his mouth deepened. Just for a minute, Hallie couldn't take in any oxygen at all.

He knew it, too. The toad. He gave her his slow grin, the one that always turned her inside out.

"Nice dress." He walked in as if he owned her place.

His eyes glittered. "Very nice dress."

"You look n-nice, too," she stammered. "Why are you here?"

"No sense in taking two cars. I figured I could ride with you. I cleared it with Deputy Dawg."

"Fine," she said. Butterflies filled Hallie's stomach and she felt lightheaded. The evening that had looked so dreary just a few minutes ago sparkled dangerously before her. "I'm almost ready to go."

"You're not ready. Your hair's wet."

"It'll dry."

He put a firm hand on her wrist. "You'll get sick, Halliday. Go on and dry it."

She shouldn't listen to him. He wasn't her keeper or her lover or her anything.

"You're such a tyrant." She made a face at him and pivoted sharply.

"Hold it." It was a command. "You are not going anywhere in that dress."

Good grief.

"Let me guess. You don't like the back."

"What back? It doesn't have a back. You're practically nude. You are nude. It's outrageous. Go change."

"It's stylish. And I'd like to remind you that you have no right to tell me what to wear."

"I'm not telling you what to wear. I'm telling you what not to wear." He thrust long fingers through his hair, giving it a tousled, sexy look. "This is a dance, Halliday. That big ox will want to put his arm around you."

"He's not a big ox," Hallie protested. At least he'd confirmed her decision on which dress to wear.

No way was she changing into the black sheath now.

He clenched his fists, and his voice grew as steely as his eyes. "He'll be touching your naked back."

"The big ox is here," Jake called out in a cheerful voice as he walked in through the unlatched door. Hallie hadn't heard him come up the stairs. "And for the record, I don't have any problem with touching her naked back."

Baz's eyes shot fire. Typical, Hallie thought. He showed no self-consciousness at being overheard calling Jake a name. In fact, he ignored the other man and glared at her.

"Change your clothes, Halliday."

"I'm not changing, Baz. Get over it."

"She's fine just the way she is," Jake added, mildly. "Besides, I'm afraid it's too late." He grinned at Hallie. "You have to wear red." He produced a lightweight plastic container inside of which was nestled an oyster-colored orchid with a bright red center. "I consulted Jolene, so I'm pretty sure it'll look perfect on the dress."

"Oh, Jake," said Hallie, "it is perfect."

"So are you." He dropped a kiss on Hallie's nose and pinned the corsage to her dress with a deft, competent move. A girl would be damn lucky to have a guy like Jake. Hallie mourned what might have been. Baz's face matched the center of the orchid.

Hallie felt the steam rising off him from several feet away, but he didn't comment on the flower or the kiss. "Dry your hair," he barked.

She did. He was right and, besides, drying gained her a modicum of control with those dancing curls. When she came out of the bathroom, Baz snatched up her coat before Jake could get it, and he held it open for her.

Then he glanced at her feet. "Very practical, Halliday. I can see you slogging through two feet of snow in those."

"She won't have to slog," said Jake, easily. "I'll carry her to and from the car."

Baz had moved to within an inch of Jake before Hallie could get the next words out of her mouth.

They were a couple of great looking men, she thought, equally tall and well built, one dark, one blond. Intelligent men, too. Though neither one was revealing that quality at the moment.

"I've got boots," she said, hastily, dragging them out of the closet. "Nobody has to carry anybody."

She put on her boots, and Jake took her arm.

"I'd be honored to carry you," he said, in an intimate voice. "You couldn't weigh much more than a sack of potatoes."

She laughed at him, and swatted him on the arm.

Baz didn't say anything else, but when Jake helped her into the passenger's side of the Blazer, Baz told her to move over on the bench seat, and she was forced to sit between the two of them for the seven-minute ride to the Garden of Eden.

"I kinda like this arrangement," Jake said, cheerfully. "Gives me an excuse to sit closer to you."

A sound came up out of Baz's chest, but it didn't turn into words.

Hallie was so busy trying not to breathe in the

devastating testosterone she didn't notice when Jake pulled into a parking spot in front of the Garden of Eden.

"Be right back." Baz opened the passenger side door.

"Where are you going?"

"To pick up my date."

His date? Suddenly it all made sense.

Sharon. Baz's date was Sharon.

Jealousy hit Hallie like a barrel of Gatorade after a soccer win. Sharon was perfect for Baz. On top of her other sterling qualities, she was originally a city girl. The two would find sorts of things in common.

"Hallie?"

She forced her mind back to the present.

"Everything, okay?"

She reminded herself she'd turned the other man down. He had a perfect right to date anyone he wanted. She found a smile for Jake. "How are Sam and Lillie?"

"Fine. Listen, I get the distinct impression you and Outlaw have a past. Not that I'm asking about that. All I want to know is if you're looking for a future with him."

"I'm not. I worked for him in L.A., but whatever we had then is over. He's just here to help out his dad." It was a lie, and they both knew it.

The sheriff shrugged. "The doc's like a lighted stick of dynamite around you. You're different, too.

Kind of restless."

She felt like pond scum. "All right. You deserve to know the truth, Jake. Heck, you deserve so much more. Your instincts are right about us. There's bad blood, and there's unfinished business."

He nodded. "Thanks for being honest with me.

My advice, Hal? Be honest with yourself." He really was such a decent man. Hallie wanted to cry.

A moment later the backdoor of the Blazer opened, and she turned to greet her friend. Sharon's rich auburn hair and her milky complexion contrasted beautifully with Baz's dark presence. The two were laughing and Hallie felt that horrible flare of jealousy again.

"Happy New Year," she said to Sharon.

To her ears it sounded like a curse.

Chapter Nine

When she first arrived in town, Hallie had spent hours in the tiny Eden Library. She'd researched Eden County the way someone else might have studied genealogy to construct a family tree. The Eden County Grange Hall had been built in the late years of the nineteenth twentieth century as a place for farmers to gather to discuss mutual concerns and to share supplies. Its location, five miles east of Eden, had been chosen because James Eden, a descendant of one of the first settlers, had donated the property "to be used for the public good."

Back then people thought Eden would grow and, ultimately, the Grange Hall would be within the town's boundaries, but the local logging industry collapsed because of a dispute between two brothers, and the woolen mill moved to a more centralized location. Eden stayed small, and the Grange Hall remained five miles away.

Nowadays the place was used for family reunions or weddings. Tonight it was decked out with evergreen swags on the knotty pine walls and twinkle lights threaded through potted plants. A glittering silver ball hung from the ceiling. As it rotated, it scattered shards of light on the dancefloor.

George Stout, owner of Big George's Appliances located on Route 2 between Eden and its larger neighbor to the north, Bangor, served as self-appointed disc jockey and emcee for local events.

His motto was "Something for Everyone" and that applied to music as well as microwaves.

Big George was playing The Big Noise from Winnetka as they walked in. Hallie's spirits lifted.

She loved big band music. Her spirits rose. Tonight marked her one-year anniversary in Maine, and she intended to celebrate.

After they checked their coats, Hallie, Jake, and Sharon joined Jolene and her date at a table while Baz scouted out drinks.

"Guess there's no point asking what happened to your hair," she said, as she gave Hallie the once over.

Hallie made a face. "Looks pretty bad, doesn't it?"

Jo shrugged. "Not bad. Just different from the way it did in my shop." She lifted a hand. "Don't explain. Let's get some punch. There's fruit or lemonade. I think both of them are already spiked."

"Thank God," Hallie murmured. She might have to spend the evening watching Baz and Sharon Velcro-ed to each other on the dance floor, but at least she wouldn't have to do it sober. He made his way across the room as if he owned it. People stepped out of his way like waves before the prow of a ship. He wasn't the handsomest man in the room, she thought, but he was definitely the most compelling.

Hallie wasn't the only woman to notice. Lots of feminine eyes lingered at the dark man in the perfectly fitted tuxedo.

Cam arrived with his date and, almost as soon as the introductions were made, Big George replaced the swing tunes to oldies from the Sixties, like the romantic

"Unchained Melody" and "When a Man Loves a Woman."

It was a signal to dance, and most of the couples did. But not all. Hallie noticed that Baz had mousetrapped Jake into a conversation down at the end of the long table. His maneuver left Sharon and herself sitting alone.

"I wonder," Sharon said, thoughtfully, "if Baz's sudden intense interest in the Eden County traffic laws has anything to do with your backless dress."

"Good grief, no. Baz is just contrary. Everyone else is dancing, so he isn't. He'll probably want to dance when Big George is taking a break."

Sharon seemed to study her. "How is it working with him?"

"Not that bad. Lots of the time he's out seeing to the farm animals, but even when he's around, there's no problem."

"You know Cameron fixed us up. I think maybe he was trying to make you jealous."

Well he'd succeeded. She was jealous and guilt-y ridden. If there was anything worse than seeing another woman with the guy you wanted, it was seeing one of your best friends in that position.

"Hmmm."

"There's nothing to worry about. Baz told me why he's back in Eden. I know he's hoping for a reconciliation. He's a nice guy, but this is just an arranged date."

"You think he's a nice guy?"

"He's a great guy. Everybody in town is saying so. Does that surprise you?"

"Back in L.A. he was so taciturn the lab techs

called him Stoneface."

"That's kind of hard to believe. He's so easy and friendly here."

"He belongs here. It's his home."

"I think it's because of you, Hallie."

Another splash of guilt hit Hallie. "I'm sorry."

Sharon laughed. "If it'll make you feel better, I'll tell you a little secret. I'm kind of interested in his brother."

Hallie followed her gaze to the dance floor where Cameron was dancing. She had to admit the younger Outlaw brother was devastatingly attractive in his tux, too.

"Who's that he's with?" Sharon indicated his blue-haired partner.

"I think it's another former Sunday school teacher. Apparently every lady in town over the age of fifty spent some time teaching Sunday school."

"You look lovely, by the way," Hallie said, belatedly. Sharon's floor-length lemon chiffon gown emphasized her lovely pale skin and auburn hair.

"Out of this world."

Sharon grinned at her. "And you look hot." She circled her punch glass with long, slim fingers and lifted it to her lips. Hallie's gaze fell on her wrist corsage of tiny yellow roses. They matched her dress.

Baz had certainly gone to some trouble for an arranged date.

"Jo looks fabulous in that little black number, doesn't she?"

"Fabulous. But she doesn't look thrilled to be with Donny Hanson." The Hansons owned and operated Eden's only body shop. Jo caught Hallie's eye and waved.

The song ended, and while Big George chose another selection, Jolene marched over to where the women sat. She inclined her head at the men.

"What's up with those two—broken legs?"

"My date is trying to keep Hallie's date off the dance floor," Sharon said.

"That sounds healthy."

All of a sudden Hallie was sick of ruining the evening for everyone else. "I'll take care of this." She pushed back her chair. She caught Jake's eye, and he excused himself. Within seconds they were on the dance floor twirling under the silver ball to the sounds of Dave Brubeck.

Jake held her lightly as though she were delicate and valuable. She smiled up at him.

"I had an interesting talk with your partner," he said, neutrally. Hallie's heart stopped. She braced herself for his next words, but they weren't what she expected. "He was telling me about your work in L.A. He said he knew then that you'd make a great country vet."

Hallie felt a burst of pride.

"By the way, where's his scofflaw of a sister?"

It wasn't just the derogatory word. It was his harsh tone.

"If you're talking about Lucy, she's in Boston visiting a college friend. Why do you call her a scofflaw?"

Suddenly he sounded like the cop he was. "I caught her speeding out on Route two 2 on Christmas Eve. Gave her a warning."

"Oh. She was probably hurrying home for

Christmas Eve supper. It's a tradition with the Outlaws."

He frowned. "Doesn't she live here?"

"Sure. I guess she was shopping in Bangor or maybe she'd taken a freelance assignment for the Excelsior. She wants to be a war correspondent someday."

"I shudder to think of her in a battlefield situation."

"I know," Hallie said, seriously. "It could be really dangerous."

"For the soldiers."

She drew back and looked at him. "What's gotten into you? Lucy's a great young woman. How did she get on your bad side?"

"She's too good for Eden."

"It's not that. She's just anxious to experience other places. She's so young. She wants to spread her wings."

He shrugged his big shoulders. "I'm not crazy about her attitude."

"Well, for your information, Sam and Lillie like her attitude just fine. Lucy and I ran into them and Mrs. Peach last Friday night at Little Joe's. The kids love her."

He made a face. "I know. Sam named his pet rat, Lucy, Junior."

"That's quite an honor."

He held her hand more tightly. Suddenly she had to know what he was thinking. "Jake? What's really going on here? Do you have a little crush on Lucy?"

"Hell, no. She's a kid. I don't want to talk about her anymore."

Hallie played the conversation back in her mind as

he pulled her closer and danced her across the floor. Jake and Lucy? It was an unlikely duo. Jake needed a mother for his twins, and Lucy was poised to dive into life. And there was that thirteen-year age difference. She reminded herself that the nine years between Baz's age and her own had made no difference at all.

As if he wanted to stop her thoughts, Jake tucked her head under his chin and whirled her around in a series of quick, precise steps. She needed all her concentration just to keep up with him. After a while he loosened his hold, and they slowed to a trot. It was then that she caught sight of Baz's strong arm circling Sharon's slim waist. Unlike herself, Sharon was tall. Her head wouldn't fit under Baz's chin, but it looked just right resting on his shoulder. They looked so good together. Like an advertisement for People Magazine's most beautiful couples.

When Jake finally released Hallie, Cameron claimed a dance. He was so skilled she didn't have to do a thing but hang on.

"Whew," she breathed, after a series of intricate moves, "where did you learn to dance?"

"My wife and I attended a lot of functions when I was at the bank in Boston. She hired a private instructor for me."

"It certainly paid off. It's so easy to follow your lead."

"I'm glad you're having fun."

"I am." She caught a glimpse of Baz dancing with Jolene. As always, her friend was talking a mile a minute. "It looks like your brother's having fun, too."

Cam laughed. "I figured it'd be good for him to get out of the house."

Hallie danced with Donny Hanson, and the mayor, and then again with Jake. Baz kept his distance, and she was grateful for that. It annoyed her that she was aware of his location at all times, and, whenever she looked in his direction, she met his steady, gray gaze.

Some forty-five minutes before midnight, she was back on the dance floor with Jake when she realized Baz was with someone new. The flamboyant blonde wore a pink dress that must have been painted on. She was voluptuous without being fat, sexy without being pretty. Long, suntanned arms twined around the veterinarian's neck, and she was pressed up against him as if she'd decided to make a rubbing of his body.

Tension raced through Hallie. Jake must have felt it. "Something wrong?"

"Just getting a little tired."

"Let's sit this one out."

She let him lead her back to the table, but she couldn't seem to take her eyes off the long, red-tipped fingers threading their way through Baz's rumpled hair.

"Hallie?" Jake sounded concerned. "You're practically vibrating." He pulled her into a comforting embrace and she buried her face in his shoulder.

"I'm so sorry."

She felt his big hand cuffing her head. "I understand, honey. Sometimes it just hits you like a Mack truck. You can't help the way you feel."

He really was the perfect man. And she was an idiot.

On the dance floor, the blonde had changed positions. She was still plastered against Baz, but her fingers were unbuttoning his jacket. Ugh.

"I'll be back," Hallie told Jake. She headed for the

refreshment table where Jo was helping herself to a glass of punch.

"You're flushed," her friend said.

"Just thirsty." She gulped down two cups of a liquid that had probably started out as lemonade, but was now about ninety percent rum. "Who is that woman Velcro-ed to Baz?"

Jolene had been born in Eden and knew everybody in town. "Diane Cobbs. Pastor Cobbs'

daughter if you can believe it. She went to school with Baz. Her name's Diane Sanderson now. She's just moved back here after a divorce."

Jolene gasped. "Am I seeing things or is her hand really inside his shirt?"

How could Baz make a spectacle of himself in front of the whole town? How could he do this to Sharon? How could he do it to his family?

How could he do it to her?

"It's like she's got her claws into him," Jo went on. "Literally. If she shoves that boob up any higher, it'll be in his mouth. I wonder if he can tell it's an implant. You'll have to ask him tomorrow at the clinic."

Hallie didn't feel capable of asking anybody anything. Her blood pressure shot through the roof as she watched Diane rub herself against her partner's crotch.

"Real subtle," Jolene muttered.

"Real slutty," Hallie said, loudly. Too late she realized the music had stopped. A pair of silver eyes locked onto hers, heat exploded in her veins. It was the final straw in a day of bad straws. She threw off the habits of a lifetime of propriety and charged across the dance floor until she reached the couple. She wedged herself between them. Diane, not expecting what amounted to an attack, fell back with an outraged bleat. Baz gave her a cool, superior smile.

"Is there a problem, Halliday?"

She glared at him.

"The Outlaws have a reputation in this town. A reputation that does not include lewd behavior in public."

"What are you talking about?" Diane's face was flushed. Hallie realized she had heavily indulged in the punch. "We were just dancing. Not that it's any business of yours."

"Dancing, my ass. You were fondling my business partner."

Baz's dark brows lifted in surprise, and Diane snickered. "Well, honey, you've gotta admit he's one helluva package."

Hallie drew in a breath, prepared to issue another scalding reprimand, but a strong arm came around her waist and pulled her back. "Let go of me, Basil. You should be ashamed of yourself," she sputtered as she tried to wriggle free.

"You're drunk, Hallie. You need some fresh air."

For an instant she thought he was going to take her outside. Instead he signaled his brother. "Get her some air. Or coffee."

Cameron reached for Hallie, and the barracuda zoomed back into Baz's arms. Hallie couldn't stand it anymore. "I don't need air or coffee. I need you to take me home."

"I'm busy."

"Well, too bad. I feel sick."

"Maybe you're pregnant," Diane said. "Dancing

and booze always made me sick when I was pregnant."

Hallie couldn't move. Jealousy gave way to a paralyzing sense of despair. She was aware of people moving and things whirling around her, and then she felt a strong arm around her waist.

"You know," Baz said, with a sigh, "sometimes you are nothing but trouble."

The next thing she felt was the sting of sleet on her cheeks. It felt cold and good. He stuffed her into the front seat of Cam's Mercedes.

"I'm so sorry," she said. "I don't know what on earth got into me."

"No big deal. It was just a drunken rant.

Happens all the time on New Year's Eve."

"It's never happened to me before. That's the last time I drink punch at a public function." How could she face her friends and her clients in the coming days? Everyone would think she was a rude, jealous, lush and they'd be right.

The engine roared; the big vehicle slipped and slid as Baz cleared the parking lot and made his way to the country road. He drove slowly, but the heavy sleet had already coated the surfaces and the car kept fishtailing.

"Shit," he muttered.

The driving conditions didn't even figure on Hallie's radar screen.

"There is one thing you should be prepared for. Everyone in Eden now thinks you're pregnant."

Before she could recover from the shock, he added to it. "Even when they find out you're not, they'll still know we're sleeping together."

"Oh. My.God."

He shook his head. "There's nothing as efficient as

the Eden grapevine."

For the first time Hallie saw some drawbacks in small town life. She wished she could click her strappy red, sleet-soaked heels and disappear.

She stared out the window. "It's sleeting."

"I see your brain hasn't totally gone on strike."

The words were dry, but his tone was mild.

"I'll fix this," she assured him. "I'll make sure everybody knows I'm not pregnant, and we're not a couple."

"Honey, no one's gonna believe you. Hell, even I don't believe you. I can't believe there's anyone who hasn't seen the sparks between us."

"Diane Cobbs Sanderson?"

"Well, maybe one person."

She buried her face in her hands. "I can't believe I was accusing you of impropriety then I took your family's good name and stomped on it. I am so sorry."

"It's not the end of the world."

He was right. She was acting like a ninny. She took in a long breath and let it out. "I'll just tell everybody who asks that I had an aneurism."

"Or, we could handle it another way."

"What way _ —a murder-suicide pact?"

"We could get married."

The Mercedes hit a patch of black ice and spun three hundred and sixty degrees. Hallie didn't even panic. She knew Baz could straighten out the car and she was right. She made a mental list of all the reasons she couldn't marry him.

She waited for a feeling of disgust. She searched for words of rejection. She thought about how she'd felt tonight when she'd seen that barracuda Diane all over him. She might as well face it.

She wasn't going to get over Baz Outlaw. His persistence was wearing her down because she didn't really want to say no.

Baz's heart pumped at twice the normal speed.

He'd agreed to dance with Diane Cobbs in hopes that he'd get a little rise out of Hallie, but he hadn't expected a complete meltdown. He considered it a very hopeful sign. But he wanted much more than a sign. He wanted her signature on the bottom line.

She was humiliated now and vulnerable. This was the time to seal the deal. "It's the best option," he pointed out.

"I've given you my reasons for why it won't work," she said. But her protest had no teeth.

"Look. It's obvious there's still something between us. Remember the Jacuzzi? And tonight you practically self-combusted on the dance floor."

He pulled into the triple-bay garage and stopped the car.

"It was that octopus. It was just really annoying to see her hands all over you."

"That's because we belong together. Come on Halliday, this is the only thing that makes sense and you know it."

She didn't answer him. She shoved open the door and headed across the courtyard. The sleet had hardened the snow left over from an earlier storm.

Her feet made loud crunching noises as she strode toward her apartment. He realized they'd forgotten her boots. Her feet had to be ice cubes.

She was inside, and he was half way up the outside stairs when his cell phone rang. He cursed, softly. They were right in the middle of delicate negotiations. He hauled it out of his pocket. "Basil Outlaw."

"Dr. Outlaw, this is Ralph Meadows. Blue's in labor and she's having trouble."

"Hang on. I'll be there in thirty minutes."

Hallie stuck her head out the door. "Is it Blue?"

"Yeah." He headed back toward the garage.

"Wait, I'll come with you."

He glanced at her dress coat, her thin dress and her heels. "In that?"

"Yes."

Minutes later, still dressed for the ball, they were in the pickup sliding down Walnut Street.

Chapter Ten

The temperature was around ten degrees, but Ralph's face was slick with sweat. It was also leached of color.

The foal was presenting feet first. Not a good position as that left the wider part of the animal, the head and shoulders to come last. Sometimes they got stuck. Hallie said a little prayer for the beautiful mare and her baby.

Baz examined Blue with strong competent hands. She was so grateful he was there. Her own birthing experience consisted of observing a black lab produce eight healthy puppies without any human intervention and catching a few episodes of A Birth Story on the TLC channel.

Oh yeah. And watching Gone With The Wind.

Hallie knelt in the straw and stroked the mare's velvety face.

"Helluva time to call you, doc," Ralpha apologized, when Baz removed his jacket and rolled up the sleeves of his tuxedo shirt.

"No problem."

Baz positioned himself and began talking to Blue. His voice was deep and calming even as he reached inside her to grab a small hoof. He pulled and Blue whinnied in pain.

The birth seemed to take forever. Hallie forced

herself to stay calm so she could convey that sense to the laboring mother. She wished she could get a progress report as the minutes rolled by, but she didn't want to interrupt the man who, she could hear, was grunting softly with the effort of his task.

"Hallie," Baz called out, "when I give the signal, push on her belly."

Hallie scrambled into position. She was aware of Baz, one foot braced against the wall of the stable, ready to pull hard, as if the colt were stranded in icy water instead of inside his mother. She examined the ripples undulating across Blue's belly, and she chose what she prayed was the right spot. When Baz called out she pushed with all her strength, wincing when the mare bellowed in pain.

"I've got two hooves," Baz said, between his teeth. "Same thing again."

While Hallie waited for the signal, she heard a new sound. She glanced to her right and saw that Janie had joined them. She was wrapped in a Hudson Bay blanket. Her face was white and drawn.

She dropped to her knees.

Oh no, Janie was in labor, too.

"Tell Ralph. He can call an ambulance."

"Not until the foal's delivered."

That would be too late. It probably was already too late. Hallie infused her voice with as much authority as possible.

"Please, Janie. Call 911. Use the cellphone in my purse."

The young woman nodded. While she placed the call, Hallie sent up a fervent prayer that both Blue and her baby would survive. Janie had enough to handle without knowing that she and Ralph would lose their farm. She calmed a little when she heard Baz's confident voice.

"Now, Hallie." She pushed down on the heaving belly again.

"Push again. I've got everything but the head."

She pushed. "Once more." She threw all her weight onto the mare. There was another equine howl and then Ralph's awed voice.

"It's a colt!"

Ralph, Janie, and Hallie stared at the little guy as he stumbled to his feet.

"Congratulations," Baz said to the humans.

Then he spoke to the mare. "You did a great job, mama. You were very brave."

Tears pricked Hallie's eyes. No wonder she loved this man. In that moment she knew it was time to stop lying to herself. She'd been mortally wounded with the infertility report, but like Baz said, it wasn't really his fault. In any case she couldn't give him up.

She'd stop short of tying the knot, though. A good, full-blown affair would have to be enough.

When his time in Eden was over, they'd separate for good. But for the next three months, she wanted him in her bed. Her blood warmed just thinking about it.

She'd tell him on the way home.

Ralph couldn't stop thanking Baz, and he couldn't stop admiring his new acquisition, so he didn't notice when Janie clutched her belly and dropped to her knees.

Hallie crouched down with her and put a comforting hand on her back. "How close are the contractions?"

"It's all one pain. It never stops."

Not a good sign.

"Hang on," she told Janie. She dropped to the hay next to Baz. "We've got another situation on our hands."

Baz looked past her and eyed the crouching woman. Understanding dawned on his face. "Ralph," he said, coming to his feet, "Janie needs to get to the hospital. Carry her to my truck."

Hallie put her hand on his arm. "No time for that. She called an ambulance, but it'll take Chester most of an hour to get out here."

"On second thought," Baz said, "why don't you just carry her into the house."

Ralph gaped at his wife, writhing on the hay.

"Omigod, why didn't you tell me?"

"Blue comes first." She groaned.

Ralph was having trouble shifting gears, but before Hallie could urge him to move, Baz scooped up the woman in the blanket. He strode across the farmyard while she buried her face in his muscular chest. In that moment, Hallie would have given anything to be Janie Meadows. Appalled at her self-centered thoughts, she sprinted ahead and tackled the situation. From the strength and frequency of the groans, she didn't think there was time to get Janie upstairs.

"Settle her on the sofa," Hallie directed.

"What can I do?" Ralph asked, anxiously, as Janie grabbed his hand and squeezed.

"We need clean sheets and towels and boiled water." Hallie looked at Ralph's white knuckles. He clearly wasn't going any place.

She heard Baz shut his phone. He knelt by Janie. "Okay, here's the situation." He used the same voice he'd used with Blue, and Hallie fell in love with him all over again. "The ambulance is on its way. Meantime, I don't want you to worry. Hallie and I are doctors. We'll take good care of you and Ralph, Junior." Her eyes were glazed. Ralph yelped as she squeezed his hand. "Will you let me take a look to see how far you've dilated?"

"Could Hallie do it?"

Baz hesitated an instant then he rose. Hallie knew he was concerned. He probably figured she'd never seen anyone's dilated cervix before.

"I can do it," she assured him.

She peeled the blanket off Janie and pushed the nightgown up to her waist. The opening between her legs was the size of the top of a peanut butter jar _— with pink flesh inside.

Hallie gasped. "I can see your baby's head.

"You're completely dilated. You've gotten through the worst part."

"It feels like the worst part is still going."

"I know. Just hang in there. As soon as we get the water and sheets, you can start to push. Ralph do you have a pair of sharp scissors you could sterilize?"

"Scissors?"

Baz strode into the room with a pile of clean sheets. "I'll find 'em," he said. "I've got water boiling in the tea kettle."

"Good thinking." She smiled at him, and he smiled back.

"Hallie? I need to push," Janie gasped. "Is it time?"

"Almost. Try panting." She demonstrated and Janie followed her lead. "Good. That's it."

For a twenty-year-old woman stuck in a snowstorm

with a couple of veterinarians and a zombie for a husband, Janie was doing great. Hallie prayed this birth would be simpler than the last one.

At least the baby's head was in the right position.

She returned to her spot at the end of the sofa.

Baz appeared a minute later with scissors and the water.

"Okay," Hallie told the young mother. "The next time you feel a contraction building, I want you to push down hard for a count of ten."

"It's coming," Janie wailed a minute later. "Oh my god, it hurts."

"Push through the pain," Hallie instructed.

"Remember, your body's doing exactly what it's supposed to do. Ralph, can you support her back and pull back her leg?"

"Which leg?"

Hallie glanced at Baz, who'd started tearing up sheets. He moved to the sofa and propped Jane's head and upper back up against his chest. "That leg," he told Ralph. "Hold it back. Yeah. Like that."

The man seemed to know exactly how to do this. She wondered if he'd watched the popular series "I Didn't Know I was Pregnant."

Janie pushed a couple of times, and then she began to cry.

"Hallie, massage the perineum," Baz instructed.

"That'll ease the baby's passage. Janie, we're a team here. All four of us are going to make sure this baby is nice and healthy. Everybody's got their job and your job is to push down in your bottom. Don't screw up your face. Use the energy down below."

"Can I scream?"

"You can scream the house down."

She did scream. And she pushed. Baz and Hallie coached her while Ralph held her leg. It seemed as if the painful process took hours. In reality, it couldn't have been more than thirty minutes. Hallie strained her ears for the sound of the siren, but she could hear nothing but Janie's intermittent shrieks. The young woman's face was as red as a radish, and her sweat-dampened hair was plastered to her skull. She let out a powerful grunt.

"She's gonna blow," Ralph said, hoarsely.

Hallie dipped her hands into the nearby water.

She wiped them off. It only took one more push. The baby's head popped out. She supported it gently and cleaned out the tiny nostrils with a Q-tip.

"One more push," she said.

"You can do it, honey," Ralph said. "Come on, push."

"Shut! Up! Next time you're doing this part."

"Next time?" Ralph shook his head. "Are you insane?"

Hallie wanted to laugh, but she didn't.

Baz moved quickly to place Ralph behind Janie's back. He instructed them both, and Hallie, too.

"Hold onto her, Ralph. That's it, Janie. Focus now. This is it. Last push. One, two three, go. He started to count. In between seven and eight he looked at Hallie. "Time to catch the baby," he said.

Suddenly she panicked. She stared at Baz. "You do it."

"You'll be fine," he said.

A moment later the child slid into her arms. He was red and wet and wiggily. He squawked and flailed his little arms. Hallie cradled him.

He was a miracle. She hadn't realized she was crying until Baz brushed away a tear. "You, okay?"

"He's perfect," she said.

"What is it?" Janie asked.

Hallie heard Baz's low voice. "Ralph, Junior."

"I have a son!" Ralph yodeled and kissed his wife.

Hallie wiped the baby off while Baz tied the cord and Ralph cut it. She swaddled the baby boy in a scrap of sheet. He stopped squealing and gazed up at her.

Then she felt Baz's comforting hands on her shoulders. "Honey," he said, in a voice so gentle she hardly recognized it, "give Janie the baby."

Oh God. She should have done that immediately. She handed Ralph, Junior to Baz who settled the child in his mother's arms. Janie looked more like a Madonna than a warrior, but Hallie knew she was both.

"Just so you know," Ralph, senior whispered in his wife's ear. "You come first. Always."

Hallie's heart filled with gratitude for the safe birth with just a hint of regret that she'd never get to experience that searing pain or that limitless joy.

She looked at Baz. The gray eyes held understanding and sympathy.

Chester made good time considering the snow and sleet. Hallie and Baz cleaned up the farmhouse and prepared the small family for their trip to Eden. Hallie barely felt the cold as she and Baz stopped in at the barn to check on Blue then made their way back to the truck.

"Thank you," she said, suddenly.

"For what?"

"Letting me catch the baby."

"You did a great job."

She leaned her head against the high seat back.

"What are you thinking?" he asked.

"I'm thinking that I'm so incredibly lucky. How many people get to attend even one birth, much less two in one night?"

He nodded but said nothing. A moment later he'd backed out of the yard and turned down the unpaved driveway.

"You're a good doctor," she continued. "You knew exactly what to do for Blue. And you were a natural with Janie."

A natural birthing coach, a natural father. He would make a great husband and dad. She fought the sense of sadness that threatened to overwhelm her.

"What just happened?"

She looked at him. "What?"

"Your mood changed. Why? What are you thinking?"

She shrugged. Her heart was too full not to tell him the truth. "I'm thinking how much you need kids of your own. And I can't give them to you."

He stopped the truck in the middle of the driveway. He reached over and unbuckled her seatbelt then he pulled her up against his chest. She buried her face in the crook of his shoulder. It felt wonderful. It felt like home. Her defenses melted, and tears dampened his ruined shirt.

She cried with relief for the babies born tonight and with regret for those she would never have. He held her until she was out of tears. "You are my family, Hallie."

She stopped crying and looked at him. "I'm tired of being sad. I'm tired of thinking about what I can't have.

This is New Year's Eve, Baz. I want to celebrate what we do have."

"Sssh," he said, not understanding. "You're exhausted, baby. Put your head down on my lap. Go to sleep."

His suggestion triggered an image in Hallie's brain. Suddenly she had a plan. "Okay. Thanks."

She snuggled down on the seat and laid her cheek against his rock-hard thigh. It was a perfect position for what she had in mind.

This was a bad idea. A really bad idea.

The feel of her cheek against his thigh made Baz grit his teeth. They were both exhausted, covered in bodily fluids, and he was operating a ton of moving metal. None of that stopped the jolts of electricity that rocketed through him every time she moved.

Hell, every time she took in a breath.

He searched out an old image from college biology. All that was happening here was a psychological reaction. Just knowing her mouth was that close to his genitals was sending an urgent signal to his left anterior cingulated cortex. The part of the brain that controlled arousal. He was aroused, all right. He gripped the steering wheel and tried to focus on something else. Normally he was excellent at compartmentalization.

Where the hell was his control?

A groan worked its way up his chest as she rubbed her cheek against him.

He hadn't had control of his life since she'd shown up at the lab last year. He felt her breath against the inside of his thigh. Christ! Was it open?

He wanted to run the truck into the sleet-sodden

weeds, rip her clothes off, and plunge into her. Hallie.

He couldn't do it. He had to wait for a signal from her. Besides, he wanted more than a hot fuck on the side of a country road at three o'clock on New Year's Day. Didn't he? He wanted her for keeps.

He explained that to the blood rushing to his groin. Pretty soon there would be nothing between his ears, nothing to keep him from going overboard.

He needed to move her off his lap before he did something unforgivable.

"Hallie?"

"Mmmm?" She adjusted her position by using her fingers to smooth their way down the inside of his thigh.

He forgot what he was going to say.

She shifted again. When she spoke, her lips moved against him, and he felt moisture. Jesus.

"Do you want something, Baz?"

He shut his eyes, the truck slipped as he forgot what he was doing. "No, no, everything's fine."

"Is there anything you need?"

Christ, yes.

"Not a thing."

"I don't think that's quite true." Her hand closed over his erection.

He jerked upward and took his foot off both the accelerator and the clutch. The truck stalled. He pumped the pedals desperately, succeeding only in flooding the engine.

She sat up but didn't move away from him.

"Flooded?"

"Yeah. It has to rest a minute."

"You know. I'm really happy for Ralph and Janie.

They have everything."

She was too close. Her fingers were still splayed on the muscles of his thigh and he had an arousal the size of Mount Rushmore.

"What's your definition of everything?" Dammit, his voice was hoarse.

"Each other, the baby, the farm."

"They'll be lucky to keep that farm. They're probably crazy to try to start a breeding program with nothing but a mare and her foal."

"There must be a stallion somewhere. That foal has a father."

A father. Robert.

Guilt, regret and longing swarmed inside him, blocking him, blocking out the lust. In a minute he'd try the engine again, and she'd sit back in her seat. They'd be home in thirty minutes. Home and in their own beds.

"Baz?"

Her fingers were between his legs again.

He put his hand over hers. "Don't, Hallie."

She peered at his face. "What just happened?"

He shrugged. "This is no place to fool around.

Anyway, I don't want to do this until things are right between us. You were right. I jumped too fast. We've been apart a whole year. People change."

"I don't want to talk about any of that tonight, Baz. I don't want to talk about the past or the future."

"What do you want to talk about?" Damn. He sounded hoarse again.

"I don't want to talk at all." She leaned into him.

"I just want to be. And I want a kiss. It's New Year's

Eve, remember? I never got my midnight kiss."

He eyed her in the darkness. A kiss would probably be all right. He slipped his hand behind her neck and brought her mouth to his. God, she tasted so good. Nectar of the gods. Without thinking he parted her lips with his tongue and explored behind her teeth. He felt the usual jolt of lust, but he could control it. It was just a kiss. He realized he was running out of air. His chest moved heavily, and he had to break the kiss.

"That was nice," she whispered. "But it wasn't exactly what I had in mind." He was still trying to catch his breath when she unbuckled his belt and opened his pants.

"Halliday!"

She gathered the throbbing swollen flesh that was his erection into her hands. "Now I get to kiss you."

He dropped his head against the back of the seat, shut his eyes, and wrapped his fingers in her curls. Sensations tore through him, and he heard a harsh groan. His? She stroked and licked and sucked and excitement coiled and jerked inside him. God, he was going to burst.

"Hallie," he gasped. "That's all I can take."

She paused, leaving him hard and throbbing.

"You want me to stop?"

"We should get home."

"Now?"

He laughed. He didn't want to go anywhere. He was home. "Soon."

"Or in the morning. I'm having such a good time I could do this all night." She took him in her mouth, and he groaned.

"If you keep doing what you're doing, I'll be lucky to last another minute." Suddenly he stopped. He didn't want a blow job in the middle of the M-15 at three a.m. He wanted her, Hallie, in his bed, every night.

Forever. "C'mon. Let's finish this at home."

It took fifteen miles for the raging hard-on to subside. Every foot of the way he wondered why she'd done it in the first place. When he'd achieved a measure of control, he asked her. "Why?"

She didn't pretend to misunderstand. "I wanted you to know something."

He waited.

"I wanted you to know I'm ready to be your lover."

Intense satisfaction exploded inside him. "That's a start, but it won't be enough. I want more than an affair with you. There's no reason we can't be together permanently."

Except for Nicole and Robert. You still haven't told her.

"Can't sex just be about sex?"

It always had been before. Even with her last year in L.A. He hadn't been thinking long term. Sex could be just about sex.

"Not for us. Not anymore. I want a commitment, Hallie."

Chapter Eleven

She loved him and she wanted him. She even forgave him for the year-long delay that had cost her so much. Couldn't that be enough?

She glanced at his hard profile.

Apparently not.

"Because you can't forgive me."

She shook her head. "It's not that. I can forgive you. I just can't go through all of that again."

"All of what?"

"Losing you."

And she would lose him when he finally figured out he needed to have kids of his own.

"That's not going to happen."

Suddenly she was ticked. "Isn't it enough that I want you now? For goodness sake, Baz. All anybody really has is now. In this 'now' I'd like to have an affair."

"Forget it."

She didn't know quite what to make of that.

She'd never heard of a single guy turning down a chance for uncommitted sex. "So it's all or nothing?"

"Yeah."

"Has anyone ever told you you're mule-stubborn?"

"It's been mentioned."

The attempt at humor had a calming effect on her. "What about a compromise?"

"No."

She ignored that. "How about if we just become a couple for a while and see where it goes? You know, like normal people."

"You mean an engagement?"

She let out an exasperated laugh. "I mean like exclusive dating. Sleeping together. Getting to know one another."

"I'm too old to go steady."

"We wouldn't have to call it that. We could call it, uh…"

"A courtship," he said. "We'll call it a courtship."

She considered that. She could have nothing at all, or she could have a three-month "courtship" with the man she loved.

"Okay. A courtship it is."

A courtship. Well, it was better than nothing. It implied marriage, too, didn't it? He decided it did now.

The darkness of the night was thinning when they finally arrived home. He accompanied her to the carriage house apartment, not sure whether he'd be invited to spend the rest of the night there.

He took her key and opened the door. Cameron was lounging on Hallie's sofa. He came to his feet.

Baz frowned. "What're you doing here?"

The shirttail of Cam's tux was out. He'd lost his bow tie. He scrubbed a hand down his face. The stubble on it matched Baz's own.

"I came to find out what the hell's going on.

Everybody's saying you got Hallie pregnant."

Baz winced. He knew the words would hurt. He wondered if this soul-wrenching loss would be with her for the rest of her life.

"Diane Cobbs started the rumor." Cam narrowed his eyes at Baz. "I'm assuming you can do something about this?"

Baz looked at Hallie.

"Cam knows about the infertility."

For some reason that made him angry. "People can bite my ass. Nobody has to know about that."

"It's not just the pregnancy part," Cam said.

"This is a small town. Everyone knows you're having sex."

"We haven't had that much of it." That was a stupid response.

"The point is it could hurt me in my business and dad in his. Mostly, it could hurt Hallie.

She doesn't have a reputation for sleeping around, and she's not going to get one."

"Damn right she's not. She sleeps with me. No one else." Shit. He was starting to sound like a caveman.

"That's very primordial." Hallie bit back a smile.

"Listen, Cam. Don't worry about this. I'll take care of

it. A few well-placed comments and the grapevine will print a retraction."

He didn't look appeased.

"We're just dating," Hallie went on. "You date people. Sharon dates people. Jolene dates people.

That's all I'm doing. Dating."

"Just dating?" The brothers spoke in unison.

"Pinkie swear," Hallie said, automatically. The brothers looked at her. "When I was in the third grade we always said 'pinkie swear' when two people said the same word in stereo. Oh, and you have to link pinkies."

The brothers looked at each other. Then Baz held

out his little finger. After a moment's hesitation, Cam hooked it with his own pinkie.

"Yup. Like that."

"All right," Cam said, rubbing the back of his neck. "You're dating. What happens when Baz goes back to L.A.?"

"We'll cross that bridge later on," Hallie soothed. "In the meantime, we're just dating."

"Courting," Baz corrected her.

"Courting?"

"You know, flowers, candy, dinner out. Stuff like that."

Hallie flashed her brilliant smile. "Look, could you excuse me? I really need some sleep."

Cam stepped aside, and she disappeared into the bedroom. Baz ground his teeth. Well, hell. At least this little scene answered one question. He wouldn't be spending tonight with Hallie.

He had a bad feeling he wouldn't be spending a lot of nights with Hallie.

Courting in Eden, Maine would demand discretion.

****

Two days later Hallie skipped breakfast at the house and went straight to the office. She was in the midst of making notes on the Meadows' mare when Baz arrived with hot coffee and Asia's homemade danish. She was aware of the scent of his after shave,

Woodsy but not too, and the strength and heat in his muscular body. Her hormones jumped when he leaned over to set the food down on her desk.

God, she'd missed him and it had only been one day.

"Thanks."

"I'd have brought flowers, but nothing's open yet."

"It's the thought that counts."

"I'd like to take you out to dinner tonight. I thought Cerrutto's might be nice. I know you like Italian food."

Her heart squeezed. Baz was so literal. He'd probably spent yesterday researching the actions appropriate to a courtship and compiling a list. It was hard not to love a guy like that.

"Cerutto's would be lovely," she said, "but I'll have to take a raincheck. Tonight's the Tribal Council meeting. I promised Molly Whitecloud I'd attend."

Baz's face looked impassive, but Hallie knew that his mind was busy searching for loopholes. He'd set his course and he was not a man to be deflected.

She figured he'd try to talk her out of the meeting or, if that failed, he'd insist on accompanying her. His response surprised her.

"Maybe later in the week."

Her eyebrows lifted and he gave her that slow smile that never failed to release butterflies in her stomach.

"I can be patient, Halliday. Just watch."

He was better than patient. He left the office at four and just before the office closed he returned carrying a pair of grilled cheese sandwiches and pickles along with a single red rose in a bud vase.

"What's all this?"

"You have to eat. I figured we'd have a little impromptu picnic before you left for the Rez."

It was a brilliant move. Not only was the gesture thoughtful in itself, it reminded her of the indoor picnic they'd had in his condo last year. It especially reminded her of what had happened after they'd eaten and suddenly her face felt hot.

Baz appeared not to notice. "I'd offer to go with you tonight, but I'm going to be busy."

Busy? "Doing what?"

"I'm planning a courtship, Hallie. And it has to be just right."

****

The tribal elders met in the meeting room of an all-purpose building that included the general store, the post office and a tiny museum of Indian artifacts.

Cameron and Hallie got a late start and arrived just before the meeting started. Hallie suspected Cam had stalled on purpose. Was it because of Molly? When they entered the room, she searched for her friend.

"I'm going to sit with Molly," she murmured.

"Fine." His voice was clipped. She noticed he didn't look in the midwife's direction.

The five tribal elders were seated in a semicircle. Mollie and the other spectators occupied plastic molded chairs set haphazardly around the room. She nodded at Hallie, but her face was drawn and tight. Tiny lines radiated from her full lips; there were purple bruises under her eyes. She'd looked like this ever since Cam joined forces with Nate Packer to build the resort and spa.

No one spoke. Hallie, unsure of the protocol, didn't want to take a chance on offending the elders.

She gazed around the room. Built-in shelves were loaded with books and exercise mats and percussion instruments. There was a whole row of tom-toms.

This was probably where the after-school classes in Indian culture were held. Reservation children were bused into Eden to attend school, but, Molly had told her, the tribe offered the extra classes to make sure the new generation learned about its heritage.

Cam stood against one wall. Jake was next to him. Hallie gave a start. She hadn't seen him since New Year's Eve. She owed him a big apology. He looked different tonight. Was it his uniform—_ or the fact that he was wearing a gun?

Suddenly the silence in the room made sense.

They'd called Jake because they expected trouble.

Just as suddenly, trouble arrived. The door burst open and half a dozen young men exploded into the room. They were dressed in loincloths, headbands, and war paint; they held tomahawks and hunting knives in their fists. A series of war whoops filled the air.

There was something wrong with the picture.

"It's like the set of a spaghetti western," she murmured to Molly.

"Exactly." There was disgust in the midwife's voice. "We're woodland Indians. Our ancestors didn't wear paint or headdresses. They didn't yell war whoops. These guys are pathetic."

Hallie suspected they were also drunk. The stench of cheap beer filled the air. Across the room, Jake looked relaxed but ready for anything. He'd never fire that revolver at a bunch of crazy kids, but, still, someone could get hurt. The war dance felt malevolent.

A heavy man in what looked like a pair of pajamas lumbered to his feet and raised his hands to stop the chaos.

"That's Davey Tall Tree," Molly said, in a low voice. "He's our chief of police."

He looked more like a Buddha than the chief of anything. Good grief. Cam had been right. The man was wearing bedroom slippers.

All of a sudden the protesters formed a tight semi-circle around him surrounding one man so he was, effectively, trapped against the wall. The whoops got louder, and they brushed their weapons against him.

It was Cam. Hallie's heart was in her throat. Jake tried to intervene, but even his authoritative voice couldn't be heard over the ruckus. And then Hallie heard a drum beat. It was a plain rhythm, like a heartbeat. The mischief makers quieted immediately. It was almost as if someone had cast a spell on them.

One by one they backed away from Cam. She searched his face and realized the blue eyes were focused beyond her _ —at the drummer. Hallie didn't have to look to know it was Molly.

The beat continued, and everyone remained still.

Finally, Molly stopped. "Go home Andrew, Tyler, Jacob. Your behavior tonight does not reflect well on the tribe. The council has serious business here. You have all been raised to respect your elders. You should know better."

The would-be warriors looked sullen, but no one talked back. They filed out the door.

Hallie thought the room would erupt in chatter, but that didn't happen. The meeting was called to order, and the council voted its approval for the Sunrise Resort. Jake nodded at her and slipped out the door when the discussion moved on to the question of needed road repair. She expected Cam to signal her to leave, but it didn't happen. He remained at his spot against the wall; he seemed to be listening to the council's agenda.

When the meeting finally ended, Hallie was able to

question Molly about the drum.

"The after-school classes are paying off," the midwife said. "Those kids knew exactly what the steady drumbeat means. It mimics a heartbeat. We are taught from the cradle to respect its message of peace."

Hallie didn't hear Cam's approach. His gruff voice startled her. "Ready to go?"

The smile disappeared from Molly's face. Molly figured it was just more of the tension she'd seen between the two, but Molly moved toward him.

"You've been hurt."

Hallie realized he was holding his fingers tightly against the opposite arm. There was a growing stain on his charcoal suit jacket. Blood?

"One of them knifed you," Hallie gasped.

"Can you drive him to my house?" Molly sounded calm.

"Of course."

"Forget it. I'll stop by Eden Memorial on the way home."

"It's more than twenty-five miles." Molly kept her voice low. "You'll pass out before you're halfway there. Also, you'll have to explain how you got the wound."

She left unspoken the fact that the incident would strain relations between Cam's project and the Rez, but Cam obviously understood. He didn't say another word, and he allowed Hallie to lead him out to the parking lot.

Molly's home wasn't far. It was located off the main reservation road on a little spur that backed up to woods. In summer, the small white dwelling looked like an enchanted cottage decorated with vines and climbing roses. In January it looked like what it was, a tiny frame cube.

Inside, the walls were decorated the clear blue of a summer sky. The earth-toned furniture was sleek and streamlined, and the cottage, like Hallie's apartment, was decorated with local handicrafts including a large, feathered dreamcatcher on one wall.

Molly instructed Hallie to have Cam sit at her postage-stamp sized kitchen table while she located hot water and her bag. She worked quietly, methodically, like the medical professional she was.

She used a soft washcloth to clean out the wound. then she laced it with an antiseptic that must have stung, but Cam never batted an eyelash as he watched the midwife work.

Last, she pulled out a needle and suture thread.

Cam sucked in his breath as she pierced his skin for the first tiny stitch.

"I'm sorry," Molly murmured.

"No problem."

As soon as she finished, Cam stood and headed toward the door. Hallie heard him mutter "thank you," and she heard Molly's equally low-key response. "No problem."

Cam insisted on driving. Hallie respected his obvious wish for silence. Occasionally she gazed at his sculpted nose and his square jaw. With that profile, he could have posed for an Indian head nickel. She wondered what had happened between Cam and Molly to have left a footprint of so much pain for so many years. As they turned onto Walnut Street and she thought about the difference between the warm, welcoming lights of the two-story stone house in town and the modest cottages and rusty trailer on the Rez.

Had the culture gap been too great?

Cam parked in the three-bay garage.

"Will you be all right?"

He nodded. "She's the only medical professional on the Rez. She knows her stuff."

Hallie remembered the timely drum. "She rescued you."

"She wanted to stop the kids from getting into trouble. She's Blackbird's Joan of Arc." He got out of the car but seemed a little unsteady on his feet. She wondered if he felt faint. After all, he'd lost a lot of blood.

"I'm going to walk you upstairs."

He didn't protest. A few minutes later, he sat on the big bed in the room he'd had as a child. There were framed posters of the major European cities.

Cam and his late wife had lived on Beacon Hill in Boston; they'd traveled around the world.

She thought about Molly's cozy cottage. She and Cameron Outlaw couldn't have been further apart, but at one time there must have been something important between them. Hallie could think of no other explanation for their hostility now.

And the concern. At least on Molly's side. Hallie didn't believe Cam's cynical explanation. The midwife had taken care of him twice. That wasn't the behavior of a woman who didn't care about a man.

It was nearly midnight when Hallie made her way up the steps to her apartment. She had a sudden, intense wish to see Baz. She'd missed him tonight. He was probably asleep now like everybody else in Eden. Anyway, she wasn't quite sure what "courtship" entailed. She had an unpleasant feeling it did not include sex.

She unlocked her apartment door and crossed to her bedroom without turning on a light.

"Halliday."

Her heart galloped. "Good grief," she said, not sure whether she was more startled or happy to see him. "What're you doing here in the dark?"

He switched on a table lamp. He was sprawled in her easy chair like a resting predator, his hair rumpled and his reading glasses perched on the end of his nose. He reminded her of Red Riding Hood's wolf masquerading as grandma.

"I've been waiting for you. Where the hell have you been?"

She gaped at him. "You're angry?"

"Do you know what time it is?"

She glanced at her Timex. "Almost midnight. Were you afraid I'd turn into a pumpkin?"

"Never mind what I was afraid of."

She heard the worry under the roar. "Baz, I was out on the Rez, with your brother."

"That's the only reason I haven't called in a missing person's report. That, and the fact that I'd have to talk to Deputy Dawg."

Hallie laughed at his disgruntled tone. "Jake was at the meeting, too."

He lunged out of the chair, and his eyes narrowed on her. In the shadowy light they looked almost black. He was no longer the patient courtier.

Hallie explained what had happened in the meeting. He looked at her broodingly. "Is Cam okay?"

Her heart caught. He was bonding with his brother. She couldn't regret it. Not even if it meant she'd have

156

to leave Eden. "He's fine. Molly Whitecloud patched him up."

"I thought she was a midwife."

Hallie's expression didn't change, but the regret in his eyes said he recognized his error. A midwife delivered babies. This baby thing would always be between them. Even if she one day got past it, he'd always be careful, sensitive. It was no way to live.

She couldn't resist taking this time with him.

She stepped into his arms.

"You shouldn't have been out there," he growled into her hair.

She looked up at him. "What bothers you? The fact that there was a disturbance, or the fact that I was with a couple of attractive men?"

"Both. Everything." He pulled her tightly against him. "Aw, hell, Hallie. This courtship thing isn't doing it for me. I need to know you're mine."

"I am yours." She twined her arms around his neck. "All yours."

For tonight, anyway.

He groaned and slid his fingers through her hair. He held her so she could see the turmoil in his gray eyes. "I love you. It doesn't change anything between us, but I want you to know. I love you." She stared at him. "I will never love anyone else."

Chapter Twelve

She loved him.

He stared at the ceiling over his bed and contemplated that. It was good to hear, but it wasn't enough. She was still resisting any kind of commitment.

Nothing has changed between us.

She might love him, but she still had no intention of marrying him. The baby business would be between them forever. Even if she could get over that, there was the problem of Nicole. He scowled as he remembered the phone call.

She claimed the boyfriend had sent her a letter threatening to take her to court if she didn't give up the child. Baz rubbed the back of his neck. He didn't know what to believe. Nicole was a situational liar.

Whenever she was in a situation she didn't like, she lied to get out of it.

She wanted him to come back to L.A.

Shit. Her call had stirred up a hornet's nest of feelings. Her neediness annoyed him and her timing was irritating, but her lack of interest in Robert was what concerned him. He felt an emotional pain that was almost physical when he thought about the baby.

Baz made a mental to-do list.

Figure out what to do about Nicole.

Ensure that Robert was safe.

Tell Hallie about his ex-wife and son.

He groaned and turned onto his back. When had his personal life become so complicated? Eighteen months ago he never had to answer to anyone.

Suddenly he was juggling a girlfriend and an ex-wife, a child, his own career, and his father's practice.

Baz's jaw tensed.

This was all her fault and, by Jesus, whether she knew it or not she would pay for it by marrying him. Very, very soon.

The next morning Baz invited Hallie to dinner again. This time he told her she could choose the night.

"I choose July 24th," she teased.

"Anytime," he said, blandly, "within the next forty-eight hours."

She grinned at him. "There's that need to control."

"This has nothing to do with control. I just like to eat out."

"Yeah. Sure. Well, okay, I accept your gracious invitation. How about Thursday?"

He hesitated. He obviously wanted to do this tonight, but since Thursday was within his two-day time limit, there was nothing he could say. Or so she thought.

"Any special reason you don't want to go tonight?"

She flashed him a bright smile. "Yep. I want to buy a new dress for the occasion."

His eyes flashed in amusement and relief.

Despite gray skies, dirtying, crusted snow and predictions of a winter storm for the weekend, Hallie's day was practically perfect.

It wasn't that every client was friendly or that the health problems she encountered were minor. It was because she was happy.

She kept reminding herself that nothing had changed, but in her heart she knew it had. Her resistance to Baz was melting faster than a snowman in Texas. She knew he needed a family, but he had all the Outlaws and he had her. Maybe they could be happy with no children. Maybe they could fill their home with abandoned dogs and cats, nieces and nephews, and children of their friends. Maybe this could work.

Baz went out to check on Blue. By the time the clinic closed he hadn't returned. Hallie agreed to meet her friends at Little Joe's. The three of them consumed thick, tomato-topped hamburgers and homemade French fries while Jolene regaled the two relative newcomers with anecdotes about the ball.

After she and Baz had left, Eleanor Oglethorpe had asked Big George to play Chubby Checker's "Limbo Rock." Jolene gave a vivid description of the geriatric set trying to see how low they could go.

There was one minor back injury and, apparently, a whole lot of laughter among the aging baby boomers.

Hallie laughed so hard she had to wipe the tears off her face.

"So," Jo said, when they'd calmed down enough to eat their homemade apple pie, "what's going on with you?"

Hallie looked at Jo's inquiring face, and Sharon's compassionate one. She valued these two friends more than she could say, and suddenly, she wanted to tell them everything.

"You were both right about Baz Outlaw. He did come to Eden to convince me to get back together with him. I'll admit I'm tempted."

"What's stopping you," Sharon asked. "You love

him don't you?"

She nodded. "You know about the endometriosis.

The part you don't know is that last year Baz and I became lovers. I knew I didn't have a lot of time to have a child. I explained it to him, and I proposed. He turned me down."

"Mercy," Jo murmured.

"As you know he got me a job here, with his dad. I thought it was over between us, and then he showed up on Christmas Eve."

"Does he know about the latest lab report?" Sharon asked.

Hallie nodded. "He says we can be happy without a baby of our own."

Jolene looked into her eyes. "What do you think?"

"At first I thought there was no way. I was so angry at him, at the situation. But I'm coming to grips with how unfair it was to ask him to solve all my problems that night. I mean we'd been friends for a while, but we'd only slept together once."

"Great heavens," Jo said.

"I've been telling him I couldn't get over this but, you know what? I think I can."

"Because you love him," Sharon said.

"Yeah."

"So what happens now?" Jo was a bottom-line type of person.

"I'm not sure. We're trying a courtship."

"That sounds dangerous," Sharon teased.

"Tell me about it. He's already brought me two meals at work. Tomorrow night we've got a date for dinner out."

"What if he proposes?"

"He already did."

"But what if this time's the real thing? You'd better figure out what you're going to do. Baz Outlaw doesn't strike me as a patient guy. He knows what he wants, and my guess is he won't slow down until he gets it. You know, Hal," Jo added, kindly, "a baby's a baby. You can always adopt."

Hallie didn't answer. She couldn't bring herself to go over the old, sad story of her childhood. She knew intellectually that not all adoptions ended badly. It was different inside her heart. "You make it sound so simple."

"It is simple once you cut through all the bull.

You love him and he loves you. Marry him."

"I don't know about love. He hasn't really talked about that."

"It's implied," Sharon explained. "No man would propose to a woman without strong feelings for her."

"Maybe he won't ask tomorrow."

Sharon and Jolene exchanged a glance. "He will," they said in unison.

"Pinky swear."

The women grinned and hooked their little fingers.

Hallie had picked Sharon up. As she pulled up in front of the inn to drop her off, the redhead turned to her. "I didn't want to mention this in front of Jo, but before you agree to marry him, I think you should ask him where he's been the last twelve months."

Good grief. She'd practically forgotten about that.

"You can't build a good marriage on secrets.

Believe me, I know."

Five minutes later Hallie pulled into the parking lot behind the clinic. The sound of her phone released butterflies into her stomach but it wasn't Baz. "Hey," Jo said. "I didn't want to make a big deal of this in front of Sharon, but I think you should find out where the hell the guy's been for the last year."

"Good thinking," Hallie said. "I appreciate the suggestion." She stared at her phone for a long minute before she went upstairs. If nothing else the events of the past year would make for good dinner conversation tomorrow night.

If she could wait that long. She had a sudden, overpowering impulse to talk to him now.

She found Lucy alone in the parlor.

"Welcome back, stranger. How was Boston?"

"Big. Cold. I'm glad to be back. If you're looking for Baz he isn't here. Asia said he called and told her he'd be really late."

"Oh." Hallie was disappointed. "Okay. Thanks, Luce."

"Hallie, wait."

The younger woman got to her feet. Her short dark hair framed a pixie-ish face. Her eyes were sky blue, like Cameron's. "How was your New Year's Eve date?"

Hallie got the sense that she wasn't asking out of idle curiosity. "It was a little weird. I had too much to drink and acted silly. I wound up leaving with Baz."

Lucy wrapped her arms around her slim waist.

"Was Jake all right?"

Hallie nodded. "He's an exceptional man. Very understanding."

Lucy's dark eyebrows lifted in surprise. "That's not how he acts with me. He's always on my case about something."

Hallie didn't voice her suspicions about the sheriff's crush. She didn't want to put ideas into Lucy's head. Instead she told the younger woman about the two births at the Meadows Farm. She mentioned Baz's cool competence in the pressure situation.

"Hard to imagine Baz delivering a baby," Lucy said. "He's such a confirmed bachelor."

"He was unflappable."

"Huh. Maybe he's got some dad potential after all."

For the first time the words didn't hurt so much.

Dad potential was the same as husband potential. Maybe she and Baz could be happy together without a child.

The next morning, she tingled with excitement. She felt like a teenager preparing for a first date. She pulled on rust-colored cords and a turquoise sweater then she checked with Mavis who assured her there weren't many clients scheduled and that Baz could handle them all.

"I'll be out for a while," she said.

He might or might not propose. She might or might not say yes. But one thing she knew for sure: she wanted a new dress for the occasion. She drove to High Street where Mavis's niece, Alma Crotts, had a used clothing shop called The Closet. On the few occasions Hallie needed something she couldn't get out of the L.L. Bean catalogue, she'd found it at Alma's.

"How was the red dress?"

"It was a great," Hallie said, honestly. "I got lots of comments on it." She didn't tell the proprietor she'd had to throw it out after she'd caught the baby.

Like most folks in Eden, Alma didn't pull her

punches. "I heard about that business between you and Diane Cobbs. You really pregnant?"

"Nope. That was a function of too much spiked punch," she said, cheerfully. "Listen, I need something suitable for a fancy dinner."

Alma showed her all the dresses in her size.

Hallie rejected a sequined white ankle-length gown and a short black cocktail sheath. Her eyes lit up at the sight of a retro shirt-waist updated with a shimmery coral-colored material, a stand-up collar and a ballet length full skirt.

"It's very I Love Lucy."

"And, coral looks good on everybody."

"I'll take it."

Alma pointed out the absence of sleeves. "You'll catch your death."

Hallie thought about the heat she always felt in Baz's arms. No way she'd be cold. "I'll just keep my coat on. "Thanks, Alma."

Excited about the purchase, Hallie inhaled the fresh cold air on Main Street and caught a whiff of the freshly baked bread at Caroline's Bakery. She selected treats for the office, then drove home. Her heart kicked when she spotted Jesse's pick up in the parking lot. She hadn't seen Baz in nearly twenty-four hours. It had felt like a year.

"Bless you, child," Mavis enthused as she peeked into the bakery box. "This is exactly what the doctor ordered." She took a big bite of a jelly doughnut.

Hallie looked at the closed door of the treatment room. "Baz in there?"

Mavis nodded.

She should probably wait until he was finished, but

the coffee would get cold. Besides, she knew everybody in town. No one would mind if she interrupted.

Her heart beat fast as she plucked two coffees out of the carrier and shouldered her way into the room. And then everything became a blur. She was aware of a sharp piercing shriek and the clatter of cups hitting the floor. She felt the sting of hot coffee on her arms, and she saw it on the walls. She finally realized she was shivering so hard she almost bit her tongue.

"Holy mackerel," yelped someone. There must be a child in the room.

"Holy shit." The voice was deeper, smoky, irritated "What the hell's your problem?"

Baz exploded into the room. He grabbed Hallie's shoulders and strafed her with wild-looking eyes.

"What happened? What's wrong? Are you hurt?"

She collapsed against him, and she felt his arms close around her. Even in the circumstances she felt safe.

"What is it," he asked, his voice gentle. He stroked her arms and back as though checking for broken bones or an open wound.

The heat that shot through her wasn't generated by his proximity this time. It was pure humiliation.

She closed her eyes and pictured the loosely coiled boa on the treatment table and she shuddered.

"She's scared of Nadine," the boy explained.

"Lots of moms are."

Hallie closed her eyes. What would Baz think of her? A veterinarian wasn't supposed to be scared of snakes.

The contemptuous comment did not come from the man who still held her.

"Jesus H.," the woman said. "I've never heard of an animal doctor afraid of a snake."

Hallie recognized the voice. Diane Cobbs Sanderson. She almost groaned. The woman was going to think she was insane. Worse, she'd probably convince everybody in town.

"She was just startled." The low rumble of Baz's voice seeped into her body, and she felt herself calming down. Of course he was completely mistaken. She wasn't just startled. She was scared to death. There was nothing to do but suck it up and confess.

"No, she's right." She inched away from her protector. "I've always been afraid of snakes."

Baz lifted her chin with one finger. There was merriment underneath the compassion in the gray eyes. "You must've had one helluva time during the herpetology rotation in vet school."

She shuddered. The other students, even the other women, had flung pickled reptiles at one another while she'd had to leave the classroom to go throw up.

"It was rough."

"We actually came here to get Basil to take a look at Nadine," Diane said.

Hallie suspected the impatience in the other woman's voice was due more to pique at the interruption than irritation at the delay. Gratitude swept through her as Baz shifted positions and made sure his body was between her and the patient.

"I really wanted to tell you what a great time I had on Saturday night," Diane said to Baz, her voice smooth and suggestive. "We fit well together, don't you think?"

"Diane, I don't believe you've been introduced to

my partner. This is Doctor Halliday Scott." He squeezed her. "We're more than partners. We're courting."

"As in Froggie went-a?"

Hallie laughed in spite of the situation.

"Sounds like I guessed right," Diane said. "You must be pregnant."

It was time to slay this dragon.

"No," Hallie answered. "I'm not."

Diane relaxed. No pregnancy meant there was still room for Baz to change his mind. "Oh. Well. Whatever." Diane smiled at Baz. "This is my boy, Tommy."

The redhead shook hands with both Baz and Hallie.

"Nadine won't bite," he said. "She's not hungry now. She just ate on Sunday."

Hallie shuddered. She could picture Nadine's victim at Sunday dinner. "I'm sorry I screamed," she told Tommy. "I do all right with snakes when I have some warning." She smiled at him. "But I have to admit I try to avoid them. I figured one of the advantages of living this far north would be the cold climate and subsequent lack of reptiles."

Geography hadn't helped her today.

"Is Nadine a good pet?"

"She's awesome," Tommy said.

"What seems to be her problem?" Baz asked.

"Ennui," Diane replied. She pronounced it e-noo-ee. "I found the diagnosis in All About Snakes for Dummies." She walked over near Baz. Hallie could smell the heavy perfume. The woman was wearing tight black capris and an orange spandex top under a short faux fur jacket. When she removed the jacket, even

Hallie had to admit she looked pretty spectacular.

Under the spandex her breasts were served up like a couple of oranges. Not the Florida oranges, either. The fat, juicy Navel oranges from the West Coast. Hallie took a moment to admire the determination of Diane's bra.

"Ennui is common in cold-blooded creatures at this time of year," Baz explained to Tommy. "Snakes hibernate in the cold. They downshift into two speeds: slow and stop."

"That describes Nadine's behavior very well," said Diane, clearly trying to get into the conversation. When Baz glanced at her she thrust out her breasts in a move calculated to recapture Baz's attention. It succeeded. Hallie watched his gray eyes glance at the other woman's figure.

"She's been off her feed lately, not up to par. So we figured we'd pop in for an examination."

That part was certainly true. Diane was after an examination. Just not one of the snake.

Baz looked at the creature. How did one even examine a snake? There was nothing there to probe or press or stick a thermometer into. Hallie heard him asking Tommy questions and praising him for his knowledge of his pet. He seemed like a great kid.

"Maybe you could tell Dr. Scott a little bit about Nadine."

"Sure." Tommy looked at her. His young eyes were kind. "I got her because my dad left, and I was sad."

Hallie's heart ached for him.

"She stays in an aquarium in my room, but she rides around on my shoulders, too. She likes to sit in my lap when I play video games. Sometimes she plays hide and seek, though. My mom gets pretty mad when I can't find her."

"I can understand that." Hallie could just imagine finding Nadine curled up in the dryer or draped over the edge of the bathtub. "What made you decide to get a snake?" When there are so many abandoned cats and dogs in the world.

"He's allergic," Diane said. "Can't have fur or pet dander."

Hallie nodded. "Dr. Outlaw's niece, Daisy, has a potbellied pig."

"Cool," Tommy said.

"I'm sorry if I scared you and your mom and Nadine," Hallie said.

"That's all right," Tommy said, with a winning smile. "The time I took her to show-and-tell, Miss Oakrum spent the whole time in the bathroom."

Baz and Hallie laughed.

"You know, Tommy, you're a lucky boy to have a mom who lets you keep a big snake," Hallie said.

"I know. You're lucky to have a pet pig. Say, Mom, think we could get a pig, too?"

Diane's lidded eyes were sending a clear message to Baz. Hallie suspected the woman would take on a litter of wolf pups if it meant she could see more of the veterinarian.

"Speaking of unusual pets," Baz said. "Last week Dr. Scott saved a baby bat. His name was Charlie and he had a broken wing."

He was trying to restore her credibility with the clients. It worked, too. At least with Tommy. She answered all his questions about Charlie. She realized her pulse was back to normal. It looked like she'd survive the snake experience, after all.

"Dr. Scott," Baz said, "I'd like you to come over here." He was inches away from the examining table.

"Why?"

"I'd like you to get a closer look at Nadine."

Her breath caught in her throat. A flash of panic-induced heat gushed through her veins. She couldn't afford to have another freak-out in front of clients. He knew that. He was holding out his hand.

She felt nauseous but she didn't protest as he pulled her next to the table. "Okay, I'm here." She kept her eyes on her hands.

"I want you to touch her."

"No." She remembered her manners. "Thanks."

"I'll help you, Dr. Scott," Tommy offered. He took her ice-cold hand in his then he put her fingers on the creature's smooth, dry skin.

"It's not slimy," she gasped. "It's smooth and hard."

"Mmmm." Amusement played in Baz's voice.

How could he be thinking about sex at a time like this?

"Everyone knows snakes aren't slimy," Diane said, obviously irritated she'd lost Baz's attention.

"That is, everyone who passed tenth-grade biology."

She was right. Hallie knew that, too. She had just repressed everything she'd learned about snakes.

Tommy returned her fingers to her. "You did a good job."

"You are a very kind young man," she told him.

"Baz? Could you carry Nadine's cage out to the

car for me?"

He didn't answer right away. The gray eyes were focused on Hallie. "Tommy's right," he said.

"You did a good job. Next time you can examine Nadine."

Hallie cleaned up the treatment room while Baz accompanied Nadine and her owners to their car.

The relief she felt at the snake's departure was only temporary. Now that Baz knew about the phobia, he wouldn't give up until she'd conquered it.

When he rejoined her, he invited her into the office then sat by her on the sofa. "Tell me about it," he said, quietly.

"I'm phobic, of course. I don't know why. I apologize for my reaction. Nadine was a surprise."

"You've never been through a desensitization program?"

She wrinkled her nose. "You mean where you expose yourself to snakes over and over, like in a reptile house at the zoo?"

"Yes."

"No. But judging from the expression on your face. I'm guessing that's something I'll be doing in the near future."

He smiled. "Yep."

"I really don't want to."

"Nadine isn't going to be the last snake you ever see. Especially in a general practice like this one."

"I suppose we couldn't just put up a No Snakes Allowed sign."

He hooted. "Every kid in town would be out searching for garter snakes to bring you. You can get the best of this, honey. You're a strong woman."

She had her doubts. "Thanks for handling it with such finesse. It's hard enough getting accepted as a female vet. This meltdown isn't going to do anything for my reputation, but you minimized it."

"What d'you think about Diane?"

Hallie shrugged. "She's got a great son."

"She's also got a great bra. I can't imagine how a piece of fabric could hold those girls up."

"I'm sure she'd be happy to show you."

He pulled her onto his lap. "It was an idle question. I'm only interested in one woman's underwear. By the way, I'll pick you up at six. I've got a big evening planned." He kissed her, and her heart rate spiked again.

This time it had nothing to do with the snake.

Chapter Thirteen

Baz slapped aftershave onto his cheeks and stared at his face in the mirror. He was uncomfortably aware that his palms were sweaty.

Proposing could do that to a man. Especially when the answer was in doubt.

He dressed in a crisp white dress shirt, his gray pinstripe suit and, because he didn't want to look too corporate America, he wore the red tie Daisy had given him for Christmas. Its diagonal strips were composed of tiny white pigs.

He was pleased with his arrangements. He'd reserved a private alcove at Cerrutto's. The chef would prepare whatever kind of pasta Hallie wanted, and Baz had already chosen a red wine to go with it.

A heart-shaped cake would be delivered at the restaurant sometime this afternoon along with vase of yellow daisies. He'd arranged for the restaurant's pianist to play the show tunes Hallie loved.

Then there was the ring. He patted his left breast pocket and tried to ignore the sharp twinge of guilt. He had no business proposing before he told Hallie about Nicole. On the other hand, his chances of success were between none and negative numbers if he revealed his secret beforehand.

Ethics versus Expediency.

In this case, it was no contest.

He decided to put the whole issue out of his mind. He'd done his homework for tonight.

Everything was perfect. All systems were go.

Everything except the weather.

He frowned at the sleet pinging against the bedroom window. The storm wasn't supposed to get here until Saturday. He'd planned to borrow Cam's elegant Mercedes, but he'd better take the pickup to be on the safe side.

A lightning bolt of desire zigzagged through him, and he felt himself hardening inside his fine wool slacks as he remembered what had happened in the pickup on New Year's Eve. If all went well tonight there might be a return engagement. This time, though, they'd do it in Hallie's bed. He couldn't wait to move her to his own king-sized bed.

It was at the top of the priority list. His lower body throbbed in anticipation.

Well, damn. He wasn't gonna be able to get past Asia and Lucy in this condition. He forced himself to think about non-sexy subjects: Hallie's fear of snakes. Hallie's reluctance to marry him. Hallie's big disappointment.

It worked. He felt a lot more sober. Almost depressed.

"Where are you going?" Lucy asked, as he strode through the kitchen.

"I'm taking Hallie out to dinner in Bangor."

"You drive careful," she warned him. "It's not a fit night out for man nor beast."

"Nor pig," Daisy said, looking up from the book she was reading to Wilbur.

"I'll be careful."

Shards of ice nicked his face as he strode across the courtyard. The outside lights illuminated the ice in the backyard trees. Didn't it do anything in Maine except sleet? He refused to let it get him down. They could always stay over in a hotel. Hell, Mother Nature was doing him a big favor. They would stay over.

Despite the cold his temperature spiked.

When she opened the door, he felt something move under his heart. Her brown curls bobbed and whirled around her wide-set golden eyes. Her dress shimmered in the artificial light. He liked the way the bodice hugged her firm breasts.

"You look beautiful," he said, astounded to hear a frog in his throat. "I love you in red."

She grinned. "This is actually coral." She twirled and the skirt belled out, revealing her shapely legs.

She hadn't put on her heels yet so she was almost a foot shorter than he.

"It reminds me of something."

"Fifties sit-coms. It's retro."

"Ah."

She sat down to put on a pair of shiny black shoes.

"I think you'd better wear boots. Sleet's coming down pretty heavily."

She made a face. "If only I hadn't left them at the grange hall." She stood and he caught her hand.

"Then I'll carry you." He pulled her to him and fitted his mouth to hers. As usual the kiss triggered an instant explosion of urgent need. He forced himself to break it off. That was just an appetizer he reminded himself. Time for the full meal later.

When they got to Bangor.

It became clear almost immediately that they

wouldn't get to Bangor. Walnut Street was an ice rink. It took twenty minutes to drive to the end of it.

Baz was grateful for the pick-up's rear wheel drive, but even with that he couldn't drive much above four or five miles an hour.

"Baz?"

"Mmmm?"

"I think we're going to have to abandon Bangor."

"Yeah." He thought about all his carefully made arrangements. "We'd never have to fight weather like this in L.A."

"I can't argue with that."

The humor in her voice restored his. Things weren't so bad. He had the girl and the ring. He could still propose.

"We could go back to my apartment," she said.

He nodded. That seemed a little anticlimactic. "Or to the house. I'm sure Asia made plenty of supper."

Definitely not back to the house.

"What's the best restaurant in town?"

She grinned at him. "You mean the only restaurant in town? That'd be Little Joe's."

A proposal in a greasy spoon? Well, at least it would be memorable.

"Baz?"

"Mmmm?"

"The place isn't important."

"You got all dressed up."

"Later I plan to get all undressed. What we do in between doesn't matter to me as long as we do it together."

Warmth flooded his soul as he looked into the golden eyes. Damn he was a lucky man. "Little Joe's it is."

They inched along High Street.

"Uh-oh," she said, "the place is packed. I forgot it was meatloaf night."

"Meatloaf night?"

"Every Thursday. Joe puts green pepper and onion in it. And a little sage. It's really good."

"Every Thursday. And nobody objects?"

"Predictability appeals to some people. Me, for instance. I like knowing the specials almost as much as I like knowing people everywhere I go. I like it that they know me."

"Don't you get bored living here? Familiarity is one thing, but nothing ever changes in Eden."

"I think that's why people choose to live in small towns. People who aren't adventure-seekers."

He heard something in her voice. "You really love it here, don't you?"

She nodded. "I'll admit I can't understand why you wouldn't choose this life. Your family is great.

The town is great. I've met more great people here than anywhere I've ever been in my life."

"Diane? Nadine?"

She punched him. "This is home for you," she continued, refusing to be sidetracked by the teasing.

"You belong to Eden."

He heard the wistfulness. "You belong here, too, Hallie. More than I do because you've chosen it."

She shook her head. He tried to make her understand. "Damn, Hallie. You're back on that blood-is-thicker-than water thing, and I've got to tell you, you're dead wrong about that. My dad, Cam, Lucy, Asia, and Daisy think of you as one of the family. I'm pretty sure even Wilbur would back me up on that."

She laughed, and he realized how much he loved that sound. He wanted to tell her they'd come back here for holidays and vacations, but he didn't want to talk about the future. Not until after the proposal.

"Why don't we go over to the inn?"

"I thought Sharon only served breakfast."

Hallie fluttered her eyelashes at him. "She does. We'd just have to wait for it."

She wanted to spend the night with him.

Well, hell. He was sorely tempted. He hesitated but decided against it. He needed her undivided attention. He wasn't sure he'd get that with her best friend nearby.

"Baz?"

"Not this time, honey."

"You're hungry, huh?" She looked around. "Well, we're in luck. We've made it to Buddy Burger."

Junk food. He was going to propose over junk food. He wondered if that'd be what she remembered from this night. His jaw tightened. He'd have to make sure it wasn't all she remembered.

"Is that a serious suggestion?"

"I like Buddy burgers. Besides, the faster we eat, the faster we can move on to whatever else is on the agenda."

His body jerked in anticipation and she giggled.

"Sold," he said, hoarsely. "Buddy Burger, here we come."

There was a large statue of Buddy revolving overhead and a pair of rainbow arches. The menu included Buddy whoppers and McBuddy sandwiches.

Buddy Holmes, the entrepreneur who'd built the

place, hadn't wanted to overlook any of the fast food icons.

Baz half drove, half slid into the parking lot.

Hallie giggled.

"What's so funny?"

"You're so dressed up. We're both so dressed up. We look like we're ready for a four-star restaurant out of Zagat's, and we're at Buddy Burger. Oh, and we're in the takeout line, so we'll be eating in the truck."

Someone behind them honked. Baz shot the other driver a look and Hallie snickered. "You've got to move up."

"That's ridiculous. Every time I put the damn thing in gear it slips. Why can't we just sit here until it's our turn at the window?"

The car honked again.

"Tradition?"

He groaned. "This'll make quite a story to tell our grandchildren."

For an instant Hallie froze. Baz damned himself to the last circle of hell. He'd ruined everything.

"Hallie, I…"

"Look." She put her hand on his arm. "If we're going to go to pieces every time a reference is made to kids, this won't work. It's time to accept things as they are. Think you can do that?"

He stared into the serious golden eyes. "Yes."

She nodded. Then she looked around. "I'd say everyone who's not at Little Joe's is here. There are six cars in front of us and two behind. This'll take a while."

Baz's lips twisted. A sense of fierce urgency roared through him. He couldn't wait until they got their food and parked somewhere. He couldn't wait another minute. He had to get his answer. Now. She was flushed and soft and she had that devilish look in her eye. Lord, he wanted her. Now.

"Baz?"

For an instant he was paralyzed by the need within him. He shifted into Park, turned to face her and took her hand. "Halliday, I regret last year more than I can say. I missed you constantly."

"As long as you brought it up, why did it take so long for you to come back?"

Why did she have to ask that now? "There's no short answer to that question. I'd like to put it on hold. We can discuss it later. There's something else I need to say to you right now."

She nodded. "All right." He heard another honk.

"Better move up first."

He shifted and pulled forward. "After you left I couldn't stop thinking about you. I stayed in contact with my dad so I could get updates on you, make sure you were okay while I tried to sort out my, uh, life. I just want you to know there was not one single day that I didn't miss you and regret what I'd said. I promise you I'll never be that foolish again. I'll never say no to you again. Not on anything important."

He took a breath. "I know you've been happier here in Eden than you were in L.A., but I can change that. You can move into my condo, and, if you want, you can have your old job back. Or, if you'd rather, you can join a veterinarian's practice. I have quite a few contacts in the area."

"You know I think you should consider staying in Eden. Your dad needs you. The whole family needs you, and I think you need them."

He scowled. "That isn't what I want to talk about tonight, Hallie."

A horn blared at him.

"Better scoot up," she said.

This definitely wasn't working out the way he'd planned. "I want you to come back to California with me."

"You said that."

Neither the words nor the slightly pained look on her face were encouraging signs. "Okay, okay, forget California for now. That isn't what I want to talk about either."

"You don't want to talk about California or the lost year or Eden or your dad, right?"

He'd blown it. He was losing her. The playfulness he'd enjoyed earlier was completely gone from her eyes. Panic erupted. He grabbed both her hands. "I brought you out tonight to propose. I had it all planned, dinner, wine, a special cake, and music. I wanted this to be the most memorable moment of your life."

Those long lashes covered her eyes and he felt as if he were on the brink of a steep abyss. What if she said no?

"What about a baby?"

Did she know about Robert?

"You know I can't have children. How d'you feel about that?"

Relief washed over him. "I feel sad. Very sad for you and for me. But it doesn't make any difference. I love you, Hallie. I love you and I want to marry you and spend the rest of my life with you."

"Could you put that in the form of a question?"

The car behind them honked again. Twice. Baz ignored it. He fumbled in his pocket and found the ring box. It took him three tries to get it open. There was no way he could get on one knee. He just blurted it out. "Hallie Scott, will you marry me?"

Tears filled her eyes and ran down her face. He prayed they were happy tears. This time, the series of beeps sounded like Morse Code. It didn't matter.

He couldn't have moved if all the drivers behind him got out of their cars and surrounded him with rifles.

All his senses were focused on this woman, on whether she could forgive him enough to spend her life with him. Sweat trickled down his back. Damn, he couldn't wait any longer. "Hallie? Will you marry me?"

A teasing look came into her beautiful eyes and he knew it would be okay. "Of course I'll marry you.

Let me have another look at that ring."

He reached for her then, and she practically leapt into his arms. Relief washed through him like a series of waves. All he could do was bury his tongue in her mouth and hold her tightly against his chest. If the other cars were honking, he didn't hear it. She felt warm and soft and eager for him, and he wanted that moment, that exact moment, to last forever. When they had to break for air he buried his face in her curls.

She laid her hand against his chest. "Your heartbeat's too fast."

"I was nervous," he mumbled, his voice thick with passion and relief. "I thought you might turn me down."

"You shouldn't have worried. I love you. I've loved you from the first day I walked into your lab and found out the other techs called you Stoneface."

"They call me Stoneface?"

Her smile lit up the inside of the cab. "I imagine they don't anymore."

The next honk was one long bleat. Baz let go of her long enough to move up. "Now, where were we?"

"We're at the window." She giggled. "It's time to order."

He reached behind him and cranked the handle.

An adolescent male voice rang in his ear. "Good evening, sir. Would you like the big fish combo tonight, sir?"

Baz stared at the color in Hallie's face and the brilliance of her eyes. "Promise me you won't change your mind."

"Sir? Sir?"

"Promise me, Hallie."

"I promise." She raised her voice. "Two buddy burgers and a couple of Cokes."

"Supersize, medium or small?"

She grinned at him. "Definitely supersize."

"Would you like fries with that, sir or, uh, miss?"

"I'd like you," Baz murmured. "Now."

Hallie giggled. "Sure," she called out, "give us the works."

Baz pulled out of the Buddy Burger and into the empty lot of the Staghead Realty Company.

"You want to buy some property?"

He lifted the bag of food out of her hands and set it behind the seat. "Let's put it this way, I want to stake a claim." He pulled her over onto his lap for a soul-searing kiss. An instant later she felt his big hand cupping one breast. Her nipple hardened and she moaned. "Oh God," he groaned, "I want you right now."

The take-out lane was mostly blocked by a row of pine trees, and, anyway, the ice on the windshield obscured their movements. No one would cruise by and wonder why there was a pickup truck parked in the lot of a closed business.

"Let's do it here."

"I don't think I've got a choice." His fingers started to work on the buttons on her new dress. He pushed down the bodice and released her lacy bra with one quick move.

"You've got awfully quick wrists. Do you do this a lot?"

"It's racquetball. Kiss me."

She slid her hands around his neck and pressed up against him. His heart pounded fiercely against her breasts. A shirt, suit jacket and overcoat separated her from his broad chest. She fitted her mouth to his, but he couldn't maintain the kiss. His breathing was heavy and fast. His urgency fueled hers. She felt that rush of warmth.

"Oh my god. I'm already wet."

"Oh, baby, baby," he groaned.

Her hands fumbled with his shirt. "Got to get these jackets out of the way."

"There isn't time."

His whole body was trembling. She made a quick decision. "Screw the jackets," she said as she unbuckled his belt and eased the zipper over the pulsing mound of his erection. And then she was stroking him.

"Honey, I can't take that. I need, I need…"

He didn't have to finish the sentence. She knew what he meant. It was a little awkward, but they managed to get her panties and pantyhose off. He was gasping with need, and she wasn't far behind.

He picked her up to settle her over himself.

"Wait," she said. "Wait."

His eyes were glazed. "What?"

"I want to wear my ring."

A moment later she found his mouth again and wiggled until she felt him inside her, until she was all around him. He dropped his head back against the seat and she began to move. It was heady, exhilarating to have sex only a few yards away from the hungry people of Eden. It was awesome to be on top, the position of power. She loved the way his fingers dug into her hips, too hard, as if he were out of control. It was wonderful to feel the friction, that perfect fit that drove them higher and higher until the now-familiar magic flung them into the air and they collapsed against each other, spent and sated.

The proposal had been perfect. She loved that he'd planned an elegant evening. She loved even more that he'd wanted her enough to propose at Buddy Burger. She loved that they'd made love in the lot of Staghorn Realty.

Most of all, she loved knowing beyond the shadow of a doubt that he loved her.

Chapter Fourteen

Hallie's face was frozen from the biting sleet.

She'd ruined another dress and a pair of pantyhose and, to top it off, she'd slipped on the ice-slick wooden steps outside her apartment and twisted her ankle.

She'd never been happier in her life.

She'd waited forever to have someone who belonged to her, and now he was here.

Baz took her key and turned it in the lock. An instant later they were inside. "Hallie, I'm sorry—"

She cut him off with a kiss, probably the fiftieth or so of the night. He winced, and she figured his lips were chapped like hers. "No apologies. It was the best night ever."

"Even though right about now you're so hungry your stomach is up against your spine?"

"Yep."

"Even though your ankle hurts?"

"Yep."

"Even though I messed up by staying away for twelve months?"

"Yep."

"Even though I don't plan to stay in Eden?"

She grinned at him. "I'm still hoping to change your mind about that."

"Hallie, I—"

"I wonder if the cleaners will be able to get that

stuff off your pants. Calling Bill Clinton."

A slow smile spread across his rugged features.

It was the smile that never failed to make her melt.

"Do you like the ring?"

Good grief. She hadn't even looked at it. She held it up to the light. "Oh, my."

The stone in the center was larger than the ones next to it but they were all emeralds. Not the dark, heavy kind of emeralds but the paler versions, the ones called green beryl. They reminded her of the first leaves of spring.

She looked up at him. "I told you last fall, a year ago last fall, that I had always liked pale green stones. That day we went to the Natural History Museum in L.A.?"

He nodded.

She studied the ring. "It's so beautiful. I can't believe you remembered it all this time."

"It wasn't as long as you think. I bought the ring in January."

"Last January? You planned to propose to me a year ago?"

He nodded. There were parentheses carved on either side of his mouth. His gray eyes had become very solemn. "There's something I have to tell you, honey. I should have done it before, but I was too damn afraid of losing you."

A premonition of disaster sent a shiver down her spine. Suddenly she was afraid of that, too, so she stalled. "Let's get something to eat first," she said.

He hesitated then nodded.

She slipped out of her ruined dress and into a soft, chenille robe. While Baz was doing what he could to salvage his clothes, she towel-dried her hair.

He grinned when he saw her. "I remember that bathrobe. A gift from Cam and Daisy wasn't it?"

Hallie held out her arms so he could see the dozens of fluffy pink pigs cavorting in a green pasture.

"I love it." He held her face between his hands and dropped a kiss on her nose. "I love you."

She touched his cheek and her heart soared.

"Whatever it is you're planning to tell me, Baz, it won't make any difference. Not after tonight. We are definitely, absolutely, positively engaged."

His lips quirked in the beginning of a smile.

"Because of the ring?"

She pretended to think. "The ring's a consideration, but I think it was the sex in the front seat that sold me."

"It was hot."

She grinned at him. "And empowering. I feel like a sex goddess." She dished the eggs onto a plate and spread some butter on the toast.

"Hallie?"

"Almost ready."

They sat at the table facing each other. The food smelled delicious, but after one bite Hallie couldn't eat. Sex goddess aside, she felt the sword of Damocles hanging over her head. There were still unanswered questions about this past year. She needed to know why he'd stayed away, but she dreaded the truth. There was no way she could enjoy her new found happiness much less breakfast.

Baz looked at her and put his fork down, too. "I can't eat, either. I have to get this off my chest. I have to find out whether this will ruin everything."

She couldn't swallow past the blockage in her

throat. She wondered if it was her heart.

"Last year, right after you left, I was miserable.

I'd decided long ago never to marry, but I missed you like the devil. I told you I bought the ring in January. It was late January. For a few weeks I thought I'd get over it."

She gripped the seat of her chair. "During those few weeks you met someone else."

It wasn't a question. It had to be someone else.

"In a way."

The lump seemed to be expanding. She couldn't suck in a deep breath.

He never broke eye contact with her; she could feel him willing her to understand and, probably, to forgive.

Please, God. Don't let this involve a baby.

She clamped her jaw shut, afraid she'd said it aloud.

"I started spending the evenings at some dive. I sat at the bar like one of those losers in the movies and drank beer after beer until I'd had enough to fall into such a dead sleep that I didn't dream of you."

She waited.

"I met a cocktail waitress. Her name's Nicole."

Hallie envisioned a shapely blonde working her way through law school on tips. "Is she pretty?" She bit down on her tongue. What difference did it make if she was pretty?

"What?" He seemed startled by the concept. "I guess. I don't know. She's a kid. We started to talk.

She's a pretty good listener." He frowned as if unsure on that last point.

Great. His girlfriend was not only a Playboy bunny and a Rhodes Scholar, she was also a good conversationalist.

"You told her about me?"

"Yeah. Some. Mostly I listened. She was vulnerable and scared, Hallie. She'd been in an abusive relationship, and she'd run away from it.

Some two-bit mobster out of Vegas., At first I was just grateful to get my mind off what I'd done to you, to us. Then I began to think about how you wouldn't just have listened, you'd have found a way to help her."

She kept her gaze on his eyes. She didn't like the darkness she saw in their gray depths. "You wanted to help her?"

He sighed and rubbed the back of his neck the way he did when he was tired or exasperated or both. The gesture looked familiar, and she realized his brother did the same thing.

"She was pregnant and scared to death that this guy would kidnap her. She needed protection, a place to stay, medical care. I could provide that."

Hallie fixated on the first three words. The damning three words. She was pregnant. The phrase sent a fist into the middle of her chest. Baz was still talking and she had to force herself to listen.

"We drove down to Tijuana and got married."

"You got married." She repeated the phrase as if hearing it again would help her grasp the concept.

"You married a woman who was pregnant."

He used two fingers to lift her chin so he could hold her eyes. She saw the remorse in his.

"Right from the start I told her it was temporary. I didn't want to be married, remember?"

"I remember." The words were faint.

He shrugged. "Something happened when I said

my vows. I looked at Nicole and I saw you. That's when I knew I'd made a huge mistake. That's when I knew nothing could stop me from coming to Eden to plead for a second chance."

"Nothing," she said, dully, "except the fact that you were married to someone else."

His jaw tightened.

Pain throbbed in Hallie's chest. She pressed one hand against it. She wanted to get away from him.

Away from here. She knew she could not. She was doomed to hear the rest of the story.

"I brought her to the condo, got her doctor's appointments, and found her a job at a florist's shop.

The job didn't work out, of course. Nicole's got major attention deficit issues. She can't stick with anything for more than a few weeks."

"She stuck with you."

"Sure. I provided everything she needed."

She looked into gray eyes that suddenly seemed foreign. "Did you go to the doctor's appointments?"

She could tell from the sick look on his face that he had. And then a new wave of pain swept through her.

"You were with her when the baby was born."

He didn't have to answer. She knew.

"That's why you were so good with Janie. You'd been through it before."

He took her hand. "I didn't know about your situation. Not that it had gotten so dire, anyway. I'm so goddam sorry about all of it."

Hallie squeezed her eyes and prayed she wouldn't start crying. Or vomiting. Or both. He remained quiet allowing her to process the information and absorb the blow.

"I filed for divorce as soon as Nicole was back on her feet."

"And the baby?"

Something flashed in his gray eyes. She recognized it immediately. She'd always been able to read him like a ten-cent novel. Baz had fallen for the child.

"His name is Robert."

Robert. He was undoubtedly beautiful. All babies were beautiful.

"He's in L.A. with Nicole. I hired a nurse and then a nanny."

Of course he did. Baz was nothing if not responsible.

"Nicole's still worried about Jimmy Dinari. He wants the baby."

"Are they in danger?"

"The condo's got a state-of-the-ar security system. On top of that, my name is on Robert's birth certificate. Legally that makes him my son."

The woman was still living in Baz's home. Her baby was legally his.

"But he's the mobster's biological son?"

"That's what Nicole says."

"Do you believe her?"

He hesitated an instant too long.

"Is he yours?"

She could tell she'd shocked him.

"No. Absolutely not." But he'd answered just a split second too quickly.

"But it's possible, right?"

The gray eyes were pools of misery. She knew he wanted to spare her this most excruciating detail.

He didn't have to answer. Of course he'd slept with

her. Women escaped reality with ice cream and romance novels. Men had sex.

This couldn't be happening. She'd been so ecstatic just minutes ago. How had the bubble burst so quickly? It wasn't quick, she reminded herself.

She'd known there was another shoe to drop. She just hadn't realized it was going to kick the hell out of her heart. She did the only thing she could do.

"You can't leave that young woman and the baby alone in L.A., Baz. They are your responsibility."

"Hallie. I love you."

"That's beside the point. You spent twenty years denying your dad and siblings. Are you going to spend the next twenty denying your connection to this young woman and her child? Would you deprive her of a husband and him of a father? They are your family now. Not me."

He grabbed her hands and squeezed. "You're my family, Hallie. You."

She shook her head. "There's no way I could be happy knowing you've left a child, Baz. You know I'm right. You wouldn't be happy, either. Not in the long run."

His hands moved to her shoulders, and he enclosed her in his arms. She could feel his heart beating fast, much faster than Molly's tom-tom.

"Don't even think about breaking up with me. You're mine. We're meant to be together. You know it, too.

You feel it."

She felt numb. For once she wasn't distracted by Baz's masculine scent or the strength in his arms.

She wasn't even hungry anymore. Or tired.

It was like she had died.

The phone rang. Automatically she started toward it. "Don't," he barked, hoarsely. "Whoever it is can wait."

She looked into his eyes and saw something she'd never seen there before. Panic. She heard herself speak. "It might be an emergency."

He grabbed the phone off the wall. "Dr. Outlaw."

He hung up and stood for a moment, with his head bent. A strong, confident man reduced to despair. Tears pricked the backs of Hallie's eyes.

"That was Lucy. They just got a call from a Miami Hospital. It's my dad. He had a heart attack on the boat."

Fear broke through the numbness and twisted Hallie's heart. "Is he okay?"

"He needs an emergency bypass. Cam and Lucy are heading down there on the first plane out of Bangor. I've got to drive them to the airport." He paused.

The news had shaken him, badly. This was his dad. His family. She made a quick decision. "You have to go with them. I'll drive you all to the airport."

"I'm not leaving you."

"I can handle the practice alone for a few days."

She hurried to her room and changed into jeans and a sweatshirt. "I'll stay in the house with Asia and help her with Daisy."

"No. I won't leave while things are unresolved between us."

His tanned face was the color of rice paper.

"You've missed twenty years with him, Baz. You need to be there now. I'll be here when you get back."

"But you won't marry me, will you? You've made

your decision on that." His face twisted into a dark scowl. "Don't you ever get tired of being a martyr?"

"I'm not a martyr. I can see just see more clearly because I'm on the outside. You can't abandon that boy. Let's get over to the house and pick up your things."

Baz drove the thirty miles to Bangor on automatic pilot. The sleet had stopped, and the salt trucks had been out. That was one thing about Maine; they had too much snow, but they knew how to handle it.

The flight wouldn't leave for another four hours, but they couldn't afford to miss it. As it was they'd get there in the middle of the surgery. His gut clenched. He needed to be there. Hallie was right about this. She was wrong about the other, though.

Dead wrong. She was his woman, not Nicole.

But she did have a point about Robert and he knew it.

And Robert was the part that hurt her most.

She might never admit it but he knew. He'd enabled

another woman to have a healthy child while Hallie's time clock was running out. She'd never forgive him, and he didn't really blame her.

****

Hallie returned to Eden, cleaned up her kitchen, and packed up a few clothes. She'd have given a lot to be allowed to stay in her own place for the next few days, but Asia could use some help with Daisy, and, in any case, the housekeeper was nervous about being the sole adult in the house. Hallie knew, too,

Asia was worried sick about her boss.

Hallie was worried sick, too.

After the clinic closed, Hallie joined Asia and Daisy for supper. The pork chops were undoubtedly delicious. Asia was a superb cook, but, once again, Hallie couldn't eat much of anything and Asia noticed.

"Off your feed, tonight?"

"I'm worried about Jesse," she said, after Daisy had left to read a child's version of Charlotte's Web to Wilbur. It was on the approved list because the pig was one of the heroes and he didn't die.

"You sure that's all that's on your mind?"

Hallie's heart hurt so badly. She wished she could confide in the older woman. Asia had a lot of common sense and a ton of experience with the Outlaw family. It would be a relief to share the burden of her new knowledge with someone, but it wouldn't be fair. Asia's first loyalty was to the Outlaws, including the Prodigal Son.

"Couldn't help but notice that new sparkler," Asia said.

Good grief. She'd forgotten all about the dancing emeralds. It was a beautiful ring, and she'd be sorry to lose it, but it was just a ring. Her heart convulsed as she thought about the future without Baz.

"Baz gave it to you, didn't he?"

"He did."

"It's on your wedding finger, too. That mean you two are getting hitched?"

Hallie sipped her coffee. She didn't need the caffeine. She was dead tired from getting no sleep the previous night and putting in a full day of work.

She wouldn't sleep well tonight. Sleep just made things worse because when she woke up she had to experience the heartbreak all over again.

"It's complicated."

"Doesn't have to be. The boy loves you. And everyone knows you're crazy about him. You never had that color in your cheeks or that twinkle in your eye when you were dating the sheriff."

Hallie was surprised Asia had noticed. "I wasn't really dating Jake. It was more of a friend situation."

"The little one's got a crush on him."

Hallie lifted her eyebrows. She knew Asia meant Lucy."I wondered about that. I think he likes her, too."

"Too much age difference."

Hallie's heart ached for Baz's younger sister It seemed as if she were star-crossed, too. Just like Hallie.

"She'll get over it when she gets that job in Boston."

"Maybe."

Baz called a short time later to report that the operation had gone well.

Hallie knew the first twenty-four hours after an operation were the most critical. The hospital staff and the three Outlaw children would keep a close eye on Jesse.

"We've checked in at a Holiday Inn near the hospital," he said, "but we're not spending much time there. You can get me on the cell any time you need me."

"I know. Thanks."

He asked her about the day's patients, and she told him.

She tried to sound normal and cheerful, but her words came out like stones dropping into a pond.

When she stopped there was silence.

"Hallie."

His tone said he planned to start in on the situation.

She couldn't bear it. Not now. Not when Jesse was sick and they were thousands of miles apart.

Not when she wasn't ready to accept what she knew she'd have to accept.

"I need to read a bedtime story to Daisy," she said. "Asia sends her love to everybody."

"What about you?"

"I send my love, too."

He was silent a moment. He knew as well as she did that love wasn't the issue anymore.

"Tell Lucy to call if she's got time. Good night, "Baz. I'll be praying for your dad."

Chapter Fifteen

Baz decided that if he spent another eight hours in the plastic molded chair he'd turn into a plastic molded chair. He got up and walked around the waiting room.

It had been eighteen hours since they'd left the Bangor Airport. Eighteen hours since he'd seen Hallie. He, Cam, and Lucy were feeling the effects of the emotional strain and fatigue.

They made sure the nurse's desk had their cell phone numbers then they headed for the Holiday Inn. He tucked Lucy into bed. She was already half asleep, but she lifted up to give him a kiss on the cheek. "I'm glad you're here, Baz. Let me know if anything changes with Daddy."

He'd spent so many years denying his own father, now he could lose the man. Was he really going to deny Robert a father? He'd never admit it to anyone, but he'd missed the baby like hell.

Goddamn

Even if he could convince Hallie to marry him, he'd still have a hole in his heart. If he didn't marry Hallie, he'd have no heart. He realized she was right.

There was no way he could abandon the kid.

Shit.

His eyes felt like sandpaper. He was swaying on his feet, but he knew he wouldn't sleep. Not with his whole world falling apart. "I'm going down to the bar," he told Cam.

His brother had already removed his shirt in preparation for bed. "I'll go with you."

They found a table in the back of the darkened room as far away as possible from the sultry brunette singing torch songs in Spanish. Baz rubbed the back of his neck, and so did his brother. They exchanged a look that said they'd noticed the similar gesture.

"Helluva day," Baz murmured.

Cam's blue eyes were bloodshot but penetrating.

"Wanna tell me what's up between you and Hallie?"

The cold fingers of fear that had gripped his heart all day formed a fist. For a moment, he couldn't get a breath. Cam waited.

"It's a long story."

"I've got all night."

Baz stared into the golden whiskey in his glass.

Until Hallie entered his life last year, he'd never had anyone with whom to share his problems until Hallie had entered his life last year. It was strangely comforting to have someone now. A brother. The concept was a little foreign. Something occurred to him, suddenly. "Are you asking because you're worried about Hallie?"

Cam blinked. "I'm worried about both of you."

Baz nodded. He gave Cameron a brief description of the relationship with Hallie that had developed over several months the previous year.

"It sounds damn near perfect," Cam drawled.

He'd leaned back in his chair, one booted foot resting on the opposite knee. "Why the break-up?"

Baz felt a twinge of guilt. "This part's a little

personal."

Cam nodded in silent understanding that it was to go no further.

"Hallie had a fertility issue."

"I know about that."

"Oh." That was disconcerting. Who else had she told?" Anyway she'd been told she needed to have a baby sooner rather than later. After the time we made love, she told me she wanted to grab her chance to be a mother after the first time we made love. The only time we made love." He stared at his drink. "She proposed, and I turned her down."

"Makes sense. You barely knew her."

Baz looked up. "You don't understand. It was her last chance. I ran her out of town on a rail. I asked Dad to hire her, and he agreed."

Cam's gaze was level.

"It was our gain. And, I think, Hallie's been relatively happy in Eden."

Baz drained the whiskey and signaled the bartender. "I was an idiot."

Cam shrugged. "You needed more time."

Baz shook his head. "That's just it. I knew right away that I wanted her, but I was scared shitless.

Our family's such a damn mess. I hadn't planned to get married at all.

"After she left I got involved with a waitress.

She was pregnant and in trouble. I wanted Hallie, but I wasn't ready to come to Eden. For some damn fool reason, I got it into my head that she would want me to help Nicole. The girl's ex was after her. He wanted his baby. I gave her the protection of my name and a place to stay until after the baby was born."

"You married her?"

He didn't miss the shock in his brother's voice.

"It was temporary. Just for legal purposes. We're divorced now."

"What about the kid?"

Baz accepted another whiskey from the waiter.

He took a healthy swallow before answering.

"They're in my condo in L.A."

"Any chance he's yours?"

"Slim to none."

Baz chugged the rest of the glass as his brother waited for an explanation.

"The marriage was about protecting the girl."

Cam's eyes were steady. "In any case he's your responsibility now."

"That's what Hallie says."

"What're you gonna do?"

"I don't know. Nicole claims the ex knows where she is. He wants the kid.

She wants me to come back to L.A. to protect her and Robert."

"Robert. That's the baby's name?"

Baz flashed on the dark-haired child, and his throat went dry." Yeah. Robert."

"You gonna go?"

"I can't. Hallie can't handle the practice alone, and, besides, I don't want to leave her. I don't think I'll ever be able to leave her. She makes me feel a kind of contentment I didn't even know was possible.

It's like when I'm with her, I'm home."

"And she's hot."

Baz closed his eyes. "Yeah."

"Forgive me for saying so, but it sounds like this is

not all about what you want."

Baz glared into his empty glass. His brother was right and he knew it.

Goddamitall to hell.

"My advice? Don't lose Hallie. She's one in a million. A woman you can trust."

"Sounds like you've known the other kind. Your wife?"

Cam's fine lips thinned into a grim line.

"Elaine's only been dead a year and a half, and all I can remember are the bad times. There were so many." He signaled the waiter. "I married her because she got pregnant. Her folks are wealthy Bostonians. She had no interest in coming up to Maine. After a while she had no interest in me."

Baz lifted a brow. "Was she a good mother?"

"I guess so. I'm not sure it's fair to judge when a house is the size of a railroad station and it's filled with servants and nannies. Parenting was only a small part of her schedule. The marriage was a mistake from start to finish."

"You got Daisy."

Cam's grim expression lightened for an instant.

"The one bright spot."

The waiter brought fresh drinks. "Bar's closing in thirty minutes."

The brothers attacked their refilled glasses.

"So who was the woman who betrayed you?"

The younger man's saturnine features twisted.

He took so long to answer Baz thought he intended to ignore the question. When he finally spoke he made no sense. "Tiger Lily."

"Tiger Lily? You mean the character from Peter

Pan?"

Cam shifted in his chair.

"It's an old story. Boy and girl meet in high school, fall in love and promise to wait for one another until boy finishes college. Boy comes home for Christmas vacation, almost sick with longing to see the girl. Turns out she's gotten a better offer and she's married to someone else."

"Shit."

"Yeah."

"It was a long time ago."

Cam gazed at him. "Twelve years. Will you have forgotten Hallie in twelve years?"

He had a point.

"Why'd you call her Tiger Lily?"

"It was my nickname for her. She lives on the Rez."

Baz was genuinely startled. "Blackbird?"

Cam nodded. "She's half native. A Penobscot couple adopted her when she was sixteen. She feels she owes them her life."

"Maybe it never would have worked."

Cam took another drink. "Probably not."

"You still see her?"

Cam nodded. "She's the midwife out there, but she's involved in all the political issues. Turned into a real activist."

"It's Hallie's friend, right? Molly Whitesky?"

"Whitecloud."

"She still married?"

Cam shook his head.

"Why not?"

"I've got no goddam idea."

"Christ," Baz said, without heat. "We're a couple of losers."

"Exhausted losers." Cam struggled to his feet.

"Let's grab some shut-eye before we head back to the hospital."

Baz realized it had helped to talk to Cam. There were worse things than having a family. If only he'd figured that out last year.

If only.

****

Normally the clinic closed at two on Saturday, but Hallie didn't turn off the computer and shut off the lights until five. She updated records, completed correspondence, and searched the veterinary websites for jobs.

Not that she planned to leave. Not immediately, anyhow. Now that she knew she had no future with

Baz, she had to be prepared. Eden was his hometown. The Outlaw Veterinary Clinic belonged to his family. She was the outsider.

Asia had phoned earlier to announce that she and Daisy were going to visit Asia's niece in Glasgow since most of the family was out of town. She'd left food in the fridge. Hallie assured her she'd stay in the big house and take care of Wilbur. Not that the pig needed much care. A few soft-boiled eggs, an occasional filet, a fresh spring salad and he was good to go.

Hallie smiled thinking about the little girl and her pet. She'd miss them. She'd miss everybody, Cam, Lucy, Asia, Jesse. She realized, with a start, that she'd made her decision. She swallowed hard several times. There was no sense in crying about this. It was time to let go.

She found Wilbur snoozing in front of the television while Julia Child whipped up some kind of French concoction. She filled his bowl with food and talked to him while he ate. Then she looked into the refrigerator. Asia had left lots of covered dishes.

Hallie closed the door, made herself a cup of tea, and sat at the round, wicker kitchen table while it cooled and finally grew cold.

She decided she'd allow herself to think about Baz while she was here in his family's home. She would cut it off once he got back to town. The musing wasn't all sad; she remembered the months spent urging the stone-faced research professor to loosen up, to come out and play. Then they'd become lovers.

She had been upset when she left L.A. last year. She hadn't spent a lot of time thinking about Baz.

She realized now, just how much he'd changed from the man she'd met a year and a half ago. He was a man of warmth and kindness. He'd found his humanity. Whatever price he paid or she paid was worth it.

****

Jesse was moved to a private room the morning after surgery. He looked frail. He'd lost the vigor Baz associated with him through all their years apart.

Baz realized his father was nearly seventy and something caught at his heart. They'd wasted all those years.

Jesse spoke with Cam, accepted a kiss from Lucy, and then he looked around until he focused on his eldest son. His smile was tremulous but full of welcome. "I'm so glad you're here," he said, as Baz moved next to the bed. "It was almost worth having a heart attack to find out you still care."

Baz lifted his dark brows. "Next time, just ask."

Jesse chuckled and grimaced. "Baz, I need to talk to you about the practice."

"You need to rest."

"I will. Let me say my piece, okay?"

Baz nodded.

"I'm not ready to shuffle off this mortal coil anytime soon, but I don't know that I'll be able to resume the practice. I know you've got a sterling career out there in California. Lord knows I'm proud of all you've accomplished, and I won't ask you to leave it. Not if that's what you really want." He paused to take a breath.

"Slow down, Dad. I'm not going anywhere."

"I'm just going to say that if you want the practice, it's yours. I can't think of anything I'd like better than to see you and Hallie running the place together."

"Dad,"

"I know. Things aren't settled between you. Maybe they never will be. So if you decide to stay, I'd like to have your word that she will always have a job at the clinic. My best advice? Make her your partner."

"Believe me. I'm doing my damnedest.

"Appreciate the offer, okay? I'll think about it. I've got some issues that I've got to clear up before I can make any permanent decisions."

"I understand, son."

The old man was exhausted from the conversation and disheartened, too. Here was one more person Baz had disappointed. He made a sudden decision. "Dad?"

"Mmm?"

"I'd like to stay. I'll see what I can do."

Jesse smiled and closed his eyes.

Baz's phone buzzed. He slipped the instrument out of his pocket. "Baz Outlaw."

"He's got a court order," Nicole sobbed. "He wants Robert to have a DNA test. The nanny quit. I can't do this by myself. I'm scared, Baz. You have to help me."

Christ. Just what he needed.

He walked out into the waiting room. "You're safe in the condo. There's a state-of-the art security system, the community is gated, and there's a guard.

Why'd the nanny quit?"

"She said she was burned out. I don't know."

Baz's mouth straightened into a grim line.

"Burned out" was the code phrase for mistreated by Nicole. He knew she'd dumped all the work on the women hired to help her.

"Robert just keeps crying."

"Crying?" Baz felt a jolt of anxiety. "Why's he crying? Does he have an ear infection?"

"How should I know? I just know I can't stand it anymore. If you won't come to L.A., I'm coming to Maine."

Baz groaned. Could this situation get any worse?

"Don't do it. I'm not even in Maine. I'm in Miami. My dad's in the hospital down here."

He could almost hear her trying to figure out how she could benefit from the situation. Nicole was nothing if not an opportunist. "Well," she finally said, "I've got to do something."

"Sit tight. We'll talk about it when I get home."

"I thought this was your home."

He'd thought so, too, but it didn't feel like home anymore. It hadn't felt like home since Hallie left last year. "I'll get back to you," he told Nicole. "In the meantime get Robert to the pediatrician."

He disconnected and scrubbed the palm of his hand down his face. He wished he could call Hallie and talk to her about this. He couldn't, of course. It was the last thing she'd want to talk about. He couldn't resist the urge to hear her voice though. He dialed her cell. When there was no answer he dialed her apartment. Then he dialed the house.

Where the hell was she?

Lucy rushed into the room. She was in tears.

"Baz come quick. Something's happened to Daddy."

He found several doctors crowded around his father's bed. Cam pulled him aside. "He's unconscious. The operation crashed. That means something went wrong, probably because of his age.

They're gonna have to open him up again."

"Goddammit all to hell."

Cam nodded. "My sentiments exactly."

The problem of Nicole and Robert and the whereabouts of Hallie would have to wait. Baz joined his brother and sister in the waiting room. He held Lucy while she cried on his shoulder.

He felt like crying, too.

Chapter Sixteen

One of Wilbur's favorite meals was chopped liver accompanied by parboiled vegetables served on a bed of wild rice. It worked for breakfast as well as supper. Luckily, Asia had prepared the dish and divided it into plastic containers. As soon as Wilbur heard the telltale "burp" he looked up from the corner where he'd slept on his Miss Piggy cushion.

"Here you go." Hallie set the food dish on the floor. Wilbur got up off his cushion slowly. He was definitely more lethargic when his small mistress was away. In addition, he had good manners. He didn't descend on his food dish like wolves on a fold.

He took small bites, at least for a pig.

When he finished, he looked at Hallie. The small red eyes held her gaze for thirty seconds. When he was convinced she wouldn't re-fill the bowl, he turned and waddled back to his cushion near the door to the cellar. He hunkered down and rested his snout on his trotters.

The pose meant it was time to replace the DVD of Julia Child with one of the Barefoot Contessa.

Wilbur lifted his head, briefly and licked his chops.

"Let me know if you need anything else," she said.

Asia had left plenty of people food, too, including containers of her hearty beef stew and navy bean soup. Hallie had to eat something. She found a slice of bread and popped it in the toaster. She made a pot of coffee.

Her most immediate concern was Jesse's health.

Baz had called this morning to tell her about the operation's crash. She prayed her friend wouldn't die, especially not now when he'd just gotten reunited with his son. She brushed tears from her cheeks and wandered into the parlor where, only a couple of weeks earlier the Outlaw family had celebrated Christmas. The room seemed cold now, the fire out, the lights low, the people departed.

Hallie sat on the surprisingly comfortable Victorian sofa and stared into the blackened fireplace. She thought about death and life, about how much Jesse was loved and needed by his family.

She thought about her lifelong dream of having a baby of her own and how, despite the impossibility of that, she'd been happy in Eden. Part of that was because of the Outlaw family, but part, she admitted, had been her own efforts. She'd found contentment in caring for pets and people, in making friendships and for, at least a little while, fitting into the Outlaw family.

Then she'd rediscovered the passion she'd experienced in L.A. For a short time, she'd rocketed past happy to euphoric. Even without a gray-eyed baby.

She still wasn't entirely certain how or why Baz got involved with the barmaid in L.A. The fact was, he had. He had taken on the responsibility of Nicole and her small son, and they were his family now. A part of her was glad he'd get to have a child.

A much larger, more selfish part of her was furious, frustrated, and hurting all the way to the bone. Baz would remarry Nicole. He'd bring her and the baby here where they could raise the boy among extended family, where Baz's interrupted boyhood could be made right through his son.

Hallie got up, put on her parka, and hiked through the darkness to the clinic. She didn't turn up the heat. She just kept her coat on while she surfed the Internet. The perfect job was out there someplace. All she had to do was find it.

Seven hours later she returned to the house.

Wilbur would be especially hungry since she hadn't been there to have a tea party with him the way Daisy would have done. Hallie needed to eat something, too. She found leftover meatloaf. She'd just pulled it out of the refrigerator when the front door chime rang again and again, as if the person on the front porch was too impatient to wait for a response. A veterinary emergency.

"I'm coming." Hallie hurried through the butler's pantry, the dining room, and the parlor. She stepped into the foyer and opened the heavy front door.

Diane Cobbs Sanderson, dressed as a ski bunny in a white fur-lined parka and matching ski pants, lifted her finger off the bell. She had an impatient look on her perfectly made-up face. Hallie looked past her. "Hey Tommy."

"I'd like to come in and see Baz."

"Please," Hallie said, stepping backward. "Come in. It's really cold out there tonight, isn't it?"

"Do you live here, too?"

Hallie ignored the rudeness in the woman's voice. "I'm pig sitting. The family's out of town. Is there something I can do for you?"

"I expected to see Baz."

Hallie made a grab for her patience. "He's in Florida. Dr. Outlaw, that is, his father, is in the hospital

213

there."

"Oh." She seemed to be at a loss for words.

Tommy jumped in. "We're going to see my grandma. She lives in New Jersey, and she's in the hospital, too."

"Oh, I'm sorry."

"She fell on the ice," Tommy explained, "and got her leg broke."

"Oh my."

"Yeah and, well, she's afraid of Nadine."

"I can't say as I blame her."

His eyes were round and serious, as if he were willing her to understand. "So we can't take Nadine with us."

Hallie felt the beginnings of a panic attack as she realized where this was headed.

"Dr. Hallie can we leave Nadine here?"

"Here?" She had a sudden vision of Nadine lounging on the Victorian sofa or curled up around Wilbur's television set. Were boa constrictors and pot-bellied pigs natural enemies? Probably.

"I don't think that would work. I'm sorry."

"If you are Baz's girlfriend why didn't he take you along to Florida?"

Hallie sighed. The woman really had a one-track mind.

"I know Dr. Outlaw keeps pets sometimes,"

Tommy said, doggedly. "My friend Jeffrey left Marvin here when his family went to the beach last summer."

"Marvin's a hotdog," Diane said.

Marvin was a dachshund, and one of Hallie's patients. "I know. But a dog is not a snake."

Her logic evidently escaped Tommy. "But she needs a place to stay."

"She doesn't need any supervision," Diane put in, finally dropping her favorite subject. "Just refill the water and keep her in a heated room."

"She won't need food until we get back next Tuesday," Tommy pointed out.

Hallie thought about opening the clinic tomorrow morning and being greeted by Nadine. She hadn't thought her life could get any more depressing.

"Please, Doctor Hallie?"

Diane's attention had wandered again. Hallie saw her eyeing the sofa in the parlor. She was probably envisioning herself stretched out there in a pair of topless lounging pajamas while Baz rested his arm on the mantelpiece and gazed at her adoringly.

Dr. and Mrs. Basil Cobbs-Sanderson Outlaw relaxing at home.

Hallie pulled herself together. "Can you and your mom bring her cage out to the clinic? I'll get the key."

They placed the snake's cage in the backroom.

There was one bit of silver lining. They weren't currently boarding any pets that Nadine might consider breakfast.

With any luck Nadine could be left alone out here until Baz got back from Florida.

"She's going to be lonely," Tommy said.

Guilt twisted down Hallie's spine. She had no intention of keeping the snake company. She got a small radio from Jesse's office and plugged it in.

"What kind of music does she like to listen to?"

"Classical. I tried to get her to listen to country, but she put her head under her tail."

Hallie laughed in spite of herself. Tommy was a great kid. Baz would be proud of her. Baz. The laughter stopped as pain jolted through her.

Hallie returned to the house, filled Wilbur's bowl, and replaced his video with one of Emeril expounding on the subject of Cajun cooking. Hallie ate a few bites of the excellent stew. She sat at the table and kept the pig company until he fell asleep, then she turned off the television and switched off all the lights except the Porky Pig nightlight near Wilbur's bed.

Hallie settled herself on the parlor sofa. She'd slept here last night, too. It was stupid, but she just didn't want to go upstairs to the family bedrooms.

She didn't want to look at Baz's room or pass by the Jacuzzi.

The doorbell jerked her out of a restless sleep.

It was probably too much to hope that it was Diane and Tommy coming back to pick up their pet.

She threw open the door to find a young woman holding a crying baby.

The girl had thick blonde hair pulled back into a ponytail, wide blue eyes, and an anxious expression on her pretty face. She had on a pair of skin-tight designer jeans and an expensive looking leather jacket.

Nicole. Hallie glanced at the furious baby.

Baz's son. Robert.

"Please come in."

The newcomer carried both a diaper bag and a cavernous designer purse over her shoulder. She bumped into the doorframe and muttered a curse.

"Let me help," Hallie said.

Instantly the girl handed her the screaming baby. Hallie cradled him against her shoulder, smoothing her hand down his small, quivering back and murmuring reassuring words. At first he fought the hold with his tiny feet and his strong little body, but after a minute or two he quieted down.

"Jeez," the girl said. "You're a miracle worker.

He's been crying since we got on the plane."

"It's the air pressure. Babies have tiny tubes in their ears. The pressure makes them pop."

"Whatever. Wow. This isn't what I expected. I figured Baz's house would be all chrome and glass, like the condo."

Hallie barely heard her. The baby mesmerized her. It felt so right to have him in her arms.

"I'm Nicole, by the way. Baz's wife. This is Robert. Are you Lucy?"

"No." Hallie had to clear her throat. "The family's out of town on an emergency. I'm Dr. Outlaw's partner, Hallie Scott. I'm keeping an eye on things while they're gone."

Nicole nodded. "I know. Miami. Baz told me. He doesn't know we're here. D'ya think he'll be pissed?"

"Of course not. Are you hungry?"

"Famished."

Hallie nodded. "Would you like to change Robert and feed him while I find something for you to eat?"

"Oh, I'm not nursing. That didn't really work out for me. Listen, why don't I just check the fridge?"

"What about the baby?"

She made a face. "Could you change him? I'm really burned out."

Hallie carried the baby and diaper bag upstairs.

His sleeper was soaked with a combination of urine and sweat, but he'd stopped fussing. He seemed to understand that relief was on the way. He reached out to touch Hallie's nose. She plucked a towel from the bathroom with the Jacuzzi, laid it on Jesse's bed, and went to work.

"You could really use a nice warm bath couldn't you?" Robert's long-lashed eyes were huge and curious. She gave him a sponge bath with a wet washcloth. She found lotion and powder in the bag and she used them. He kicked his feet and blew a bubble. She peered at his tiny features. Did he look like Baz? She couldn't tell. Or, maybe, she just didn't want to know.

"Robert," she whispered. "You are so beautiful."

She was in the middle of slipping a clean diaper under his bottom when a stream of urine hit her in the face. She yelped at first then she laughed.

"Guess you didn't like being called beautiful."

She dressed him then made her way down the back staircase. She found herself giving Robert a guided tour. "This was originally for the servants back in the days when they had servants. Asia uses it mostly now. You'll like Asia. She always smells like fresh bread, and she's gonna love you."

She spoke as if Robert had to learn all about the Outlaws, as if he would be living in Eden permanently. Somehow she felt certain he would. He and his mom and dad.

"You know," Nicole said, when Hallie entered the door into the kitchen, "there's a pig in here."

"His name is Wilbur. He's a pet."

"I'd really like a taco."

"Would you settle for meatloaf?"

"Sure. I didn't mean to be difficult." She grinned at

Hallie. "I'll warm up the food if you give Robert this bottle."

"No problem."

Hallie warmed the bottle then she sat at the table and fed the baby while Nicole put together a meal of meatloaf, potato chips, and beer.

"Tip it like that," Nicole advised when she didn't get the right angle for Robert's mouth. "It took me awhile to get the hang of it, too."

Robert sucked greedily at the bottle.

"He's really hungry."

"Pretty much all he does is eat and sleep. And poop."

"That will change," Hallie said. "Pretty soon he'll be sitting up then toddling around."

Nicole looked at her as if she wasn't holding her breath waiting for those two stages of development.

"I thought it would be more fun, you know? I thought it would be like somebody to love me. It's boring and it's lonely."

"Being a single mother can't be easy," Hallie said. She watched Robert's rosebud mouth work the nipple. "He seems like a good baby." A perfect baby.

"You should spend the day alone with him. He always wants to be picked up or changed or something."

"I've heard babies are hard work."

"You don't have any children?"

"No."

"Do you want to?"

"I'm pretty busy with the veterinary practice."

"Ya know what I'd like? I'd like to be a stewardess on a plane. That looks pretty exciting. You get to go all over the world for free."

"It would be a difficult career with a small baby."

She shrugged. "Or else I'd like to be a waitress on a cruise ship. Can you imagine how much fun that would be?"

"Not really."

"You meet all kinds of men when you're working in a bar. That's where I met Baz. He came in every night and got toasted. but he was always so nice to me. And then he married me and I thought all my problems were over."

"They weren't?"

"No. My ex, Jimmy D, he's trying to get Robert. He told me he'd follow me out here." A look of fear flashed in her big, blue eyes. "He wants the baby because his wife can't have kids, and he's Italian. He has to prove he's a stud."

"Is Robert his son?"

Hallie's heart pounded hard as she awaited the answer. Not that it mattered. Baz was Robert's father in every way that counted.

Nicole shrugged again. "I'm not sure who his father is." Hallie suspected she was lying. "Baz is his legal father, but Jimmy says he's getting a court order for a DNA test."

"I think he has to have your permission to get a DNA sample from the baby," Hallie said, quietly.

"Not if he kidnaps him."

Hallie's heart seized up. She looked at the long dark lashes against the smooth baby cheeks. She couldn't bear to think of Robert being kidnapped.

"Is Baz dating anyone? He told me he was gonna get married as soon as our divorce was final, but I figured that girl wouldn't wait for him. I know I'd have dumped his ass."

The house phone rang. Hallie reached over to pick it up. "Outlaw residence."

"Thank God you're there."

Hallie tensed. Worry leapt in her gut. "Is it Jesse?"

"No. Nothing's changed on that. We're still waiting to see how the second surgery came out. I was just worried about you. Where've you been?"

"I've been here."

"You didn't pick up before." She heard a soft curse and knew he hadn't meant to yell at her.

"Sorry, honey. I'm beat."

She visualized him rubbing the back of his neck, and she almost smiled.

"Listen, I didn't call to yell at you. I wanted to let you know there's a chance Nicole will show up."

"More than a chance. She got here a little while ago."

"Is that Baz? Let me talk to him, will ya?"

Hallie handed her the phone.

"Hey hon," she said. Hallie had never called Baz "hon" in her life. But then she hadn't been married to him for nine months. "It was hell getting here.

Your dad's partner is real nice. She's been taking care of Robert."

Hallie heard the rumble of Baz's voice.

"I know you told me not to come, but I didn't feel safe in L.A." Her voice turned petulant. "I like it here. When are you getting back?"

The voice was that of a cranky teen-ager, but the words came from a young wife, impatient for her husband to return.

Hallie glanced at the ring. The green beryls winked up at her. She'd take it off tonight and leave it in Baz's dresser drawer.

The nipple slipped out of Robert's mouth. His belly was full and he was asleep but Hallie knew there was one more thing they had to do. She lifted him against her shoulder and patted his back lightly. His surprised burp was the most gratifying thing she'd ever heard.

Nicole handed the receiver to her. "He wants to talk to you."

"I'm so sorry, Hal," he said. "So goddam sorry. I can't believe I set you up for this."

"It's not a problem. We're doing just fine here."

"Hallie, I…goddammit."

Her heart twisted. There was no way out of this.

He knew it, too.

"When do you get back?"

"Cam and I will leave tomorrow afternoon if everything's okay with Dad. Lucy has offered to stay here because we both need to get back for work."

And for their families. They both had families who needed them.

"I'm going to let you go. Robert needs to get to bed."

He was silent a moment. She knew he was trying to figure out what to say. An impossible task, really, since he didn't know what he was going to do.

But Hallie knew. "Bye, Baz," she said.

"Hang on, hang on. There's a cradle in the attic.

"My dad made it, and he held onto it for his grandchildren." She was surprised at the slash of pain that arrowed through her at the word cradle.

"Fine. Bye." She hung up.

Nicole deposited her dishes in the sink while Hallie told her about the cradle. "I can look for it if you want to hold Robert."

Nicole's eyes looked troubled as she stared at Hallie. "You're the one, aren't you? The one he wanted to marry?"

Hallie shook her head and handed over the baby. "I'm the one he didn't want to marry."

Chapter Seventeen

Hallie had planned to spend Sunday looking for jobs. She'd found several small practices looking for assistants. One was in Glacier, Alaska. Another was in Inkspot, Texas. The one near the Arctic Circle had one obvious advantage. There would be no possibility of running into a snake. If she made her decision purely on the reptilian aspects she would definitely go north to Alaska.

She searched the Pacific Northwest. She'd always wanted to see Seattle and maybe live on one of those islands up there. Maybe the best thing would be to choose a spot and just drive there.

Surely she could get a job doing something even if it was just walking dogs.

She discovered she was too busy to spend any time on the computer. Nicole was a talker. She had lots of questions about the Outlaw family and about Eden. It was almost as if she knew her life would be here.

"The family is fantastic," Hallie said. "Cameron is Baz's brother. He is a widower with a daughter named Daisy. Then there's Lucy. She just got out of college, and she's applying for jobs at some of the newspapers around the country."

"I wish I could've gone to college."

"That's always a possibility."

"I couldn't afford it. Now I've got Robert." She

sounded resigned.

"I'm sure Baz will help you with tuition and babysitting. What would you like to study?"

"Oh, anything. I mean all you hear about is panty raids and beer parties and fun stuff like that."

Hallie blinked. "Community college is a good alternative."

"I know, I know. I had a girlfriend for a while, another waitress. She was taking cosmetology at community college. I think I'd be good at that. Or nails. I guess you went to college, didn't you?"

Hallie nodded. "I was very lucky. My father left me some money when he died."

Nicole sighed. "I never really knew my father. I mean, my mom said he split when he found out she was pregnant. There were some guys in there. Quite a few guys. But none of 'em took. Mom finally got tired of living in a rusted out trailer on a road outside of Plummet, Oklahoma. She found out about this commune in Northern California. That's where she is now."

Hallie's heart went out to the young woman.

She'd had a hard childhood.

"Ya know, it's really nice here. I mean, except for the cold. When I first met Baz, he told me he never planned to come back to Maine. I guess he changed his mind when he found out you were here."

Hallie didn't know quite what to say to that.

"I know you two were together," she said. "He talked about you in the beginning. Not so much after that. Mostly we talked about the baby. He got me a doctor and vitamins, and we went to childbirth classes. There was this one really hot guy in the childbirth class.

Kenny. He had the greatest eyes.

He asked me to go out for a beer one night but there was no way."

"I would think not."

"Baz would never have let me have a beer. 'No booze,' he said." She imitated a scolding voice. "It's not good for the baby."

Hallie couldn't help smiling. "He just wanted you and Robert to be healthy."

"Yeah. Well, we were. I got high blood pressure, ya know? I had to stay in bed. He hired people to come in and take care of me when he had to go to work. If I'd been on my own I'd've definitely lost Robert. I might even have died."

Hallie's throat clogged. She visualized Baz taking care of the young woman. Nicole didn't know it but she'd been in the safest possible place.

"So why didn't you guys get married when he came back?"

Hallie shrugged. "It didn't seem like the right thing to do. Now I realize it was because Baz had another family."

"What family?"

"You. You and Robert. You're his family."

"I guess. In a way. It's not like we're in love or anything."

"Love can grow." It was hard to talk.

"Did it grow for you and Baz?"

Hallie nodded. "For a little while."

Nicole tilted her head to one side. "You know, Baz once said you were the kindest person he'd ever met. He called you an inspiration."

"Well, he didn't know me all that well."

She smiled to indicate that was a joke, but Nicole didn't laugh.

"I think you'd make a good mom," she said. "Do you think you'll have children some day?"

"No. No, I can't have children. I have a condition called endometriosis. Stuff grows inside the uterine wall so a fertilized egg has no chance to attach."

"It's weird to think we were all just fertilized eggs at one point, isn't it? I guess you could adopt a child."

Hallie smiled. She didn't want to debate the merits of adoption. Not now. Not with this young mother. "Tell me something. This guy, Jimmy. Is he dangerous?"

"Oh yeah. I mean, at first I thought he was kinda hot. He's good looking and all that, and he's got lots of money. Then I found out he was married, and I was so like pissed. You know? I mean, not that I wanted to marry him, but jeez he coulda been honest with me. When he found out about the baby, he just wanted it in the worst way. He was willing to pay me and everything. I said no. I mean, I wasn't even sure I'd have it. He wouldn't give up, though. He was on my butt every day."

"Why do you think that was?"

"It's cause his wife can't have a kid. She's sterile or whatever."

"Barren."

"Yeah. Oh, I guess it's the same for you.

Anyway, they wanted a kid real bad, and Jimmy wanted his own kid. He's Italian. He said it's real important to Italian men to be able to become fathers."

"What did you mean you weren't sure if you were going to have the baby?"

"I figured I'd get an abortion. I mean, I'd had three before this."

"Nicole!" Hallie just couldn't help herself. "Don't you know about birth control?"

"Yeah but…I don't know. The pill makes me sick. Besides, I never have insurance. Anyway guys forget to use condoms. I decided to keep the baby after I met Baz."

That answered one question at least. "So you were already pregnant when you met him."

"Yeah." The girl didn't look her in the eye, and, once again, Hallie found herself wondering if she was lying.

"I knew I'd be okay with him." Her voice softened. "I mean he was real strict but he was kind and he always took real, real good care of me. I knew he'd make a good dad, too."

"Did you realize he would feel responsible for you?"

"Yeah." She looked down. "He kept saying it was temporary and all that, but when you've met enough guys, you get a pretty good feel for the ones that'll stick around. I figured he'd never just cut me loose.

Then when Robert was born, I knew. You should have seen the look on his face when they pulled that baby out of me. I didn't want to hold him, but Baz did. I think he held him all night."

"Excuse me a minute." Hallie hurried into the bathroom. She couldn't seem to stop the tears from leaking out of her eyes. She and Nicole were sisters under the skin. They'd both recognize the father potential in Baz Outlaw. Too bad only one of them would get to keep him.

There was a knock on the door. "Hallie?"

"Be right out."

"Did I make you cry?"

Hallie opened the door and smiled at the girl.

"Just a little. I knew Baz would make a good father, and I was right."

"Are you in love with him?"

She considered lying but she decided against it.

"Pretty much."

"He's in love with you, too, isn't he? I mean you're much closer to his age and all that."

"You don't have to worry about me, Nicole. I'm getting a new job. I'll be moving away."

"Oh." She looked sad. "Where're you going?"

"Alaska. Probably."

Nicole made a face. "Sounds even colder than here."

Hallie chuckled.

"Baz talked about you on our wedding day.

When we were standing in front of the judge or whatever he was. When it was time to say my name, he said Halliday. I didn't understand. I mean it doesn't sound like a normal name."

Robert's cry was the most welcome sound in the world.

"Could you get him?"

"Be happy to." Hallie took the back stairs two at a time. She wanted to make the young woman feel welcome, but she'd heard about all she could take.

She changed Robert and carried him downstairs.

"Uh, Nicole, unless you have a supply stashed somewhere we're running short of diapers. I'll go up to the store."

"Oh, no, let me go." Her eyes sparkled and color flooded her face. She was like a kid getting out of school for the summer. Hallie dug a credit card out of her purse and handed it over.

"Do you know how to drive a pickup?"

"Sure."

"Ferguson's Market is on the corner of Main and—"

"Don't worry. I'll find it. I've got a nose for shopping."

"Better get some more formula."

"Right. Sure." She stared at Hallie for a moment. "I wish I'd had a mom like you."

After Nicole left, Hallie sat in Lucy's room and watched Robert sleep. He was so perfect with his dark lashes resting on the curve of his cheek, the fuzz of light brown hair on his head, and the tiny fingers that stuck out of the wrists of his sleeper.

With very little effort, she could fall in love with this baby. Probably she already had. It was something of a revelation.

Maybe the blood tie wasn't that big a deal.

Maybe it wasn't really so important to share allergies and a tendency to pronate. Maybe she'd been wrong all this time. Not that it mattered.

Robert wasn't hers. He'd never be hers. He already had a mother. And a father.

"You are a very lucky boy, Robert Outlaw. You've got a mommy with a good heart and the best daddy in the whole world. I predict you'll have a great childhood."

Robert screwed up his face, and Hallie heard a soft explosion. She grinned.

"Good timing. We've got one diaper left."

****

Cam looked up from his newspaper and stared at his brother. "You've paced the length of the airport half a dozen times. What's up? Why are you so nervous?"

"Why? Because my ex-wife and my son are at the house with my girlfriend."

"They'll be fine together. Everybody loves Hallie."

"Yeah and she loves everyone. I'm scared to death that by the time I get back Hallie will have adopted both of them and they'll go off to live in the commune with Nicole's mother."

Cam grinned. "Afraid you'll get left out?"

Baz scowled. "I'm not afraid of it. I know it. I know Hallie. She's made up her mind. She thinks my place is with Nicole and Robert. I'll never be able to talk her into marrying me."

"Wait and see. Things have a way of working out."

"Very philosophical. You didn't take that attitude last night."

Cam fell silent and Baz cursed himself. His brother was just trying to help.

"It's not just that. Drama is Nicole's middle name. Trouble follows her wherever she goes.

Usually in the form of this guy Dinari. I don't like it that the women are alone with the baby." He rubbed the back of his neck. "I've got to get back there."

Cam looked concerned. "Do you have any reason to think he'll show up in Eden?"

"I got a call from his lawyer. He was required to give me a heads up when Jimmy got a court order to get Robert's DNA tested. If he can get biological proof the kid is his, he won't have much trouble convincing the courts to give him at least visiting rights."

"Wouldn't that solve your problems?"

"Huh?"

"Robert is really Nicole and Dinari's business. If they take the boy, you'll be free to marry Hallie."

"It isn't that simple."

"Why not?"

Baz heaved a huge sigh. "I feel responsible for the baby. Nicole's an airhead and Dinari.'s a mobster."

"You feel responsible or you love him?"

Baz glared at Cam, but he didn't argue. He loved the little guy. Shit.

"You could give him a good life. You and Hallie."

Baz stared at his brother. "I can't have Hallie and Robert both."

"Why not? People get divorced all the time. They don't have to lose contact with their kids. Our situation was just weird because Mom was whacked."

"You don't understand. Hallie wouldn't want to be a stepmother. Hell, she doesn't even want to adopt. It's been her lifelong dream to have a kid of her own. Robert would remind her of my betrayal and what it cost her."

"I think you're selling her short. Hallie loves rodents and pigs. There's no way she wouldn't fall in love with a baby."

A small flicker of hope ignited in Baz's soul. Was it possible? Could he have both of them? Then he remembered the threat of the mobster. "Damn. What if Jimmy shows up?"

"Surely he won't hurt his own baby. And why should he hurt Hallie or Nicole?"

"She'll try to be a hero. You know her. She'll fight

him, and he'll wind up hurting her. Goddam."

"Call Jake. He can check on them."

Baz didn't like that option. The last thing he wanted was for the sheriff to hang around Hallie.

Well, the second to the last thing. Mostly he wanted to be sure she was okay. "All right. Fine." He placed the call. The sheriff promised to check on Walnut

Street every half hour.

"Now call her. If they're in danger, you've got to let her know."

The phone rang at 4 four o'clock. Hallie's stomach roiled. She picked up the phone. "Is Jesse all right?"

"So far, so good," Baz said. "Lucy's still with him. Cam and I are in the airport in Atlanta. We missed our connecting flight. The earliest we can be home is midnight."

"Okay."

"Things sound quiet there."

They were quiet. Hallie was just sitting in the rocking chair admiring the way Robert was able to ball up his fist and stick it in his mouth. "Nicole went out for diapers."

"Lord. I hope you didn't give her a lot of money."

Hallie thought of the credit card. "I didn't."

He was silent a moment. "What am I going to do?"

"The right thing, of course," she said, firmly.

"You always do the right thing, Baz."

"Not always."

She knew he was talking about last Christmas.

"I think it's time to let that go."

"I can't let you go."

Her chest was filling and she was afraid her voice

would shake. "We should talk about this later. When you get home."

"Will you be there?"

"Yes. You didn't think I'd just bolt, did you?"

"It crossed my mind."

"Robert's hungry. You and Cam have a safe trip. I'll see you later."

"Wait. There's something I've got to tell you.

This guy who's after Nicole? He may be heading for Eden. He's got a court order for a DNA test, but he can't get one if Nicole and I refuse to let him have the baby."

"You think he'll try to steal Robert?"

"I think there's a real good chance. He's a bad guy. You and Nicole and Robert need to go somewhere safe. Like maybe a motel."

"You want us to go to a motel in Bangor?"

For a moment neither of them spoke. Hallie knew he was thinking of the night they'd both tacitly understood they'd be spending the night in a Bangor motel. The night he'd proposed at the Buddy Burger and they'd celebrated in the front seat of the truck cab in the parking lot next door.

"I think we'd be safer here," she said, her throat dry with unshed tears. "I'll talk to Jake. He can drive by every so often."

There was another silence. Hallie knew Baz was trying to come up with an alternative to the sheriff.

She knew he couldn't.

"I already checked with him. He said he'd patrol the house. Lock all the doors and windows."

"You really think he's coming tonight?"

"I've got a bad feeling about it. Hallie, whatever

you do, don't get hurt. If he's got any kind of weapon, give him the baby. He won't hurt Robert."

"I'm not giving him the baby. No way. Forget it, Baz. Listen, I'll keep them both safe for you."

"I know you will. It's you I'm worried about."

"I'll take care of myself, too. I'm pretty good at it, you know. I've been doing it a long time."

"Hallie?"

"What is it—the baby's crying?"

"I love you."

He heard an odd, choking sound then the line disconnected.

I love you, too.

A short time later Nicole bounded into the house with half a dozen shopping bags.

"I stopped at White's. It's pretty old-fashioned. This town needs a boutique bad. And a Starbucks. Anyway, I scored some clothes. What they lack in style they make up for in flannel."

She pulled a powder pink parka out of a bag.

She'd gotten a pink and blue tam to go with it and a pair of fashion boots with spike heels. Hallie didn't even want to think about those boots on the ice.

"I got a couple pair of jeans and some wool pants. They were having a sale on cashmere sweaters."

"You got four?"

"Three. The eggplant one is for you."

Tears pricked the backs of Hallie's eyes.

Everything was making her cry today. "That was very sweet of you."

"Well, it was your credit card."

"How about Robert? What did you get for him?"

"Three white sleepers and some T-shirts. They

didn't have much. I had to buy a pink snowsuit."

Hallie laughed. "Robert's got enough self-confidence to wear a little pink once in a while." She started to hand the baby to his mother. "Why don't you play with him while I fix supper?"

"I could fix supper. Or we could get a pizza."

Hallie visualized an unknown deliveryman coming to the door. "Maybe tomorrow night for the pizza. I'll just see what else Asia left in the fridge."

"You can take Robert with you. I always put him on the floor when I've got something to do. He doesn't roll off that way."

Hallie didn't mention the fact that floors in Maine tended to be very cold. She nodded, approvingly. "That's a good point."

She found a cardboard box in the pantry and set Robert up inside with one of Wilbur's pig-themed pillows. He could watch Wilbur, and he could watch Hallie. He seemed perfectly content.

"After I put my new clothes away, could I go out back and see the clinic?"

"Sure."

"Where do those outside steps lead?"

"To my apartment."

"Oh, wow. Can I see that, too?"

"Why not? Key's on the hook by the back door."

Hallie tried to decide when and how to tell Nicole about Baz's premonition. She didn't want to scare the young mother, but they needed to have a plan to defend themselves and Robert. Straight out seemed like the best bet.

"Baz called," she said. "He thinks there's a chance Jimmy D. will show up in Eden tonight."

Nicole's eyes suddenly looked solemn. "I think so, too."

"Why?"

"Because I called him. I told him I'd be here."

Tears leaked out of the big blue eyes. "I want Baz to take care of Robert, but if he won't, JImmy can have him. I know you think I'm the worst mom in the world, Hallie, but I just can't hack this anymore."

The girl rushed at her, and Hallie opened her arms.

"I don't think you're a bad mom, Nicole," she said, softly. "Nobody ever said parenting was easy, and you're very new at this."

Chapter Eighteen

Several hugs and a box of tissue later, Nicole ventured out to the clinic. Hallie breathed a sigh of relief. Drama and chaos seemed to follow Nicole like the cloud of dust behind Pigpen. Hallie enjoyed the younger woman's company but found it exhausting.

Or maybe the exhaustion came from trying to repress her broken heart.

"It is what it is," she told herself.

She'd survive this and she'd thrive. That's what she'd always done. She opened the refrigerator door.

Maybe there was something in here she could make into tacos or some taco-like food. She'd just started to investigate when the back door slammed open.

Oh, God. Nicole had found Nadine. Hallie hurried over to comfort her. "I'm so sorry. I completely forgot to tell you about Nadine."

"Who?"

Nicole seemed remarkably un hysterical for someone scared half out of their wits by a reptile.

"The boa constrictor. We're boarding her for a few days. It must have been a terrible shock. I know it was for me the first time she showed up at the clinic."

"You mean the rainbow snake? I'm not scared of her. I saw lots of snakes up at my mom's commune."

"Oh. That's lucky, I guess."

"There's like a foot of water in the clinic. I think a pipe broke or something."

Hallie sighed. "You'll have to watch Robert."

Nicole made a face. A moment later Hallie stepped into the clinic. It wouldn't be necessary to build an ark, but the floors were completely covered with water. She hurried back into the house and called Jolene. The hairdresser would know who to call.

"My cousin Danny's a plumber," Jo said. "I'll send him over on the double. Jeez. In this weather the whole place'll turn into an ice cube in no time flat. By the way, how's Jesse?"

"So far so good. I'll call you when I hear more."

Hallie hung up the phone. The first thing Danny would do is turn the electricity off which meant the building would get very cold very fast. It was no place for a coldblooded creature like Nadine. They'd have to bring the big snake into the house. She opened her laptop and did some quick research.

She couldn't find any evidence of boa constrictors dining out on pot-bellied pigs, but there were several entries about adult pythons consuming Wilber's brethren. Still, when Danny arrived with his son, Danny, Junior, she asked the two to bring Nadine's crate into the mudroom.

No point in tempting fate.

Hallie accompanied Danny to the clinic where they turned off the water and the electricity and tried to find the source of the leak. Half an hour later Danny, senior, decided a pipe had burst. He agreed to return in the morning to fix it.

By the time they walked back to the house Hallie was shivering. That position in Texas was starting to look better and better. She thanked the plumber for coming on short notice then she opened the back door

"Maybe I could show you around town while you're here," Danny junior said to Nicole. "Have you got a number or something?"

Hallie peered at the teen. His lips looked bee stung. Nicole snatched a sheet off Asia's notepad, scrawled on it, and handed it to the plumber's son. "It was nice to meet ya," she said, with a sassy smile.

"I'll call," Danny said. "Good bye, Dr. Scott. That's a real cute baby you have."

"Thanks," she mumbled. The instant the plumber and his son were out the door she rounded on the younger woman. "What on earth are you thinking? Danny's just a teenager."

Nicole shrugged. "So? I'm a teenager, too. For a couple more weeks."

"Oh my god." Hallie had thought she was four or five years older. She should have known.

"I lied to Baz when I met him."

Hallie wondered if Baz had any idea of how close he'd come to statutory rape.

"He knows now. I had to put it down for real when I registered at the hospital."

"Well, that aside, you aren't thinking of dating Danny, right?"

A belligerent look appeared in the clear blue eyes. "Why not? It's not like I'm married anymore."

"But you're a mom."

"Yeah." Nicole squirmed a little. "Danny thought Robert was your baby, and I let him think it. I haven't been out with anybody in forever. I can't remember the last time I got kissed." She grinned.

"It felt so good."

Hallie was so outraged she started sputtering.

"What about Baz?"

"What about him?" Nicole glared at her. "He's not sitting around pining for me. I'll bet you ten bucks he's done it with you. Probably lots."

Hallie's dismay must have shown on her face because Nicole quickly backtracked. "And that's okay. I mean, I know I was married, but I never felt like a wife. This whole thing with Robert...I mean, I love him and all, but I'm not ready for this. I'm too immature."

"You're overwhelmed right now," Hallie said.

"You just need some help, and you've come to the right place. There's lots of family here in Eden."

"They're not my family."

"That isn't true." Hallie tried to find the right words. "You are connected to Baz through Robert and because you were married to him. Everyone here will love you, Nicole. Wait and see. Give this a chance."

Nicole tilted her head to one side. "Give what a chance?"

"This. This situation. You here in Eden with Baz."

Hallie sat in one of the wicker chairs, and Nicole took the other. "You're saying Baz and I should remarry, aren't you?"

Nausea roiled in Hallie's stomach, but she had to be honest. "I think it would be best for both of you and Robert."

Nicole shook her head. "I don't get it. I thought you and Baz had something going." Her face tightened. "Is this because you don't want Robert?"

The question shocked Hallie. "This isn't about me. Baz needs to be a full-time father to Robert. He can do

241

that best in a family."

"We don't love each other."

Hallie thought of her childhood with a single, uncaring parent and Baz's with a single, withholding parent.

"He was your knight in shining armor. How could you not love him?"

The girl shrugged. "He never loved me. He took care of me and all that, but I always knew there was somewhere he'd rather be. Now that I've met you, I know why."

Hallie didn't know what to say to that. Besides, she couldn't form any words. Tears leaked out of her eyes and trickled down her cheeks.

"Don't cry," Nicole said. "This will all work out for the best."

Hallie sniffed and Nicole got up to get her a tissue.

"Just for the record," she said, wiping her nose.

"I don't think you're immature at all."

Hallie found a frozen pizza in the freezer. She added olives and sausage to it, and, when it was heated, she sprinkled it with fresh parmesan cheese.

"This is better than tacos," Nicole enthused.

"You're a good cook."

Hallie laughed. "Maybe I'll get my next job at a Pizza Hut."

Nicole stopped chewing. "You're joking, right? I mean, you're not really gonna quit your job to bus pizza."

"The practice isn't big enough for three doctors. I won't leave until Baz's dad is fully recovered though."

"Isn't the dad like a million years old? He could retire."

Hallie tried to imagine vital, gregarious Jesse Outlaw retired. She couldn't do it. Not that it mattered. She, Hallie, couldn't stick around Eden. Whether Nicole liked it or not, Baz would do the right thing. It would be easier on all of them if she took off.

After supper they put Robert in his cradle in Nicole's room while they discussed strategy. "The smart thing would be for you and Robert to go over to the Garden of Eden. My friend Sharon could look out for you there. Then, if Jimmy shows up, the baby won't be here, and he'll just go away."

"Or he'll take you as a hostage."

"That seems unlikely. I mean, Baz isn't going to trade Robert to get me back."

"I want to stay here," Nicole said.

Hallie nodded, slowly. The more she thought about it, the less she liked the idea of splitting up.

And it was sleeting again. Nicole didn't need to be on the road in this weather. Not unless it was absolutely necessary.

"In that case," she said. "I have a plan."

Nicole helped her pull Nadine's cage into the kitchen.

"I feel like that kid on Home Alone. You know, when he's booby trapping the house for the water bandits?"

Hallie smiled but didn't reply. She was mentally reviewing the plan. Would it work? Was there any chance the Vegas gangster would be able to get his hands on the baby?

"I felt a little like that kid when Baz left L.A."

"The Macauley Culkin character?"

"Yeah. I mean, there I was in this big, fancy condo,

and I spent all my time takin' care of this baby. It was like unreal. You know? Like not my real life."

Hallie put her arms around the girl. "You're not alone anymore."

Nicole spent the rest of the evening watching back-to-back episodes of Runway. Hallie put Robert to bed in the cradle up in Lucy's room. At ten o'clock, Nicole went upstairs, and Hallie returned to the parlor. She decided to sit in the rocking chair in the parlor because she could see out the front window. If Nicole's ex-girlfriend approached the house she'd call Jake.

She considered passing the time with the latest copy of Paws, Claws and Pincers, but she didn't want to turn on a light. She needed to stay focused on what was going on outside the house. No matter what happened tonight she wouldn't fail Robert.

Around eleven an odd swishing sound jerked her alert. She held very still, and she heard it again.

Swish-swish. Swish-swish. With her heart pounding hard, she got up and followed it through the house.

Swish-swish. The sound came again. And again.

Hallie's heart sprinted. She inched open the swinging door in the butler's pantry. Over in his corner, Wilbur raised his snout, but when she failed to head toward the refrigerator, he lowered it again.

Hallie barely noticed. Her eyes were on the rainbow-colored creature in the cage. Nadine twisted and flipped like an Olympic gymnast.

Swish-swish.

For a long minute Hallie watched the colors shimmer and change in the dim light shed by Wilbur's nightlight. Something had broken through Nadine's ennui. The warmth of the house? Or was she inspired by the presence of the other beings here? Whatever it was, she was a new snake.

Hallie too, had come a long way. Less than a week ago she'd shrieked at the sight of the boa.

Tonight she was fascinated by it. It just went to show that people could change. Nicole could change. She would grow into her role as a mother and a wife just as Baz would become a great father and husband.

It occurred to her, not for the first time, that things happened for a reason. Nadine had shown up in her life to help her overcome long-held irrational fears. Nicole and Robert had come into Baz's life to help him find his way to the family that he'd denied himself.

Hallie closed the butler's pantry door and returned to the parlor. Other than the occasional swish-swish, the house was so quiet she could hear the seconds tick off on the grandfather clock in the hall. Periodically she'd see the sweep of Jake's Blazer headlights as he drove by. It was a comforting sight.

By eleven thirty she'd begun to think that they'd overreacted. Jimmy D. wasn't coming tonight. In the silence, her cell phone sounded like Gabriel's trumpet. Hallie's heart exploded as she pressed her hand against it. She was more tense than she'd thought. "Hello?"

"You, okay?"

"We're fine. Nothing happening here."

"I wanted to let you know we're on our way back from the airport," Baz reported. "Be there in half an hour. Make that twenty minutes."

For some reason Baz's anxiety communicated itself to her. Cold fingers etched a path up her spine and she shivered. Suddenly she knew Jimmy would be here.

The only question was whether Baz would be here, too.

"Hallie…"

She heard a faint click and her stomach clenched.

Someone was trying to open the door.

"I've got to go," she whispered.

"I need to talk to you."

Hallie couldn't answer. Her attention riveted on the doorknob. An instant later she saw it move.

Jesse's lock had been useless. Hallie flattened herself into the shadows and watched as two men slipped into the foyer.

"Hallie? Halliday?"

Good grief. She disconnected the phone, but it was too late.

"There's somebody in there," one of the men said.

Hallie clicked on a small tabletop lamp.

"May I help you gentlemen?"

The smaller man appeared to be around forty.

He wore a cashmere wool coat and a fedora. His onyx-colored eyes narrowed on Hallie. Jimmy D. His companion was bald and well over six feet tall with shoulders as wide as the staircase. Baldy was clearly the muscle. He wore a lightweight jacket over an enormous gut. Neither man appeared to be armed.

"Where's Nicole?" Jimmy's voice was husky." I'm here to get my baby."

Hallie heard the possessiveness in his voice, and she felt a wave of sympathy. If she'd had a son she'd come after him, too. She disregarded the question.

"I'm afraid we haven't been introduced. I'm Doctor Halliday Scott. I work with Dr. Outlaw." She looked at him, politely, obviously waiting for him to identify himself. He did so grudgingly.

"Dinari."

Hallie nodded. She looked inquiringly at the other man.

"This here's Bluto."

Hallie wanted to keep them talking. She couldn't let the men leave the house with Robert; she had a much better chance of stopping them with help from Baz or Jake. She listened for another car out on the street, but the night was quiet.

"Look, I don't wanna waste a lot of time. I've got a court order here."

"Does it permit you to break in to my house?"

He seemed startled.

"It's for a DNA test for the boy. Where's Nic?"

"Upstairs. A DNA test sounds like you aren't certain Robert's your son."

"I am certain. I just need the proof so the courts will give me the kid."

"It's unlikely they'd take him away from his mother but aside from that, how do you know Robert isn't Dr. Outlaw's biological child? After all, Nicole was married to him."

"He's my kid." Jimmy D. scowled at her. "The timing's right."

"You know gestation isn't an exact science," Hallie pointed out. She kept her voice low and calm.

"I'm his father, dammit. I'm the one that got her pregnant."

There was something in his tone. A defensive note. Hallie played a hunch as the puzzle pieces clicked into place. "He isn't yours is he, Jimmy?" She kept her voice gentle." It isn't your wife who's infertile. You're the one who can't have a child."

Jimmy D. turned puce. He let out a series of curses and denials that made the hair stand up on the back of Hallie's neck. They also convinced her she was right.

"If you are certain Robert is your biological son then you don't need to take him tonight. Why wake a sleeping baby? We can meet you tomorrow at Eden Memorial Hospital. We'll have the test done then."

"Celeste can't wait," Bluto put in. "She painted the baby's room blue, and she's got a mobile with teddy bears hanging from the crib." He pronounced it "mobil."

Hallie kept her eyes on Jimmy. "I sympathize with both you and your wife. It's very difficult to find out you can't have a child. I know. I'm barren, too."

But Jimmy did not appear to be interested in Hallie's fertility issues.

"Dammit woman! Just get Nic and the kid!"

Not yet. She needed to stall another minute or two.

"Infertility's a problem for a lot of people," Hallie said, casually. "It's no reflection on me as a woman or you as a man."

"I told you, it's not me. That kid upstairs is my flesh and blood. I'm tired of bein' jerked around. I want him now. You've got one minute to hand him over. Otherwise we'll go up there and get him ourselves."

He'd actually been remarkably patient for a gangster. Hallie knew she'd pushed him as far as she could. It was time to activate the plan. She prayed it would work as she headed for the stairs.

"I'll get him," she said.

A moment later she stepped into Lucy's room.

Nicole was dressed in her new pink parka and her fashion boots. Robert was in her arms. He had on his pink snowsuit. Hallie smiled, in spite of the threat downstairs. Maybe he was Baz's son. Pink suited him. She scooped up a bundle of blankets and headed back along the landing to the front staircase.

Behind her, Nicole tiptoed to the back stairs.

The fake baby would only buy Hallie a few seconds, but that might be enough. She talked to the fake Robert as she made her way, slowly, down the steps.

The mobster's patience had run out. He vaulted up the steps and reached for the baby. "Jesus Christ," he yelled, "the bitch is tryin' to trick us. Nic's gotta be goin' out the back."

Bluto took off with Jimmy only a few steps behind him. They made their way through the big house in a matter of seconds. Hallie stood very still and prayed.

An instant later a bloodcurdling shriek reached her ears. She smiled.

The plan had worked.

She called Jake.

Chapter Nineteen

Curses exploded out of Baz's mouth as he questioned the universe." "Where in the hell is the law when you need it?"

"We're almost there," Cam soothed. "Just focus on the road."

Baz floored the rental car. He'd give a lot to have his Porsche wheel under his hands, but the old Buick was steady on the ice. Shit. Fear tasted like bile in his mouth.

What if it was too late? What if he was too late?

Again? His timing had stunk this past year.

"Baz, man, you're driving like a maniac."

"I know she's gonna try to stop him."

"She won't do anything foolish. She won't let Nicole and the baby get hurt. Jimmy D. has no reason to hurt Hallie. They'll all be fine."

Hallie would protect the others. It was her nature. The fear clawing at his guts wasn't just about her physical safety. "She's gonna run."

"Who? Hallie?"

"I know her. She's got it in her mind that Nic and I should make a family for the boy."

"You can talk to her. Work it out. You're going over the yellow line."

"The hell of it is, she's right." He frowned at the road ahead. "I owe the kid. I guess I owe Nic, too.

Hallie's all I've ever wanted and I'm gonna lose her."

Cam stopped. Understandable, Baz thought.

There was nothing left to say. A burst of panic shook him. "I'll give her up," he muttered under his breath, "if she can just be safe."

****

Hallie pushed open the door that separated the dining room from the butler's pantry. She paused for an instant, in front of the glass-fronted cabinets that housed the Outlaw family's dishes and pressed her ear against the door to the kitchen.

All she could hear was a kind of whimpering.

She was tempted to stay on her side of the door until Jake arrived, but she couldn't do it. She had to be sure neither of them had followed Nicole.

She sucked in a breath and pushed open the door. Jimmy D. faced her, his palms flat against the wall next to the sun porch door. He looked like a corned cartoon character. His attention was riveted on the center of the room at a rainbow-colored boa constrictor coiled on top of the wicker table.

Bluto was embracing the refrigerator. His huge body shook as he continued to whimper. Wilbur stood next to him.

"I see you met Nadine."

"It's a damn python," Jimmy bit out in a shaking voice. "It's gonna eat us."

Bluto's whimpers turned into a whine.

"Highly unlikely. Nadine was fed yesterday. She won't be hungry again for about a week. In any case, she's not a python. She's a boa."

"Shit, boss," Bluto wailed. "That means it'll

squeeze us to death."

Dinari let out a harsh curse.

Bluto sounded plaintive. "Why's that pig looking at me?"

"You're next to the fridge. Wilbur is interested in any activity that involves the fridge. He's waiting to see whether there's a midnight snack in the offing."

"You think you're pretty damn clever, don't you? You got your damn creatures here to take us hostage so Nic could get away with my boy."

"You're not hostages. You can leave the room whenever you want."

"Why the hell should I trust you?"

"I wouldn't lie to you, Mr. Dinari. Not about something like this. Just as I'm sure you wouldn't lie to me about Robert's parentage."

He glared at her. "What difference does this make to you? It's no skin off your nose if I take the kid."

"You're wrong about that. Robert is Baz's son, and I love Baz."

The dark eyes flared for a minute. "You're the one, aren't you? Nic told me that's why he came out here. You think you're gonna marry him now and get the baby into the bargain?"

"No. Robert belongs to his biological parents. That's not me. It's not you, either."

He looked at her pleadingly. "I told Celeste I'd bring him home."

"I understand. I'm very sorry for you and your wife, but Robert isn't a possession. He's a person who needs years of nurturing and guidance. He needs parents, grandparents, aunts, and uncles. He needs his family."

Suddenly, right there with the boa on the table, the pig guarding Bluto and Jimmy's sullen face in front of her, she recognized a truth. A feeling of protectiveness swamped her senses. She loved Robert. All her objections evaporated like sugar in the rain, and she knew, in that moment, she could be part of his family.

"Robert should be with his natural parents,"

Hallie said, softly. "But there's room in his life for people who love him. Do you love him, Jimmy? Does Celeste? Or is this about your masculinity and her longing for a child?"

The man didn't respond. He looked away from her.

"It's not that I don't understand. You have to understand. Robert deserves to be with people who love him regardless of blood ties."

Jimmy's question surprised her. "You love him?"

Hallie nodded.

"Too bad you're not the mom. Nic can't handle this."

"She'll grow into it."

"She's got a butterfly tattoo on her butt, and her nipples are pierced. That's why she couldn't nurse the kid."

Hallie shook her head. She didn't want to hear about Nicole's shortcomings. "You should both go.

The sheriff'll be here any minute. Dr. Outlaw is on his way home, too."

"You sure it's safe?"

"Yeah. Go on out the back."

"Dr. Scott?"

"Yes?"

"I won't try to get the baby again."

"I know."

Hallie was relieved to see the last of Jimmy D and his sidekick, but she was left with a problem. It wasn't that she didn't trust the Internet, but she wasn't fully confident Nadine wouldn't try to hurt Wilbur. Or vice versa. She couldn't leave the two alone in the kitchen.

The sound of the front door opening came as a huge relief. "Hallie?" Baz's voice ricocheted off every wall in the house. She winced. The place had good acoustics.

"In the kitchen."

"Are you all right?"

"I'm fine. I could use some help though."

Nicole danced around the parlor.

She was like a female Peter Pan, Hallie thought. Athough. A blithe spirit not ready to be shackled by adult responsibilities.

"That was so cool! Man, we got Jimmy good. I couldn't believe the plan worked."

"It was an awesome plan," Cam agreed.

Baz slumped on the sofa his brooding gaze on Hallie. She sat in the rocking chair holding Baz's sleeping son.

"Hallie and me are a great team," Nicole went on. "The only thing is, I just wished I coulda seen those two bums hugging the wall." She howled with laughter. "You should've taken a picture, Hallie."

"To tell you the truth," she said, "I felt a little sorry for them."

Nicole stared at her. "Why?"

Hallie shrugged. "Jimmy was desperate. He's held onto the myth of his fatherhood for so long he's started to believe it." She gazed steadily at Nicole.

"And you encouraged him. That was cruel, you

know. Infertility is a tragedy to people who suffer from it."

"Hold on." Baz's eyes narrowed on her. "Are you saying Jimmy isn't the father?"

Hallie looked at Nicole who suddenly tried to avoid eye contact with her. "He's been telling people it's his wife who's got the fertility problem, but it isn't. He's sterile."

"He knew he was shooting blanks," Nicole said.

"He thought it was a miracle when I got knocked up."

"Like I said. You encouraged him."

"Well, what was I s'posed to do? I couldn't take care of the kid by myself."

"Nicole." Baz's voice was deep and intimidating.

"Who the hell is Robert's father? Is it me?"

Her pretty face twisted. "I'm not sure."

Baz's curse was so loud it woke the baby. Nicole froze, and Hallie winced.

"Baz," his brother cautioned.

Baz ignored him. "You're just a two-bit manipulator. You're shameless, and you're a damn poor mother."

"She's not, you know."

Baz glared at Hallie.

"She could have handed Robert over to Jimmy. I imagine he'd have been happy to pay her a chunk of money. Or she could have had an abortion. She has taken excellent care of the baby right from the start."

"No way. When I met her, she was boozing and living in a dump."

Hallie nodded. "Exactly. She took care of Robert by bringing you into his life."

Baz went very still. A moment later he looked at Nicole. "Tell me the truth. Am I Robert's father?"

The girl's eyes filled with tears, and she shrugged her shoulders. "Maybe. There were a coupla others."

No one spoke for a moment. Then Nicole moved to the rocking chair. She sat on the floor next to Hallie.

"I want you to have him," she said, softly.

Hallie's throat hurt from holding back tears. She knew a generous gesture when she heard one. Nicole might be bored with the day-to-day tedium of motherhood, but she loved her little boy. All her actions proved it.

"I appreciate that. But I know you'll be sorry someday. You'll regret giving up your child, and Robert will wonder why his birth mother left him with someone else. He'll never understand. You've got to trust me on this. Blood is always thicker than water."

She heard a soft curse coming from the sofa.

Nicole shook her head. "I made up my mind before I came out here. I can't do this alone. I was going to l eave the baby with Baz."

"You and Baz can raise him together."

"No." Her eyes were earnest now. "I don't want to raise him. I don't want to marry Baz any more than he wants to marry me. Blood may be a big deal, Hallie, but having two parents who love a kid…well, I think that's more important to him."

Hallie was touched by her words. She was so tempted to take the gift Nicole offered. She looked at Baz. "You need to talk to her," she said, in a low voice.

He nodded. "What do you want, Nic?"

He sounded like a benevolent uncle. Hallie got up. Suddenly she couldn't stand any more. "I'll put Robert in bed," she said and started for the doorway.

"Stay," Baz said. "This concerns you, too."

"I'll take Robert up." Cam slid the baby out of her arms.

"He needs a diaper change," Hallie pointed out.

Cam's glance was kind but ironic. "Believe me, I'm an old hand at this."

For a long moment, no one spoke or moved. They were like three figures in a snow globe, but instead of snow, there was tension.

"I think it's time to figure out the best setup here for the one person who can't speak for himself."

He paused, as if hoping someone else would take over. Hallie knew that wasn't it. He was pulling his thoughts together, constructing his argument. Baz Outlaw knew what he wanted now, and he was going about it in an organized and methodical fashion. It was the researcher in his blood.

"I'll start with my own role in this. I took on the role of father without giving any thought to what it really meant. It was undoubtedly a result of my years separated from my own father. It illustrates the importance of having a role model, and, while I have no doubt there're thousands of men who could do a better job with Robert, he is stuck with me because I choose him."

Tears gathered behind Hallie's eyes. Baz had come so far in the eighteen months she'd known him.

She was so proud of him.

"I promise to do my best to raise him as an honest man who appreciates his family. To do that, I plan to move to Eden permanently. That way Robert will have all the advantages of an extended family."

Hallie shouldn't be surprised. She knew Baz would do the right thing once he figured out what it was.

He looked at her and she smiled. "Ideally," he said. His voice was hoarse; he cleared his throat. He started again. "Ideally, a child should have a father and a mother. Robert is a very lucky baby because there are two women who love him unconditionally.

The only question that remains is in what capacity."

"I hate to interrupt you," Hallie said, "but Nicole is his mother."

Nicole's blue eyes seemed fathomless as she gazed at Hallie. "You can give him so much more Than I can."

"Material things, you mean?"

"Don't you see? You can give him a mother who loves not just him but his father. You can give him a mother who longs to be a mother." She tilted her head to one side. "Do you remember when I told you I'd had several abortions? I didn't do it this time.

Don't you see? Robert was meant to get here. I had him for you. Kinda like Mary and Jesus, know what I mean?"

Hallie's laughter mixed with tears and suddenly she was sobbing. She pulled Nicole into her arms.

When Baz put his arms around them both, Hallie felt an indescribable sense of joy. For the first time since she was thirteen, she was part of a family.

Baz rested his cheek against her curls. He was a lucky man. Hallie loved him, and she was going to be his wife. And he had a son. Robert Outlaw. His son.

Hallie's son. Her happiness melted what was left of the icy fortress around his heart. He smiled at Nic.

He was very proud of her and so grateful.

When the cloudbursts had stopped and everyone was calm, Hallie finally spoke. "I don't want you to sign away your rights to Robert," Hallie told Nicole.

"He should know you loved him enough to give him a stable home with his father, but that you wanted to stay connected. I'd like you to live here, too."

Nicole glanced at Baz. He lifted his brows as if helpless. She might as well know he wouldn't risk his good fortune over a signature on a piece of paper.

"I'll tell you what," Nicole said, finally. "You adopt Robert, and I'll make this my home base. I mean, not right now. I can't wait to just, you know,

be free. But later, I'll come back here. Deal?"

Baz and Hallie exchanged a look.

"Deal," Hallie said, finally." You'll always have a family here. A home."

Nicole giggled. "It might be a little hard to explain all this to Robert. You know, this is my mother, and this is my other mother."

Hallie laughed. The sound was full of happiness that made Baz's blood sing.

"I've been hung up on titles as long as I can remember," Hallie said. "But I can change. As soon as he's old enough, we'll tell Robert about you and about all you went through to make sure he got a wonderful life."

Enough waterworks, Baz thought. "Speaking of change. How'd Nadine wind up in our kitchen?"

"She started out in the mudroom," Hallie said.

"Before that she was in the clinic," Nicole put in.

"Then there was a broken pipe, and, by the way, the clinic is underwater."

He blanched. "Underwater?"

"Jolene's cousin is coming to fix it tomorrow," Hallie assured him.

"I still don't understand. How'd you get Nadine in the first place? What about your snake phobia?"

Hallie wrinkled her nose.

"Diane had to go out of town. Actually, that might have been a ploy. She was really disappointed you weren't here. I mean really disappointed."

Nicole grinned at him. "You're such a stud, Baz."

A moment later Nicole excused herself. Baz took Hallie in his arms. She felt so good, soft but strong.

A woman a man could count on. "I know you wanted a baby of your own," he whispered.

She looked up at him, her face shining. "I never told you the rest of that wish. I wanted a baby that was ours. Yours and mine. I have to tell you I wouldn't trade that little boy for any other baby in the world."

Baz had no words for that. He pulled her into his big body and closed his arms around her. He buried his face in her springy hair.

Chapter Twenty

Baz cupped Hallie's face in his hands. Emotions zephyred through him. He couldn't tell whether they were relief or ecstasy, or lust, or some combination of all three. He lowered his mouth to hers. He intended to give her a quick kiss, just to seal the deal, but the contact hit him with the impact of a speeding comet.

All at once his tongue was in her mouth, and her arms were around his neck. Instantly, he was hard and ready.

"Bed," he panted. "Now." He grabbed her hand.

"Your apartment."

"No can do," she gasped. "Electricity's off."

He didn't waste time on a curse. "Upstairs then. My bedroom. Hurry." He placed her hand on his crotch.

"I see your point."

"Don't make me laugh, Halliday. I'm ready to burst."

He held onto her hand and started up the stairs.

She stopped him twice to sprinkle kisses all over his face and at the bottom of his throat where his tie would normally be.

"Ah, baby, that's so good. So good."

"I'm just so happy," she said.

"I know. Me too. I'll be even happier when we're lying down."

She grinned at him. "Lost your sense of adventure? Remember how fun it was to make love in the truck cab?"

"That was different. There was no chance of running into any family members there."

"Upstairs it is," she murmured.

He sent up a prayer of thanks even as he wondered if he'd make it to his bedroom.

They reached the landing only to be greeted by an irritated wail. "Shit," he gritted.

"I'll check him. It'll just be a minute."

He had become well acquainted with those "little minutes." They involved diaper changing, bottle heating, feeding time, burping time and Hallie-singing-her-son-to-sleep time.

"I've got a better idea."

He knocked on Cam's door. "I'll donate five hundred dollars to the Eden County Chamber of Commerce if you take care of Robert for half an hour."

Cam stared at him.

"Okay. A thousand. For twenty minutes."

Cam's lips twitched, but he managed not to smile. "No problem."

An instant later they were inside his room.

Another instant later and he was inside her. "Oh, baby, baby," he groaned. "It feels like it's been a year."

She smiled her million-dollar smile, and her eyes turned golden. "It has been a year. Thank God you said no last Christmas!"

He knew she was thanking him for Robert.

"I'm glad you appreciated it," he said, between kisses, "because it was the last time. I never plan to say no to you again."

****

Daisy was thrilled when she heard about the heroic efforts of Nadine and Wilbur. Especially Wilbur. She made him a little cape out of one of Robert's baby blankets and called him "Super Pig."

She was less enthusiastic about Robert.

Fortunately, Robert was fascinated with her. He kicked his feet and grinned every time she came in the room. Hallie played lots of hands of cards with the little girl. They talked about her role in raising her tiny cousin. Hallie had great hopes that she'd get used to "that noisy baby" in time.

Nicole gravitated toward Asia. Hallie was delighted to see the teenager helping out in the kitchen and confiding the details of her dates with Danny, junior, to the housekeeper.

One morning, a week from the night Baz and Cam arrived home, the family was at breakfast.

Daisy was, as usual, reading to Super Pig and Robert was listening intently. The adults were finishing their coffee, loathe to leave the warm, bright, love-filled kitchen, when the back door opened.

"Surprise," cried Lucy. "I'd like to introduce you all to the new and improved Jesse Outlaw!"

After a spate of laughter and hugs, Hallie introduced Jesse to both Nicole and Robert. It was a chance for her to practice the story that she'd tell the rest of the world. Jesse questioned no part of it. He just welcomed Nicole with his usual warmth, but his eyes glowed when he saw Robert.

"If you're not feeling overwhelmed yet, there's something else I'd like to tell you."

"Lay it on me, son."

"I'd like to stay in Eden. If you can use me, I'd like to work at the clinic."

"Well." Jesse stroked his chin and pretended to think. "I've heard good things about you, boy.

Trouble is, I've already got an assistant."

"We've got an answer for that." Hallie shifted

Robert in her arms. "We thought I could help with the books and paperwork while the two of you handle the practice."

Jesse shook his head. Hallie stared at him. She couldn't imagine he'd say no to Baz.

"What I meant was I don't need an assistant any longer. I'm interested in some free time. Got a number of younger family members I'd like to hang with." He winked at Nicole.

"What about Wilbur?" Daisy demanded.

"Family members," he corrected himself, "and pigs. My offer is this: you and Hallie own the clinic jointly. I'll help out when needed. Be glad to babysit, too."

"You'll have to stand in line for that," Asia said.

The phone in the butler's pantry rang. Hallie was closest so she excused herself to answer it.

When she returned to the kitchen a few moments later everyone looked at her.

"That was Jake. Mrs. Peach's sister fell and broke her leg. So Jake needs a housekeeper-slash babysitter-slash-nanny for a month."

"Forget it," Baz growled. "You're not available."

"Oh, he didn't ask me. He said he told Sam and Lillie they could choose someone they liked." What he'd actually said was that he'd made the mistake of letting the kids select their caregiver. She looked at

Lucy. "They picked you."

Lucy appeared tongue-tied.

"You should do it, Luce," Cam said. "The money will help with your move."

Baz frowned. "You don't have to go. I mean, if you'd feel uncomfortable staying there or something, it's no big deal."

"I think you should do it," Hallie told Lucy. She was convinced there was some kind of chemistry between Lucy and the sheriff. They should check it out. She had become a big believer in chemistry.

"Oh my gosh," she said to the man who would soon be her husband, "I forgot to tell you. I made an appointment at Eden Memorial for you. It's on Monday."

"An appointment for what?"

"A DNA test. It's no big deal. They take a scraping from inside your cheek and another one from Robert. It takes about a week to get the results."

Baz glanced at the baby in her arms. "Cancel it. We aren't going."

"Don't you want to know whether he's your son?"

Baz lifted the child out of Hallie's arms. "I already know. Robert is my son. Just like he's your son. You don't need to know whether he has your blood type, and I don't need to know whether he has my tendency to pronate. He's ours." He looked around the roomful of people. "He belongs to all of us. Just like we all belong to each other."

Hallie's eyes filled with tears of happiness. It was happening a lot these days. She knew Baz had decided not to check the DNA because he wanted them both to be in the same position. He wanted her to know that it wasn't blood that held a family together.

Hallie felt his strong arm around her shoulders just as Robert blew a bubble. She had the man and the baby she loved and she intended to take care of them for many, many years.

"We'll coin a family motto," Baz said, his voice thick with emotion. "Water is thicker than blood."

"And love," Hallie added, "provides the most unbreakable tie of all."

A word from the author...

I'm from a family of readers and writers, which is great for conversation around the dinner table but not as great when there's a broken gasket in the toilet tank or the garage door is stuck.

My career has included newspaper journalism, freelance humor writing, and technical writing. I've loved fiction since I met Dick, Jane, Sally, Spot, and Puff in the first grade. It has come as a pleasant surprise in recent years to find I love to write about small town people who, through extraordinary experiences, find unexpected depths of passion, jealousy, hatred, and heroism.

My hometown is Ann Arbor, Michigan. I live now in an emptying nest in Northern Virginia with my husband Pete, a retired journalist, and our geriatric golden retriever, Lucy. Our adult children have fulfilled their early promise of being our best friends, although none of them can fix a broken dishwasher, either!

www.annyost.com
www.annyost.blogspot.com

www.ingramcontent.com/pod-product-compliance
Lightning Source LLC
Chambersburg PA
CBHW060530260626
47161CB00003B/842